About the Author

Peter Knyte was born and grew up in North Staffordshire, England, but now lives in West Yorkshire, where by day he passes himself off as a mild-mannered office worker, while by night he explores whole worlds of imagination as an intrepid writer.

When not tapping away at his computer he spends his time slowly transforming his garden into a nature friendly habitat, motorcycling, rock climbing, snowboarding and cooking.

The Embers of Time is his third novel.

For more information about Peter and the worlds that he is exploring please visit:

www.knytewrytng.com

Other titles by Peter Knyte
The Flames of Time
The Ashes of Time

Through Glass Darkly
By a Blue and Crimson Light

The Ghosts of Winter

Forthcoming titles by Peter Knyte
A Shadow on the Sky (Glass Darkly series)
Death & the Creator – short story

THE EMBERS OF TIME

PETER KNYTE

Copyright © 2017 Peter Knyte.
Re-released 2019
Peter Knyte asserts the right to be identified as the author of this work.
All rights reserved.
First paperback edition printed 2017 in the United States and United Kingdom
A catalogue record for this book is available from the British Library.

Paperback ISBN: 978-0-9930874-8-6
eBook ISBN: 978-0-9930874-9-3

No part of this book shall be reproduced or transmitted in any form or by any means, electronic or mechanical, including photocopying, recording, or by any information retrieval system without written permission of the publisher.

Published by Clandestine Books Limited

For more copies of this book, please contact:
info@clandestine-books.co.uk
For general enquiries or to report errors, please email:
info@clandestine-books.co.uk

Interior designed and set by Clandestine Books
www.clandestine-books.co.uk

Cover art by Piere d'Arterie

The Embers of Time

Clandestine Books Limited
Peter Knyte

DEDICATION

For H. Rider Haggard, Alexander Dumas, Jules Verne,
Bram Stoker, Nikolai Tolstoy, A.A. Milne, Jonathan Swift,
Mary Shelley, John Buchan, John Wyndham and Anthony
Hope for the years of entertainment and inspiration.

ACKNOWLEDGMENTS

With special thanks to John and Tasha Williamson, Lisa Bath, Philip Hall and Shirley M. Addy for the invaluable feedback and proofreading of this title, which has improved it in countless ways.

I hope I can return the favour sometime.

DISCLAIMER

This book is entirely a work of fiction, and while it plays fast and loose the names of historic figures, places and events, no part of this book should be viewed or understood to be factual, or attempting to be factual in any way. This story is set on other worlds of imagination, which at best may bear a superficial similarity to our own, and in all probability, will be wholly different and bear no resemblance to any actual people, personalities, locations, circumstances or events whatsoever.

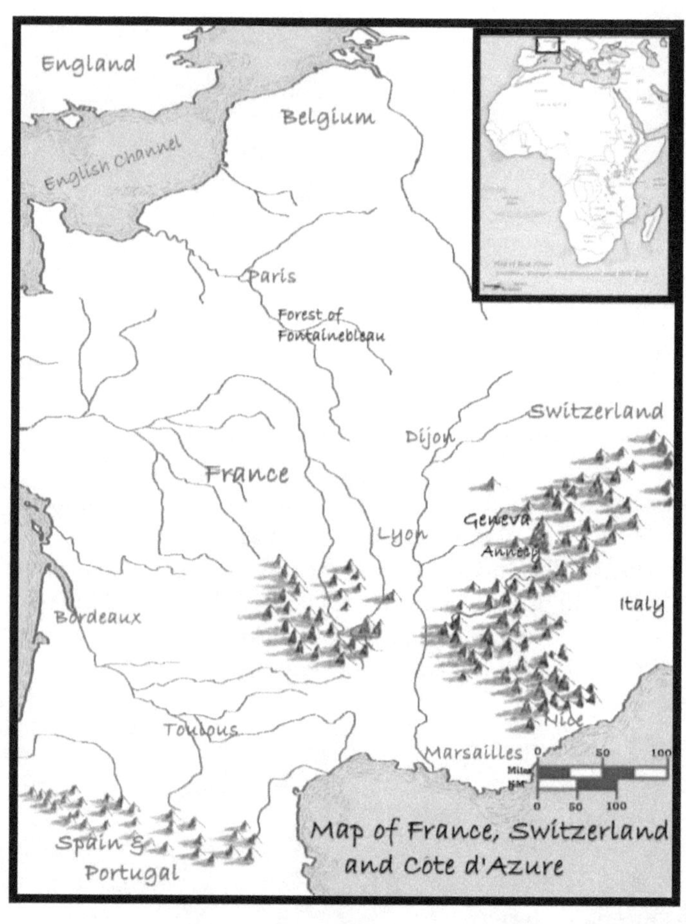

Map 1 – France, Switzerland and Côte d'Azure

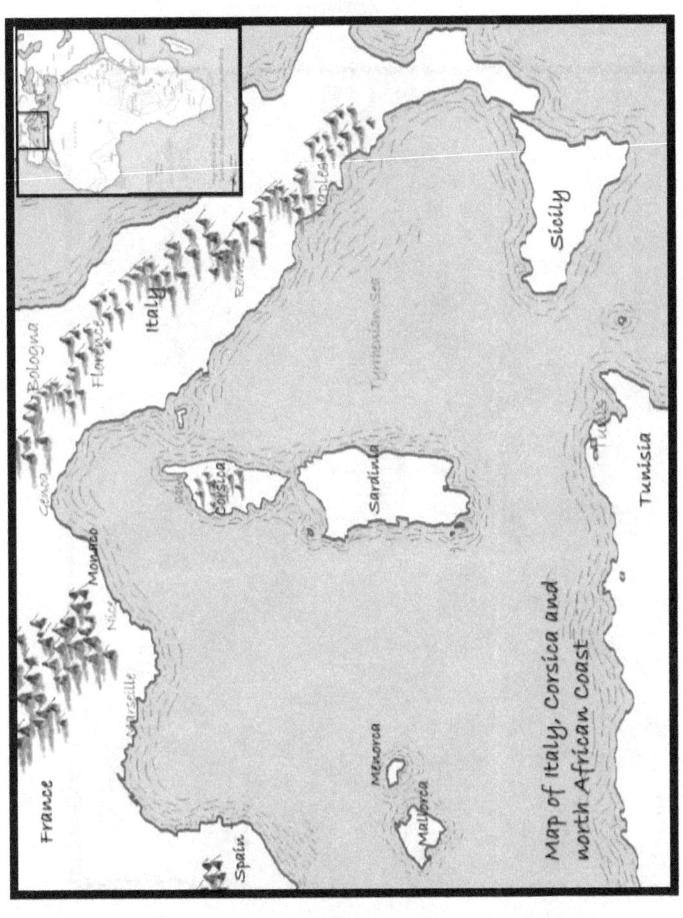

Map 2   - Italy, Corsica and north African Coast

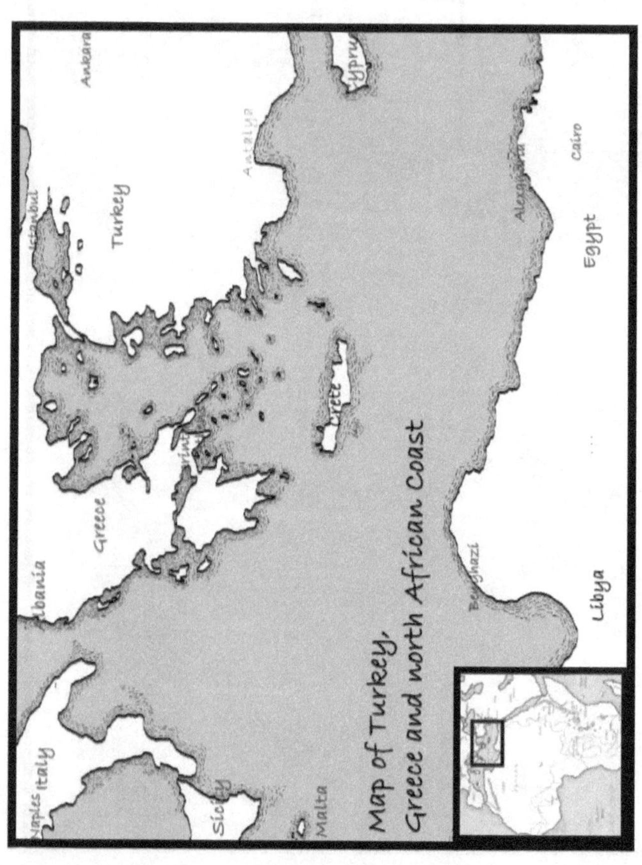

Map 3 – Turkey, Greece and north African coast

THE CHASED

I WAS THIRSTY, THE AIR WAS DRY, and the sound of the drums was all around me, racing against the thundering in my chest as I strained to keep my legs moving. The hunters were close behind me, and I could smell the copper tang of blood as I raced to get away from them.

Panic clawed at the edges of my mind as I crashed blindly through the bush. Unable to see where I was going, hoping my pursuers would lose my trail in the tangle of long grass and thorn bushes. But I was getting weaker, the pain in my side, from the spear wound, sapping my strength and dragging me down.

I stumbled, unable to get my legs back beneath me, and nearly went down, but somehow managed to stagger a little further, as much sideways as forward, and then it was all over. I crashed to the ground, legs flailing, unable to get back up, my lungs burning and heart breaking with the effort.

The hunters were close, I could hear the sound as they too crashed through the bush, closing in on me, with more spears in hand…

My skin was covered in sweat. The bedclothes plastered around me as I awoke in the small room that had once been my father's bedroom, at the house in Shropshire.

For a moment I thought I still heard the sound of the drums, fading into the distance, only to realise it was the pounding of my own heart.

I had been back for almost a year, the remains of the summer flying past, succeeded by the warm regret of autumn and the cold grey of winter.

This place had never been my home, and the life I lived here had never been my own, it was just assumed by me and everyone else that I'd find my place here, a routine, within its gentle ebb and flow.

But that was before I'd gone to Africa.

Before the dark red soil had mixed with my blood, and before the dreams had come drifting through the ether on the soft rhythm of distant drums to find me.

The time had almost come when I had agreed to meet once more with those friends I'd left behind in Africa, when we'd all agreed to come back together again and decide what, if anything, our fate was to be.

I didn't think it would be a hard decision for most of us. More than once, Harry, Jean or Marlow had expressed their doubts about ever being able to return to their old lives with friends and relatives. Even though these were people they loved, admired and missed, they somehow knew they could never go back to living amongst them, not without giving up some essential part of their own being.

I honestly don't think I'd really understood them at the time, my own home life holding so little by way of family or friends. But now I knew what they'd been talking about, and what Marlow had meant after he faced and killed that lion with just a sword in his hand.

Life back at my father's house would have been quiet and comfortable, and in time might even have become pleasant, but that rich red soil and those impossibly wide horizons had changed me, and the very idea of 'just' a pleasant life now left a bitter taste in my mouth.

There was still a little time before we had promised to meet up again at Jean's house in Paris, certainly time enough to put my affairs in order; to sell or let the house, to move the few private things that I could not bear to part with, and of course to once more pack my things.

The things I would need for a prolonged, if not

permanent, life away from England.

My solicitor was to take care of the house and its belongings, including the furniture and contents, with a signed authority to manage it as he would any other form of long term investment. The exceptions were my father's journals, and now also my own, which had been boxed up and stored away securely.

I had no way of knowing whether that mysterious organisation, which employed those dangerous young women, was still waiting and watching for any indication we were resuming our search, but discretion would cost only a little extra time. So, while I was preparing for my journey to France and then on to who knew where, I also went to the trouble of doing a few things around the house and garden to throw any potential watchers off the scent.

I began by planting some new fruit trees and laying some much-needed hedging. I also arranged for some decorating to be done inside the house, all the while ordering in my equipment and supplies through my local post office.

In order to further disguise my preparations I also made open enquiries about travelling to America through a local travel agent, even timing my train journey to London to coincide with a similar train leaving for Liverpool.

Whether my little subterfuge would be of any interest to anyone I had no way of knowing, and even if it did work for me, it would only take one of the others to be less cautious, and what little advantage it might deliver would be lost.

Jean, of course, could do little to hide our arrival at his home, but he would, I was sure, manage to disguise his own travel preparations.

The end of April finally arrived, which was when we had agreed to re-unite, and I walked out of my house for what was likely to be the last time, and into a waiting taxi cab.

As the car slowly pulled away and I looked back at

the place where I grew up, I found my mind concerned only with what might lie ahead, rather than what I was leaving behind.

The idea of once more meeting up with my friends, after the unfortunate way in which we had been forced to part company, preyed upon my mind.

Time and again, I found my thoughts returning to the question of whether our friendship would be the same, or whether our time apart had caused it to wane.

The journey down to London and then on to Paris was a simple one, and while I tried to be vigilant for any sign of those dangerous young women who worked for the mysterious Order, I knew if they had even half the ability of Selene, Miriam or Thea, I would have very little chance of spotting them.

I had only ever visited Paris once before while I was a child, travelling with my father many years previously. Unfortunately, my few memories of the trip consisted almost entirely of the fine French pastries and sweets which at that time had completely absorbed my attention, and which had, for a short while, convinced me that being a French pastry chef was surely the most glamorous and attractive of all occupations.

It was a pleasantly warm spring afternoon by the time I alighted from the train in the cavernous Gare du Nord train station, and then made my way to the exit with my bags.

I was a little peckish after the journey, and was considering stopping off for some lunch as I walked out of the station onto the bustling Rue de Dunkerque, when I spied an elegant little patisserie positively glowing in the warm afternoon sunshine.

My childhood fascination with exactly the type of pastries that would be contained within this bright jewel of a shop immediately brought a smile to my face. A smile which very nearly turned into laughter, when I considered how easily my second visit to this great city could result in very similar memories to the first.

But I did laugh a moment later, when I saw Peter McAndrews come strolling out of the self-same patisserie, with a very handsome-looking box of the bakery's produce.

'Peter!' I called out, before I even realised what I was doing.

'George!' he yelled back.

All semblance of our low profile entrance into Paris ruined in a moment.

'I just couldn't help myself,' he said, after crossing the street and holding up his trophy. 'I was waiting here to grab a cab over to Jean's place, and the next thing I knew I'd crossed the street and ordered half the shop.'

I confessed I had very nearly done exactly the same myself, and then as we fell into a light-hearted conversation about our shared childhood memories of Paris's great pastries, I knew my doubts about our old camaraderie had been pure foolishness.

We shared a cab over to Jean's house on the Ilse St-Louis, our bags and cases crammed in around us, with all the while the delicate white box of pastries placed prominently on top.

I think Peter was a little relieved to have run into me before getting to Jean's house, and to have dispensed with any potential awkwardness.

'So, George,' he began, looking a little more serious as we drew closer to the river and Jean's house. 'Do you think everyone else will still be the same? Jean, Harry, Androus, Rob?'

'I do,' I said, meaning it. 'If anything I think Harry and Rob will be even more eager to continue the search than they were before. Jean will be his usual pragmatic self, so will probably have spent some time considering all manner of eventualities that the rest of us haven't even guessed at, and Androus, I think he may just have stopped seething about the destruction of the scroll and the theft of his notes, but will otherwise be adamant that the truth must be revealed.'

'I see,' Peter replied, looking rather serious. 'So you don't think Jean will be upset?'

He had me for a moment, and could have strung me along for much longer, but Peter, unlike Jean, had at least a trace of civility when it came to his jokes.

'He won't be upset that I've brought cakes to his home?' Peter continued, before slipping effortlessly into an almost perfect imitation of our Gascon friend.

'You are perhaps concerned I will not feed you, mon amie. Never has Gascon hospitality been so cruelly misjudged…'

I could not help but laugh at the impersonation, despite having been taken in so easily, because I could imagine Jean getting into exactly that kind of melodramatic huff about it… before going on to thoroughly enjoy the very pastries that had so terribly insulted his household.

It took about half an hour in the cab from the train station to Jean's house, and we had started to discuss what we had each been up to for the past year when we arrived.

Jean lived in one of the tall old town houses made of pale stone that can be seen almost everywhere in the city.

It sat, rather grandly, overlooking the gently flowing waters of the Seine, and beyond that, to the increasingly infamous Rive Gauche, which seemed over the last few years to have become a positive Mecca for artists, poets, writers and philosophers from all over the world.

Jean must have seen our car arrive, because no sooner had we paid the driver than he was on the pavement at the bottom of the steps shaking our hands and leading us up to his front door. It was unimaginable to think of him ever changing, and as we greeted one another with warm embraces I realised, that with the exception of being a little less tanned and in his city clothes, my friend appeared exactly the same as he had when we parted all those months ago.

At the sight of Peter's box of cakes though, we both learned we had completely misjudged him.

'Ah, you have succumbed to the siren call of Madame Villandry's pastries, I see,' he commented, with a broad smile. 'A wise choice, my friends, and perhaps also just what the doctor ordered.'

Intrigued by this odd comment, we shuffled and stumbled our baggage and trappings into his house, with the assistance of a couple of Jean's staff, and were then ushered through into a spacious lounge, where we could sit and talk properly over coffee and sandwiches, provided by his housekeeper.

We did not have long to wait to discover the cryptic meaning of Jean's comments about the pastries.

Apparently both Androus and Harry had arrived the day before, and had popped out a couple of hours earlier, before Peter and I arrived, to stroll around one of the local museums.

I could barely believe it when they returned and Harry walked in through the door. He was practically a shadow of his former self, having lost a lot of weight in the last year.

We greeted one another as the old friends we were, and then settled down with fresh coffee and the cakes Peter had brought, to hear what had happened to Harry.

'It was the broken collar bone that started it all,' he explained, tucking into the sandwiches and then pastries with a will.

'I convalesced in Nairobi for a few days after Peter and Androus returned to their homes, as I'm sure you remember, but after I was discharged from the hospital a week or so later, I decided to travel back to the United States and catch up with a few folks, while my ribs and collar bone finished healing.

'Well, I decided to travel through the Mediterranean on the way to Le Havre or Portsmouth. Wherever I could get the next birth across the pond, but I stopped off along the way in Cairo, then Tunisia and Morocco just to break the journey up a little.

To begin with, when I started to feel lethargic, I presumed I'd just eaten something that didn't agree with me. I was after all trailing around some of the less frequented sites of antiquity along the way, and visiting some of the quieter restaurants and hotels in the process.

'We've all suffered with an upset stomach from time to time after eating something we probably shouldn't, and for the first few days I thought it was just a dose of the usual, so thought nothing more of it. I took it easy, made sure I stayed well hydrated and didn't stray too far from the hotel.

'But despite resting up, after another couple of days, it seemed to suddenly get worse, and by the time I got onto my Atlantic crossing, I'd developed a mild fever followed by chills, even though the weather was quite warm.

'Anyway, after another day of feeling terrible, I thought I'd best take myself off to see the ship's doctor.

'He was clearly an experienced old hand, and after taking one look at me, he starts asking if I've spent any time in Africa, or near to swampy ground or places with a lot of standing water.

'Well, half the old troglodytic Roman sites I'd visited in Tunisia were swimming in stagnant water, which still hadn't dried up after the winter, at which point I remember what a pest the midges and mosquitoes had been, after which, the penny finally drops.'

'Ah, le Paludisme,' Jean commented, shaking his head slightly. 'It was the malaria, mon ami?'

'Precisely,' replied Harry. 'But because I didn't twig to it straight away I'd given it the chance to get well-established before I even went to see the doctor.

'He prescribed the strongest medication he had available, but the next thing I know, I'm waking up several weeks later with my family and friends around the bed, looking at me as though my time on this mortal coil is up.

'The doctors told me afterward, that the pain killers

I'd been taking for my collar bone had probably masked the real start of the fever, and given the parasite time to affect my brain, which despite treatment aboard ship, had swelled up, resulting in me slipping in and out of consciousness for a couple of months.

'By all accounts they were seriously concerned about me for a while there, with me at one point even falling into a coma. So, if I hadn't gone to see the ship's doctor when I did, who knows what might've happened.

'Well, needless to say, after a couple of months of lying around on my back I was as weak as a kitten, and could barely sit up in bed for the first week, let alone walk. On the plus side my collar bone had healed nicely, it just took a few weeks before my arm was strong enough to hold a glass of water without shaking.

'It's been a slow and steady journey since then, but I'm getting my strength back now, though it's probably going to take a little while before my old clothes fit me properly again,' he said, patting his rather hollow-looking stomach.

We talked amiably for a while longer, as the rather slender Harry quietly polished off a handful of sandwiches followed by eclairs, tarts, then macaroons and dacquoise, much to our mutual wide-eyed enjoyment.

None of us had asked about Marlow yet, but as the last of the afternoon light started to fade with still no sign of him, I finally felt I could wait no longer.

'I don't suppose any of you have heard anything from Rob in the last twelve months?' I asked simply.

'I exchanged a couple of letters with him while he was in northern Spain, a few months back,' Harry confirmed. 'Enquiring about my health, and informing me he'd continued to travel.'

'I myself had heard nothing until a week ago, when I received a telegram from the very tip of Sicily,' Jean added. 'Telling me he would be here, but would probably not arrive until a little later in the day, and asking me to prepare a few things.'

'Did he mention what he was doing in Sicily?' asked Androus, rather quizzically.

'Only that he was on some tiny little island which was positively covered in Carthaginian archaeological ruins, and he was learning a bit more about archaeology, by helping with the continuing excavations.'

'Ah yes, this sounds familiar, but I cannot recall its name,' Androus replied. 'Harrison, can you remember it? '

'I recall it was just across the water from Marsala, and that the entire island had been bought by an Englishman so he could excavate it,' Harry replied, 'But I can't recall the details.'

'I believe it is Motya that you're thinking of,' chipped in Marlow from the doorway, obviously having just arrived.

'Ah, Robert, welcome,' replied Jean, springing to his feet to usher his friend into the room. 'You found my secret key without any problem?'

'I did, my friend,' responded Marlow holding up the key in question, much to everyone else's curiosity.

'I'll explain the details of my stealthy visit a little later,' he promised, handing the key to Jean, and then sitting down in one of the spare chairs.

'It is very good to see you all again, though I see that some of us have a tale of their own to tell,' he joked, looking at the new, slimmed-down Harry.

We talked a little more about the archaeology he had been helping with on his Sicilian island, and quickly recapped Harry's brush with malaria, before Jean herded us through to his dining room, and a delicious meal he had arranged, which by his own admittance was comprised mostly of traditional Gascon fayre.

As it had a hundred times before, the conversation rambled its way around the table, splitting and dividing any number of times. Jean regaled us with his countless forays into the latest artistic, philosophical and cultural thinking that he had been liberally submersing himself in on the other side of the river.

Peter then countered with news of the more practical developments in his home city of Edinburgh, the Athens of the north, with its almost simultaneous clearances of the city centre slums and the opening of both a new city museum, and the even more highly anticipated public swimming baths.

I had little to contribute beyond my planting of a few trees, but I was content to simply sit and listen to my friends, once more united, and engaged in the gentle exchange of raillery and nonsense.

I didn't have a particularly good vantage point from which to observe Marlow, but I managed to steal a few glances along the room all the same, and discovered him doing much the same as me, quietly sitting and enjoying the company of his friends.

Our meal was, in true French style, a long and unrushed affair with one course after another of rustic but delicious food, accompanied by equally fine wines, before the obligatory coffee and cognac to finish. Even the half-starved Harry apparently was satisfied by the end of it.

As pleasant as the conversation and the meal had been though, we all knew there was something we needed to discuss, and it was Jean our host who finally broached the subject, as he slowly toured the room refilling everyone's coffee.

'I feel I must once again offer my thanks to you all for coming to my home, and allowing me to enjoy a last wonderful meal here for what may be some time,' he said, smiling faintly as he looked around the room at each of us.

We all knew, of course, to what he was referring, and one by one offered a silent toast to our host in return.

'It has been a year, my friends,' he continued, thoughtfully. 'And as I look around this room I believe I see hearts and minds unchanged from when we parted. But perhaps it would be wise for us to be sure and discuss the topic a little first. Shall I open the windows so that we can listen once more for the sound of those distant drums?'

'For my part, Jean, there is no need,' replied the ever enthusiastic Harry. 'Even while I was convalescing back in the States there were quiet times when I swear I could still hear that soft rhythm on the night air.'

'I dreamed of them on the very night before I left England to travel here,' I admitted, quietly. 'And have done so on countless other occasions during the year.'

'Even I have occasionally half heard or half remembered the cadence of some incredibly distant tribal drumming,' confirmed Androus.

'And you, Jean?' asked Marlow, quietly. 'You who have often been the voice of reason, reminding us to be sceptical.'

'Ah Robert, it is true I am gifted not only with a great and passionate heart, but also with a precise and logical mind,' he replied, with a playful twinkle in his dark eyes. 'But it is also true that I am first and foremost a philosopher, and as such over the past year, I have continued to ask myself the question, of whether my mind has been sufficiently open to the strange and unusual things we experienced on our adventure together.'

'And let me guess,' broke in Harry, with an equally impish glint in his eye. 'Your mind is still undecided, but it can now see both sides?'

'Really, Harrison, for a man of such academic achievement your understanding of philosophy is still far too simple. But as chance would have it on this occasion my thinking has been greatly improved by a number of discussions I have had during our little sabbatical, and I must concede, that however inexplicable some of the things we experienced were, there is without doubt, both truth and value in this search, and as such I cannot in good conscience allow you to continue alone.'

'Thank you, my friend,' replied Marlow. 'Your support means a great deal to me.'

'Well, if we're all agreed that we should continue,' Harry summarised. 'Surely the next question we must try to fathom is where we begin? We have, after all, lost the vast majority of our information and research.'

'We could head back to the temple we found near to Great Zimbabwe to recover all the information captured on the walls,' Peter offered.

'I would certainly like to visit this site that you have described to me,' replied Androus, with unrestrained enthusiasm.

'I have already travelled back there, just to confirm it remains undisturbed,' responded Marlow. 'And I could find no indication it had been tampered with in any way.'

'Robert, that is a very dangerous part of the world for you to have travelled to alone,' commented Jean, clearly concerned.

'You're right, my friend,' conceded Marlow. 'But I was in a dangerous frame of mind at the time, and as dangerous as it might have been for me, I think you will agree it would have been an impossible location for our adversaries to have followed me.'

'All the same, mon ami…'

'I mention this,' Marlow continued, looking at Jean steadily for several moments, 'So that you are each able to weigh my next suggestion in the full knowledge that there is a genuine alternative.

'However, in contrast to the temple, which I suspect may contain a copy of what was written on the scroll carved upon its walls, the location I have in mind is one we're already aware of, and where a full set of the ancient lapis tablets are located, along with countless other artefacts that may be of relevance to our search.'

'Robert, I think perhaps you are mistaken,' began Androus, slipping into his professorial manner. 'My memory may not be perfect, but I assure you we have already sought and found all the sites we were able to identify from the scroll.'

'I do not think Robert is talking of the locations listed on the scroll, Androus,' replied Jean with an unreadable expression on his face.

'Forgive me,' responded Androus. 'But if the place you are thinking of was not listed on the scroll then how could you possibly know that there is a full set of tablets located there?'

'I know they're there, Androus, because it's where the people who took them from us take all their recovered treasures,' Marlow said simply, before standing up and walking over to retrieve the brandy decanter and glasses from the side table in the corner of the room.

'Let me be clear,' he said, putting the decanter and glasses down in the middle of the table and pouring a glass for each of us. 'I know that the tablets we found in Africa were taken back to the Vatican City in Rome. I know which archive they were interred in, and I'm suggesting we should break into the vaults where they're stored and take them back, along with anything else we find on site that may help us in our search or may make up for the destruction of the scroll.'

I watched stunned as Marlow then slowly poured a glass of the brandy for himself before sitting back down at the end of the table to wait for our questions.

TO GROUND

B UT… BUT…' I was aware of someone saying, before I finally realised it was me.

'I must admit I know more than a few historians, and archaeologists, who would give their right arm for the chance to look around those vaults,' Harry finally said, cutting off my rather inept attempts at speech.

'You realise you're suggesting an out-and-out criminal enterprise,' added Peter, slightly incredulously. 'No shades of grey or moral middle ground in the eyes of the law, especially in Italy.'

'I do,' replied Marlow, simply.

For several moments nobody spoke, we each looked at one another and then back at Marlow, thinking there must be some mistake or joke in what he was saying.

Finally, it was Jean who broke the silence.

'Natural justice, this is what you are suggesting is it not, Robert? You are proposing we even the score with Madame Agostine and the strange order of young women which she seems to command.

'I am not averse to this idea in principle,' he continued. 'But as Peter has already pointed out, that is not how it would be seen in the eyes of the law if we should be caught.'

'You are correct on all counts, my friend,' Marlow finally replied, with a gentle smile. 'But I am of course suggesting we complete our little burglary without getting caught.

'As for the other points you raise…

'Firstly, the ethical question. Please do not mistake me, my friends. I am not suggesting they have wronged us therefore we may wrong them in any way we see fit. In my eyes the question is a simple matter of justice.

'This Mother Agostine and the organisation that works for her, they beat us to the tablets on Crete by forcing Luke to betray us. They failed to do the same in Corinth even using the massive leverage they clearly had with the authorities, and they failed again with the tablets belonging to Nelion.

'Now if they'd beaten us to any of these sites fairly, by doing their research, following the evidence and discovering the tablets for themselves, then right now I would not be suggesting this course of action. But they have not, they have lied and cheated and stolen from us, and I propose only to correct the injustice of those deeds, if we are able.

'Specifically, that means reclaiming not only Nelion's tablets, but also those from Crete and the remains of those from Corinth, as well as any notes or paperwork which were not thrown into the fire.

'The recompense for the wanton destruction of the scroll we can talk about later if you wish.'

For a moment Jean looked as though he wanted to interrupt, but Marlow held up one of his hands while he continued speaking as a gentle request to be allowed to finish.

'Secondly, there is the law, and here Peter, I believe you are only partially correct.

'I say this, because the items we will be attempting to recover were stolen from us in the first place, and because there is a legal record of many of these artefacts being in our possession in Corinth, with at least one impartial academic witness, who would be able to confirm our ownership.

'There are additional bits and pieces of evidence, which I believe would at the very least plant the seed of doubt in the minds of any jury, as well as possibly sparking the interest of the international press.

'In contrast, the Vatican would either have to admit the existence of what is clearly a very secretive part of their organisation, or it would have to spin a web of equally detailed and convincing lies.'

I listened slightly awestruck by the case he was building, still not quite able to believe that he was talking about breaking into the vaults of the Vatican, one of the most sacred sites in the western world. But as he continued, I gradually started to overcome my shock, until I was able to think about what he was saying objectively.

Despite having lost a lot of the artefacts and Androus' notes and translations, we did still have quite a lot of evidence to prove we had in fact found and possessed these items. Not only that, we could also offer precise and accurate directions to a number of unique archaeological sites, each of which would help to corroborate our story.

We'd paid for board and lodgings at many of these places, with witnesses who could verify parts of our presence there.

We had also spoken to the authorities on more than one occasion, and while a large amount of the evidence we'd collected had been destroyed or stolen, there were items which we hadn't bothered to take with us. The photographic negatives of the pictures we'd printed, or copies of the photographs which we'd accidentally printed twice, not to mention some of the rubbings or early sketches taken of the artefacts which probably still littered different processing areas within the Armenian Library in Jerusalem.

It could work. . .

Morally I don't think any of us had a problem with the idea of taking back what was rightfully ours, but that would be of little consolation if we were to spend countless years in prison.

The more I thought about it, the more I realised the Church would never allow us to see any kind of formal hearing or trial, because at its root, they were in the wrong to begin with, so even if they were happy covering up the truth, in the face of the evidence we could muster, victory couldn't be guaranteed even by an organisation the size of the Vatican.

The others had started talking again as soon as Marlow had finished, but I'd missed what they were saying while I was wrapped up in my own thoughts.

It appeared Marlow had made a good case, and what had previously been so shocking was now being tentatively and objectively considered.

Harry as always seemed to have been swept away by his enthusiasm, but he was still thinking the idea through out loud.

Jean was sitting back and listening to the various

points being made, while at the same time keeping a watchful eye over Marlow, who was just sitting there answering the questions being put to him.

I don't know why it suddenly occurred to me, but I realised that neither Marlow or Jean were attempting to sway the conversation one way or the other, they'd both made their cases and were sat content to let the rest of us decide for ourselves.

'Why aren't you trying harder to persuade us?' I finally asked, looking at the pair of them.

'Observant as always, George,' Marlow replied simply.

'In truth, I need all of you to test me on this one. There is no vision or insight guiding me this time, and I feel far from indifferent about the way we were treated in Kenya.

'For supposedly civilised people to blackmail us with Harry's wellbeing was unconscionable, but to wantonly destroy a unique ancient artefact as well, was pure unadulterated brutality.

'To be blunt I can't put my feelings aside on this issue in order to weigh our options as objectively as I would like, and what I'm proposing takes us very close to the line between right and wrong. So, I'm not trying harder to persuade you because I need you to help me make my own decision.'

It was one of the frankest statements I think I'd ever heard from Marlow or any of my friends, and in saying what he had, in the way he had, it immediately changed the tone of our conversation.

None of us had forgotten how Mother Agostine had bartered with Harry's life, but in the heat of the moment I don't think it had really struck me just how uncivilised her conduct had been, but now, as I considered Marlow's words, I realised he was right.

Jean remained silent for a little while longer as we talked and considered the different dimensions of the matter, but eventually he shared his philosophical insights with us.

'George, you asked me a few minutes ago why I, like Robert, was sitting back to observe the conversation rather than engaging and attempting to sway your views one way or another.

'Well, I am now perhaps ready to answer you. . .

'You recall the lovely full-bodied wine we had with the cassoulet earlier on this evening, from Blaignac in the Auvergne. I believe you were all kind enough to comment upon how much you enjoyed it. And here now we enjoy a lovely Armagnac brandy from Limoges, an area not so far away from the home of our wine.'

'Can you truly bring every topic of conversation back to the consumption of food and drink, Jean?' Harry asked smiling.

Dismissing Harry's comment with a waft of his hand, Jean pressed on.

'The brandy, I think you will all agree is also of a fine quality, that sits well upon the palette, especially after a delicious meal. And yet, I do not always prefer to have brandy after a meal, occasionally I prefer nothing more than another glass of wine.

'Now, what has this to do with our current dilemma? I hear you say, Harrison. Nothing could be more straight-forward. Both the wine and the brandy are delicious, but is it right that we should consider which of these drinks to consume based upon which is the more likely to result in an aching head the following day? No, of course not, to do so would be to disregard the fine qualities of either, and just as importantly the mood as it takes us.

'It is I think the same with the proposition which Robert makes to us. If we are to decide which is the morally correct course of action we must do so irrespective of the consequences. It is only once we have decided upon our proper course that we should consider how to mitigate any risks to ourselves or others.'

'Well said, monsieur, well said,' replied Androus.

'But perhaps you will also share with us what you consider the correct course to be?'

'The answer to that particular question has been obvious to me from the very first,' replied Jean, without hesitation. 'To reclaim that which has been unfairly and unjustly taken from us, is both fair and just, and for myself I would have no hesitation in embarking upon a path that will achieve these aims.

'As for the secondary consideration of how we mitigate the risks to us of acting properly.

'It will, in my estimation require a significant amount of planning and good luck to achieve, but I truly believe we are capable of that planning, even if we cannot control our good fortune.'

We continued to discuss the matter for another hour or so, but with our thoughts focused upon the lines suggested by Jean the debate became considerably simpler.

From our own perspective, it was practically an open and shut case, but considering the gravity of the decision we were about to make, Peter suggested we also consider the perspective of Selene and her companions, and in particular whether there could be any rational justification for their actions.

This was an altogether more difficult proposal. But after throwing the topic around between us, it also came down to a simple point.

'In essence,' Peter began, looking around the room. 'The only thing we can think of that could in any way justify the actions of Mother Agostine and her organisation, is that of the greater good. If they genuinely had reason to believe that what we were doing would be harmful to society, then they would be justified in taking those artefacts from us in the way they did. Is that what we're saying?'

'We are certainly arrived at the most subtle element of the question,' agreed Jean, thoughtfully. 'But I would suggest "A genuine reason to believe" is still too imprecise a term in this circumstance. For some people, genuine belief, comes far more easily than perhaps it does to others. As such I would suggest a firm and absolute certainty is the standard.'

'Is such a level of certainty possible though?' Harry queried, in response. 'To me, that level of knowledge would be the equivalent of a parent stopping their child from placing a hand in the fire. How could anyone know with that degree of certainty what our search would even lead to, let alone result in for others.'

'Precisely, mon ami!' replied Jean. 'For myself I do not think such a level of knowledge is possible, and consequently I would assert that this Mother Agostine has acted unjustly, because whether deliberately or not, she has acted upon her own personal beliefs rather than the certainty that what we attempt will result in harm.'

I could see everyone thinking upon these words of Jean's, and then one by one each of us came to the same conclusion.

If the actions of this strange religious order, led by Mother Agostine, and supported by Selene, Miriam and Thea could not be rationally or morally justified, then by the same measure we would be morally entitled to take back the artefacts that had been taken from us, even if that meant going to Rome and taking them from the very vaults of the Vatican itself.

INTO THE SHADOWS

WE'D SPENT SEVERAL HOURS over dinner and discussing what to do next, so by the time we'd finally agreed to Marlow's rather breath-taking proposal, it was almost midnight. This, after an early start and several hours of travel, I must admit was making me think of retiring to my bed.

As always though our host was one step ahead of us.

'My friends, it has been a most lively and enjoyable debate, and I would like nothing more than to suggest we continue on with our discussion, but I appreciate you must now be thinking how a comfortable bed would be a very pleasant thing.

'And this is indeed what I am about to suggest, but at Robert's urging, I have also unfortunately to ask that when you retire for the evening, you do so prepared to rise again in the early hours of the morning, so that we may slip away from here under the cover of darkness, and with luck also the morning mist.'

'You believe your home is being watched by our adversaries then?' asked Harry simply.

'Yes, I know it to be so,' replied Jean. 'Though I must confess to only discovering as much by pure chance.

'I had been talking to a very promising young poet who, like so many of his countrymen, had come here from America to immerse himself in the cultural delights of fair Paris. On this particular occasion I was wanting to discover his inspiration for a pleasant ode to beauty he had written.

'Imagine my surprise when he explained he had recently had the incredible good fortune to have three young ladies of stately, even noble bearing move into the large apartment beneath his own, and while he had distinctly heard them talking in Italian, a language of which he had only a little knowledge, upon greeting them one morning he also discovered they spoke flawless and unaccented English.'

'And you discovered where this gentleman lives I suppose?' asked Marlow.

'But of course. He lives directly opposite the front door to this house on the far bank of the river.'

Even though I had taken my own precautions in

travelling to Jean's house, I realised in that moment that a part of me had never taken the prospect that we were still being watched seriously. And now, confronted by the evidence that we were, I was shocked.

'They must clearly suspect their warning to us won't keep us in check indefinitely,' I suggested.

'You think that by leaving in the small hours it will be enough to lose them?' Peter asked, more to the point.

'Perhaps not, but I have made arrangements that will make it difficult for them to pursue us, even if we are observed.'

Jean had arranged for the majority of our luggage to be spirited away during the course of the evening, while we dined in plain view of our adversaries in his dining room overlooking the river. All the while, working on the assumption that we would be leaving his home in the small hours of the night, irrespective of the route we might choose to follow after that.

We still had the essentials with us, so when it came time to rise again just before four o'clock in the morning, it was only a matter of quietly getting dressed, then making our way downstairs to the scullery on the ground floor at the back of his house, in the clothes we wore and with a single bag in hand.

It was a cloudless night, with just a thin sliver of moon and a sprinkling of stars to light our way, but the river mist had already started to rise, and while much of it remained bounded by the river banks, the occasional wraith-like tendril made its way up onto the island to glide spectrally through the darkened streets.

We would certainly have been an odd sight in the eyes of any gendarme who might have happened upon us. Half a dozen well-dressed and clearly well-to-do gentlemen strolling amiably through the night-shrouded streets with luggage in hand.

Fortunately, we encountered not another soul as

Jean led us confidently through the side streets and alleyways from the back of his house to the riverbank on the opposite side of the island, where a river boat was moored, its cabin lights shining brightly in the gloom.

Seeing us coming, the skipper of the boat stepped ashore from the shadowy top deck to quietly greet us and usher us down into the cabin. A moment later, after the engine coughed quietly into life, we could see through the portholes that the boat was slipping away from the river bank and out into the steady current of mist-covered water.

'Most ingenious my friend,' commented Marlow. 'Even if we had been followed through the streets, it would be very difficult for us to be followed on the water without our pursuers having previously arranged for a boat.'

'Precisely, Robert,' replied Jean. 'But we will not be aboard for all that long. After a little less than an hour we will arrive at a mooring in the Sevre area of the city, where I have arranged for my car to be waiting for us.'

Jean was careful with the details of where we would be heading in the car, perhaps concerned that our adversaries might somehow be able to eavesdrop upon our conversation.

For the rest of us, despite everyone still being a little tired from the early start, it was exciting to be travelling again, even if we didn't know where we were going.

Jean's plan went without a hitch, and more importantly without any trace of pursuit. Our riverboat dropped us off at a sleepy little yacht club, where a large saloon car was already parked waiting for us, the keys to which had been placed in the exhaust pipe.

We ferried our various items of luggage from the boat to the car and within five minutes were heading south through the last of the pre-dawn darkness, to a destination still unspecified.

Jean had taken the first turn at the wheel to navigate the complex route through the city suburbs and out into the countryside. At which point after he'd been at the wheel for an hour and with the sky now noticeably lightening on the horizon, Harry took a turn. Now freed from his burden of driving Jean was able to turn back to the rest of us to explain where we were going.

'My apologies for keeping you in the dark about our destination my friends,' he began. 'The house we are heading to belongs to a close acquaintance, who I would be very reluctant to involve in the enterprise we are engaged in.'

'That said, now that we are away from Paris, with no sign of pursuit I am happy to disclose a few more details. Firstly, our destination today is about another hour's drive from here, a quiet little village called Arbonne-la-Forêt which as the name may suggest is hidden away within the magnificent forest of Fontainebleau.'

'And will the lady who owns this house be there also?' asked Harry, from behind the wheel.

'Harrison, I do not believe I said that my acquaintance was female. . . But as chance would have it she will not be at home on this occasion, as the house is used only as a weekend or short vacation retreat, to escape the bustle and noise of the city.

'The forest is extensive, and the game hunting often excellent, so I have requested the use of the house in order to entertain my friends who I have mentioned in the past, and with whom I have spent so much time hunting in Africa. We are outside the game hunting season of course, but I have persuaded the owner that you would all still enjoy the forest even out of season.'

I think Harry and Peter would've dearly liked to find out a little bit more about the nature of Jean's acquaintance with the owner of the house, but that moment didn't feel like the time to press him.

The rest of the journey seemed to slide by the car windows quite slowly, and both Androus and Marlow nodded off for a short time, with me very nearly joining them as we were comfortably nestled in the back amongst the various bags and cases. But, as I'd never seen the forest of Fontainebleau before my natural curiosity kept me awake, watching out for any sign of what I imagined to be a fearsome ancient treeline on the horizon that might indicate its perimeter.

In actuality, the forest began more gradually, the occasional copse of trees amongst the fields slowly multiplied with the passing miles to form small woodlands, until somehow without me realising, we were driving along roads lined on both sides by mature trees, their great arching limbs forming a canopy of branches high above the road.

Arbonne-la-Forêt appeared to be a slightly bigger village than I'd imagined from Jean's description with a few hundred houses of differing ages, including some which appeared to be very old. Most were set back from the roads behind old stone walls or high fences and gates, and the house which Jean was taking us to was no exception.

Suddenly Harry was asked to pull into the side of the road while Jean went to open a broad set of wooden gates that led from the road onto a short driveway.

The house was built in a rather rustic alpine style with a stone built foundation and ground floor layer, topped off with timber clad walls above on the first and second floors, right up to a broad sloping roof with a couple of attic windows. There was also a wooden balcony projecting out on both the first and second floors, that ran right around the property except at the back of the house where it turned into a broad covered veranda, which provided ample space for both sitting and dining.

The grounds around the house appeared to have been carved out of the surrounding forest, with the garden behind the house being fenced in by a small wooden palisade that acted as a nominal barrier to the open woodland beyond. Here and there, large erratic boulders littered the garden, smoothed and rounded by their long journeys and now covered in moss and lichen to create a very picturesque and antique ambience in the place.

We unloaded the luggage from the roof and interior of the car and deposited our belongings in the bedrooms, before congregating in the kitchen for hot cups of tea and coffee.

While we made ourselves at home, Jean and Peter popped out to the local bakery and returned with a veritable hamper full of croissants, pain-au-chocolat, fresh bread, eggs, bacon, cheese, butter and milk, which we breakfasted upon heartily, before moving through to the lounge to digest.

I'm not sure how long it was before I dropped off to sleep in one of the comfortable armchairs, but it was long enough to see Jean place his fresh cup of coffee down on the stand beside his armchair, and then immediately nod off to sleep, leaving the coffee to its own devices.

We were clearly all tired from our early morning start, but after I'd dozed for a little over an hour I awoke feeling much refreshed and above all in need of a fresh cup of tea. So, leaving everyone else to their slumbers I made my way back through to the kitchen and made a small pot of tea before heading back out onto the veranda at the back of the house to enjoy the sunshine.

Now that the sun was fully up I could see the day promised to be bright, and I was sorely tempted to hop over the fence at the end of the garden in order to take a stroll through the woods, but I decided to wait for a little while in case someone else fancied doing the same.

The house was situated in a lovely spot, and it was just warm enough on the veranda for me to sit comfortably with my tea while I watched the birds and squirrels going about their business, though for several minutes I was kept on the edge of my seat by the sight of a large black cat with white shirtfront and cuffs climbing up onto the half derelict rooftop of an old barn, which I'd previously noticed the local squirrels using as a shortcut between two big sycamores.

Jean came out onto the veranda with a fresh cup of

coffee, just as one of the busy little creatures jumped from one long tree limb onto a tall wall, which it ran along before then hopping onto the barn's rooftop, at which point I was forced to direct Jean's gaze toward the unfolding drama.

'Ah yes,' he commented. 'I have sat here and watched exactly the same scene unfold upon several occasions, but I have only witnessed Daniel to be victorious in his hunting once, and even then, he nearly fell from the rooftop in the process.'

'You're on first name terms?' I couldn't help but ask with a smile on my face.

'But of course, we wily old hunters can spot one another from a distance. That and the lady of the house likes to feed him tinned fish while she is here!'

Daniel was once again unlucky in his hunting, this time outsmarted by his adversary who popped into one hole in the barn's roof and out of another while Daniel sat swishing his tail in vexation above.

Jean was in the mood for stretching his legs also, but rather than walking through the woods at the back of the house, which he explained were actually only a few hundred meters deep at this point, he suggested we have a stroll down through the town to book a table for an evening meal at a small restaurant on the far side of the village.

It was just approaching noon when we returned, by which time everyone had roused themselves from their naps, and moved through to the kitchen, were they were chatting amiably to one another around the big rustic table that sat squarely at its centre.

We'd passed a greengrocer on the way back from the restaurant and Jean had picked up a few vegetables to rustle up some winter broth for our lunch.

The topic of conversation as we entered had predictably already turned toward the task at hand, and how we might go about our attempted burglary of the Vatican vaults.

Harry was sharing his thoughts and barely missed a beat as we walked in off the veranda.

'Of course, we've got to get there first,' he was saying. 'And that could be difficult if they're on the lookout for us.'

'Yes, but *where* will those lookouts be positioned,' asked Peter. 'They obviously can't watch everywhere, so the first question would have to be. What will they think we're up to once they realise we've given them the slip in Paris?'

'Well, as I recall,' responded Androus, coming over to take a look at the haul of vegetables we'd brought back with us. 'If we'd failed to find what we were after in Corinth, we pretended we were going to head over to Andorra or the Basque Country of northern Spain, so that would surely be a target.'

'Mombasa and Nairobi would have to be on the list as well, in case we returned to East Africa for some reason?' contributed Jean, as he began to prepare the vegetables.

'Jerusalem, Haifa, Cyprus, Rhodes, they'd all have to be on the list of places we've visited and that we might therefore return to,' added Marlow.

'So, we think they might send their people out to practically everywhere we've already been, plus the places we pretended to have an interest in, but they might not expect us to go straight to their home in Rome?' I summarised.

'I think perhaps we are not giving our adversaries the credit they deserve,' suggested Jean, in an oddly cheerful way as he started to chop the onions with a practised precision.

'If the shoe were on the other foot, and we were the ones who had been given the slip in Paris, what would we do?' he continued, pointing his knife quizzically at each of us as he spoke. 'Would we simply sit and wait to find out where our adversaries were going?'

'Of course,' replied Harry. 'If it were us we'd stake out known acquaintances, family and friends, and maybe even use a little charm to find out if they knew anything.

'Chuk is probably the key for us to begin with, because he has the greatest knowledge of what was on the scroll, and is also the most able to translate anything new that we might find. So, staking out the library in Jerusalem would have to be a strong candidate still.'

'Perhaps, perhaps,' countered Jean, working his way through the celery and carrots with an air of infuriating nonchalance. 'But as I believe you were in the middle of saying, Harrison, when George and I returned… we have to get where we're going first. Surely knowing where we are starting from, it would be easier to simply watch the different routes and methods of transport that we might use to leave Paris and the surrounding area?'

'And together we do make quite a conspicuous group,' added Marlow.

This gave us all pause for thought. We knew our adversaries had official connections in Greece, so it was more than possible for them to have similar sway elsewhere, and how many groups like our own could possibly be travelling around France at any one time.

Suddenly I was feeling much more like a fish in a barrel, than the mouse which had just slipped out from under the cat's paw.

And there was Jean almost humming to himself as he prepared our lunch, as though he didn't have a care in the world.

'You already have something planned don't you?' I blurted, as I suddenly recognised the merciless workings of Jean's sense of humour.

'George!' he exclaimed in exasperation. 'Of course I have a solution already worked out, but you could at least have allowed me the pleasure of watching my friends perspire a little before forcing me to reveal it!'

'I know I asked if you could find a way to get us away from Paris,' Marlow asked. 'I take it this house isn't the final step in your preparations.'

'Robert, really you are almost as bad as George here. I have half a mind to forget my carefully laid plans and force you all to work out the solution to this problem yourselves.

'Fortunately, we Gascons are not so petty. So I forgive you both.

'Now,' he explained, while continuing to labour over the soup. 'The key to our particular dilemma is time.

'In attempting to escape the net which our adversaries will doubtless be trying to surround us with we have two choices. We may either move very quickly, and attempt to escape the reach of the net before it falls. This is possible, but in the process attracts much attention as very few people travel in this way.

'Alternatively, we may travel very slowly, allow the net to fall where it will, and then slip through the holes like the small fish which are of no interest to the fisherman. This creates nothing but a headache for our adversaries, because once the net is cast it will take a great deal of time and persuasiveness to keep it in place, and there will be a great many fish to deal with which are caught accidentally.'

'Alright Jean, so we saunter, stroll, amble or wander in the approximate direction we wish to take, but which direction is that and where do we go?' asked Peter, clearly far from being convinced.

'Patience my friend,' replied Jean. 'I have arranged for us to use the house of another close acquaintance, which sits on the shores of Lake Annecy in a village called Veyrier du Lac.

'It is quite charming at this time of year, and the local wine is the most perfect refreshment after several days of walking, which I am sure you will all enjoy after sitting so idly for the past day or two.'

I could see Harry was trying not to smile as he listened to Jean's talk of the lake and house he'd arranged for us to stay in next. But he didn't quite succeed as he voiced the question which I was sure the rest of us were dying to ask.

'And this house on the shores of Lake Annecy belongs to another… close acquaintance of yours?' he asked, almost dead-pan. 'But not the same female friend who owns the house we're currently staying in?'

'That is correct, Harrison,' Jean replied with just a hint of pique in his voice. 'Do you not also have numerous acquaintances with whom you occasionally exchange favours?'

'Yes, yes, I suppose so,' Harry replied, clearly reluctant to be distracted. 'And this other close acquaintance of yours, will she also be absent from her home when we get there?'

'Yes, Harrison, the owner of the house in question is also a female acquaintance, and no she will not be at home in Veyrier as she prefers to spend the winter and spring months a little further south in Monaco.'

Our trip was certainly illuminating another side to Jean's life, but as curious as I was sure we all were to find out more about these close female acquaintances of Jean's, there was only so far we could press him, especially as we were only learning of them because both Jean and his acquaintances were choosing to do us a significant favour.

While he finished making the soup, Jean explained the plan he'd conceived to slowly get us to Annecy, which essentially involved him dropping each of us off on different sides of the forest so that we could make our way either individually or in pairs to our destination, but via slightly indirect routes that would make us seem much more like tourists on walking holidays.

He encouraged us to put in quite a few miles on foot, as this would without doubt be the single most difficult means of transport for our adversaries to track, but we could break this up with short hops via bus or train.

Once we were all on our way, Jean would wait for several days and then drive the car and most of our luggage over to Annecy on the pretence of being on a business trip, where he would await our arrival.

We were each to take at least a week to get to the new house, but preferably no more than nine days without telephoning to let Jean know. The house had its own telephone extension which he was also able to provide, along with the address.

We continued to discuss the plan Jean had suggested, but by the time the soup was ready a few minutes later we'd thought of no obvious problems, so while we ate we moved the topic back to more general subjects, knowing that as pleasant as our reunion had been we would shortly be heading off in our own separate directions once again, though this time for only a week.

The following day arrived all too quickly, we'd each spent a little time the previous afternoon preparing for the journey by separating out the essentials we'd need to carry with us, leaving everything else to be brought over by Jean in his car.

I had volunteered to be one of the group that would travel alone, and was dropped off early in the morning along with Marlow in the north-western corner of the forest.

Jean had stopped for a moment to point out the paths we should each take through the forest that would in a few miles take me to a town called Melun, while Marlow, after a slightly longer walk, would arrive at a smaller town called Montereau.

As the three of us stood there about to head off in our different directions, it felt unnatural to be parting again so soon after reuniting, that I couldn't help but wonder whether we'd made the right decision back in Paris.

All that remained though was to shake hands and wish one another good luck.

BENEATH OPEN SKIES

EVEN IN APRIL, the forest of Fontainebleu was a strikingly beautiful place to walk through. The path I followed, while a little over-grown in places, was easy walking, and while I noticed the grass and earth near the path had been freshly turned over in places, I saw no sign of the elusive wild boars that were no doubt responsible for it.

I walked for a little over an hour to reach the edge of the forest, and from there another hour and a half along field boundaries and country roads before I entered the historic town of Melun.

It was an attractive place, built largely of a pale honey coloured sandstone that in the bright spring daylight appeared to glow with a welcoming warmth.

There was still a good hour until lunchtime, but I was thirsty. So, after crossing the bridge over the river into the town proper, I entered a friendly looking hotel with a good view of the street, for a cup of coffee.

The hotel manager was more than happy to oblige, and in the process asked where I had travelled from, and what my plans might be on such a pleasant day.

I explained to him that I was on a walking holiday, and had just set off after visiting a friend of mine who lived in one of the villages within the nearby forest.

After commending me upon such a fine way to spend my vacation, my host asked if I would be interested in a few recommendations for routes and places that I might consider visiting.

Too late did I recognise the glint of the enthusiastic

rambler in my hosts eye, and before I knew it he'd joined me at my table, and it was a full hour before I was able to tear myself away, albeit with an old map he'd kindly given me and several pages worth of detailed recommendations for places to visit on a generally eastward route.

Having stayed for longer than I'd intended I was now ready for some lunch, but not wanting to stop again so soon I bought the makings of modest picnic from a little street market on my way through the town.

I found the footpaths which the hotel owner had recommended, and within half an hour I was back out into the open countryside and on my way to Provins, another lovely old town that had apparently once been at the centre of all things champagne. From Provins I managed to catch a lift to Troyes, and from Troyes I had an exhausting and very wet walk to a small hamlet just outside Chaumont.

The walking had been wonderful while the weather had remained fine, but as soon as the rain came in, it changed the prospect considerably, and I started planning my course so that I could drop back onto one of the bigger roads, where I could more easily hitch a ride or catch a bus if need be.

The weather picked up again as I travelled from Chaumont to Dijon, but I arrived in Dijon half way through the afternoon on the sixth day.

I'd put off having lunch on the way because I'd thought the city was a little closer than it actually had been, so, feeling famished, I looked for somewhere nice to eat and resigned myself to travelling no further that day.

In truth, my legs were also needing a rest after several long days of walking, so all in all I was happy to have a nice lunch and call it a day.

For the previous couple of days I'd been contemplating the best route to Annecy. I was approaching from the north, and could either skirt around Switzerland to the west by travelling down to Lyon, then across to Annecy from there. Alternatively, I could keep heading east and walk over the Jura mountain range that fringed Geneva to the north. This would avoid any official record of my entry into Switzerland, providing nothing for our adversaries to find.

The route over the Jura mountains was also more direct, but I had no idea how hard a climb it would be, while travelling around Switzerland via Lyon was more of a known quantity, but would involve a lot more buses and trains if I wanted to arrive in Annecy on time.

On the off-chance that I might stumble across another local enthusiast, I asked the owner of the small guesthouse I was staying in, whether she would recommend the walk through the Jura mountains to Geneva, but in contrast to the font of knowledge I'd discovered in Melun, all I received for my enquiry this time was a polite shrug.

I considered canvassing a few other people, but as the weather looked increasingly set to be fair, I decided not to advertise my route any further, and early the next morning caught a bus over to a small village called Clairvaux les Lacs.

The bus took a good couple of hours, but I'd risen early so still had most of the day ahead of me.

Interestingly, Clairvaux was clearly one of the main jumping off points for walkers in the area, so as I strolled toward the mountain range I not only blended right in, I also had a few people I could discreetly follow.

While the mountains in the distance were quite impressive, I was relieved to see the walk up from Clairvaux was a fairly gentle looking incline, so I set off at my now normal pace, following first one group and then another that seemed to be heading in the right direction.

My legs, while still a little tired, felt much better for the added rest they'd had the previous day, so I made good time, and by early afternoon it looked like the summit was within reach.

I'd brought what had become my staple walking lunch with me again, in the form of a small fresh loaf, a little cheese, a small bottle of cider, and some dried fruit. Once I'd passed the last lot of people that I'd been following, I stopped at the next sunny spot to eat and enjoy the view down the hill back toward Clairvaux.

My bread and cheese were barely a quarter eaten when I spotted a couple of older gentlewomen making the steady ascent along the same route that I had just followed.

They weren't rushing, but they were chatting amiably as they climbed, a clear indication they must both be quite fit, and they greeted me with a cheery bonjour as they passed, which I returned with a small wave of my makeshift sandwich.

I don't know what it was about them that made me thing they we going all the way to the top, perhaps it was the easy stride and steady conversation while they walked up a good long incline, but I decided to follow them from a discreet distance.

With that in mind I had another mouthful of bread and cheese, washed down with a little cider, and then set off in pursuit.

My guides were relentless in their pace, and in no time we'd broached the ridge of the mountains and I was able to look down upon the shimmering jewel of Lake Geneva beyond, with its picturesque city of the same name lying serenely at one end.

I'd never visited Switzerland before, but if the view from the ridge was any indication, it was surely a country I would like to come and explore further at some point.

It wasn't just the contrast between the cloudless sky, the mountains and the surprisingly blue waters of the lake, or the attractive old buildings that dotted the shoreline, though each were lovely in their own right. Put these elements together with the clear spring air and bright sunshine, and the beauty of the place became almost intoxicating.

It was at this point, and with this view before them that my two elderly guides decided to take their own lunch, which resulted in us once again trading greetings as we passed.

There were several paths leading down from the ridge on this side of the mountain, but with no indication that the weather was deteriorating, and Geneva itself looking no more than another couple of hours away, I decided not to take the most direct route, in favour of a path with a better view, where I found a nice spot to sit and finish my own lunch..

If Jean had been with me I knew he'd have insisted on stopping at least once, if not several times in order to make a sketch, but in his absence, I simply enjoyed the walk and made a mental note to ask him if he knew the area when next we met.

My two elderly guides must have either turned back after their lunch, or taken a different path to the one I'd chosen, for I didn't see them again, but I followed the path down the mountain without issue, although my legs knew they'd had a good stretch by the time I walked into Geneva.

There was at least an hour of light left in the day by the time I reached the centre of the city, and on an impulse I decided to head over to the quayside to watch the sun as it set over the water.

While my walking provisions had been more than adequate, the one thing I'd been missing was a flask for a hot drink, so as I reached the quayside I was hoping to find somewhere that might serve a decent cup of tea.

Fortunately, the waterfront around the end of the lake appeared to have an abundance of restaurants and hotels, many of which even at this time of year had chairs and tables set up outside to allow their customers to sit and enjoy the glorious view.

As it was still too early for most people to be dining, the restaurants were quiet, with just a few people here and there having coffee, so I had no trouble finding a table with a good view.

While I sat waiting for my pot of tea to arrive, I

began to relax and watch the world go by, observing a few of my fellow patrons, and soaking in the glorious panorama across the lake..

It was just as my tea appeared, and I was pouring myself a much-needed cup, that I noticed a familiar figure walking across the quayside in front of me, before stopping at a park bench close to the water to sit and enjoy the view.

It was Marlow, but he was a little too far away for me to politely call out to him, and I knew he was more than happy to simply sit and watch the sunset by himself, so I resolved to leave him to it for a few more minutes until the sun had sunk behind the mountains, before I went over to join him.

I was doubly glad I'd stayed put a few moments later when, from the other end of the quay, a large saloon car pulled up, and with an equal mix of excitement and dismay I watched as three familiar looking young women emerged, accompanied once again by their servants.

Miriam was unmistakable with her long flowing red hair, as was the shorter form of Thea beside her, but instead of Selene the two women were accompanied by another young woman of either Arabic or north African descent. But while I was sure I hadn't seen this young woman before there was no mistaking the confident stride, and self-assured manner of another member of that strange religious order.

For a heart-stopping moment I thought they'd somehow managed to follow either myself or Marlow as they walked across the quayside toward us.

I'd been glad of the quiet restaurant when I arrived but was now all too aware of how exposed I was, sat at the very front of the outdoor seating area, only a few yards away from where these two young women who knew my face so well would pass by if I didn't move. At the same time if I stood up I would surely be attracting attention to myself.

They were less than thirty yards away from me now, and only slightly further away from Marlow, and there wasn't a thing I could do about it.

I sipped my tea, desperately trying to act as inconspicuous as possible, when the waiter returned to see if there was anything else I might want, by chance standing directly between me and my approaching doom.

I knew my only hope was to keep him standing exactly where he was, in the hope that Miriam and Thea would pass by without noticing me.

In desperation, the only thing I could think of was to ask the waiter if I could order something sweet from the dessert menu, as waiting staff would often memorise the list of puddings and desserts to recite to customers rather than walking off to bring back a printed menu.

My waiter was no exception, and without missing a heartbeat at my request, he simply began to list the various tarts, cakes and puddings that were available. It was a formidable selection, but by pretending to be struggling to choose I was able to keep him stood exactly where I wanted him until Miriam and Thea had walked past, obviously deep in conversation.

I ordered a tarte aux myrtilles from the patient waiter, thinking it would be best to stay where I was for another few moments until our adversaries had disappeared to wherever they were going. But just as I was beginning to relax, the trio seemed to start arguing about something and stopped in their tracks to thrash it out while their servants stood waiting behind them.

Unconcerned whether anyone overheard them, presumably because they were speaking in Italian, they made no attempt to lower their voices, so I could distinctly hear every word they were saying. How I wished my grasp of Italian were better. As it was though, I could just about pick out that they were arguing about whether to move on from Geneva or to continue their search for another day.

More interesting still, while it was clear they were looking for someone, it sounded like their quarry was female, as I was sure they kept referring to what 'she' would or wouldn't do next.

My mind was spinning with the possibilities, as they once more moved off and turned into the entrance of a hotel to continue their conversation.

The moment the coast was clear, I wanted nothing more than to get as far away from this place as I could, collecting Marlow on the way.

As if to grant me my second wish for the day, my waiter returned empty handed with an apology that the tart I'd requested had not yet arrived from the bakery. At which I acted a little disappointed, paid the bill for my tea and left.

Marlow, completely oblivious to the drama which had just unfolded, was surprised and pleased to see me, until he saw something in my expression that alerted him to the fact there was a problem. So when I told him we needed to leave straight away, he simply picked up his haversack and walked with me.

I waited until we were a good two hundred yards away along the quayside and had the cover of a small park before I even dared turn around and look back at the hotel.

After quickly explaining the close encounter I'd just had with Miriam, Thea and their new companion, I described the conversation I'd overheard between them and then suggested we should make ourselves scarce, which Marlow fully agreed with. But with the light now fading and the evening fast upon us it was a question of where we could realistically get to.

We started walking toward the south, the general direction of Annecy, hoping Miriam and her colleagues wouldn't have headed into a hotel if they weren't intending to stay there for at least half an hour.

We ducked through parks and down the quieter looking streets, talking through our options as we went. We could call Jean, but with our adversaries so close any prospect of him coming to meet us could be very risky. We could split up again, and head in different directions, and perhaps try to find a bus or train. We even discussed trying to find a taxi that would take us some or all of the way to

Annecy. It was probably only an hour away by car after all.

After putting a few streets between us and the quayside, we agreed the best course of action would be to simply keep moving. My legs had started to stiffen up while I'd had my tea, a sure sign I shouldn't do too much more walking before giving them a good rest, which I explained to Marlow.

We were still undecided about what to do in the longer term, when we stumbled across a few people waiting for a tram, which arrived just as we were passing.

On a whim we jumped on with the crowd to an area called Bardonnex, in the hope that we'd be hard to spot crowded in amongst the commuters.

The tram was quick, comfortable and efficient, and within twenty minutes we'd reached the terminus for the service in Bardonnex, a good eight or nine miles away from the quayside and our adversaries. There were a lot of other people coming and going at the terminus, so we didn't feel too conspicuous walking amongst them, strolling along with the crowd until we got our bearings.

Bardonnex was a well-kept and bustling little centre that had probably been a village outside the city at one point, before being subsumed within the greater whole. But it had a good selection of local shops, from newsagents and coffee shops to grocers, butchers, a tailor, tobacconist, and even a few guest houses and restaurants. There were also a couple of civic buildings including a small police station.

As we moved along with the crowd, trying to look as anonymous as possible, we managed to have a quiet discussion about what to do next.

'What do you think, George?' Marlow began. 'Should we go to ground or keep on moving while we've got a bit of cover.'

'Difficult to be sure either way,' I replied, thinking out loud. 'If we go to ground it gets us off the streets and we might be able to find out how we could get over the border. On the other hand, the light is fading and there are quite a few people around which gives us some good cover, and you never know we might just…'

We couldn't help but smile at one another at the sight of the sign which had just come into view ahead of us indicating we were approaching the border with France.

I don't know what it would've been like at other times in the day, but now while everyone was heading home from their day's work, there was a steady flow of people travelling in both directions across the border with no sign of any officials or border security anywhere. We just strolled across with everyone else into the small French town of St Julien-en-Genevous.

The crowd of people we'd been following started to split up now, and while there were still plenty of people around, we were once more faced with the question of what to do for the evening.

With the border behind us there was nowhere for our adversaries to camp out in order to spot us going past, so we started to relax, and after discussing our options again, we decided to try and find a small hotel where we could find rooms and a meal for the evening.

It didn't take long to spot a suitable place, set back off one of the village squares, only a few yards away from a local post office that had a sign in the window telling the world that it also had a public telephone inside. The post office was closed for the evening, but it did mean we could call the number which Jean had given us for the house before setting off again in the morning.

We checked into the hotel, which I was pleased to note also served delicious Savoyard cuisine in its restaurant, and I was finally able to give my weary legs a rest.

It was still fairly early in the evening, so I agreed to meet Marlow in the restaurant an hour later, giving us both a little time to go and freshen up before dinner.

After the drama earlier in the day, our stay in hotel Le Sauget couldn't have been more relaxing. Dinner was both delicious and very filling, consisting of a delicious cheese that was partially melted on a special stand in front of an open fire, before being scraped onto a plate of cured meats, vegetables and salad, and served with fresh bread. It seemed such a simple thing, but after a long day's walking it was delicious, and I savoured every mouthful.

While we ate, we exchanged the details of our travels over the past few days in getting to Geneva. Marlow it turned out had a very similar experience to myself, opting to walk for long stretches of the journey, though he'd managed to fall in with the owner of a river boat who'd carried him into Lyon, where he'd checked into a hotel that an English school trip were staying at overnight, before travelling to Geneva with them in their private bus.

Just before I'd seen him at the quayside, he'd spent the best part of the day trapped with a bus full of schoolgirls and their teacher, who'd offered to drop him off in Geneva if he'd tell them a bit about his travels in Africa along the way.

It was all I could do not to laugh out loud when he explained how the headmistress had completely ensnared him into entertaining her teenage charges for the entire trip.

'It's not amusing, George,' he insisted. 'Even now I still don't know how she did it. I wasn't even planning to travel via Geneva from Lyon, but somehow she… volunteered me!'

We relaxed by the fireside in the hotel lounge after our meal, with a glass of cognac each, before the conversation turned back to our encounter with Miriam, Thea and their new companion, and the strange snippets of conversation that I'd overheard and understood.

'In all honesty,' I began, trying to figure things out as I talked. 'It almost sounded like they weren't looking for us at all, but rather some female target.'

I don't know what I'd been expecting from Marlow in response, but it certainly wasn't the prolonged pause and the distracted stare into the depths of the fire before us.

'Rob, do you have some kind of idea about what

might be going on here?' I eventually asked quite bluntly.

'Yes, I'm afraid I know considerably more about it than I've let on,' he eventually confessed.

I knew better than to push him when he'd already come so far.

'I believe they're likely to be looking for Selene,' he said simply, before explaining.

'I've been struggling to figure out how to mention this to all of you, but an explanation is now clearly overdue.

'After we lost the scroll and the tablets back in Kenya, I walked in the wilds for a few months, staying with whoever would have me while my mind struggled to make sense of what we had started, and what had happened to us along the way. I experimented with the fire ritual again and again, and tried to persuade shaman and charlatans alike to help me.

'Eventually, I realised I was looking in the wrong places for what I sought, so I gradually started to make my way back into civilisation. Travelling first to Nairobi, then Mombasa, and eventually to Cairo, where I started to study and learn everything I could about the mythical and historic figures we'd encountered, as well as the societies in which they lived.

'I'd settled into a comfortable routine, I was learning how to read the earliest forms of cuneiform at the university, as well as studying maps of the ancient near east right across to India.

'Of course, I also tried to discreetly find out as much as I could about the Church of Rome and the early history of the Jesuit order.

'It was then that Selene found me. Initially, I think she just intended to warn me off from the activities I had become engaged in, but rather than simply threatening me, she attempted to reason with me and convince me to give up the search.'

He paused for a moment to order another brandy for each of us from the waiter who had come over, and I had to fight the urge to interrupt him, rather than just allowing him to continue at his own pace.

'Well, we met on numerous occasions, and to begin with she stuck to her attempts to convince and persuade. Gradually, without either of us realising, the persuasion turned into discussion, and oh so slowly into respect.

'She was incredibly reluctant at first to tell me even the name of her order, let alone what their goals were, but inch by inch I learned a little more, until eventually in one of our discussions she admitted the destruction of the scroll in Africa had haunted her. That the stated goals of her order were to find and hold such artefacts until such a time as the world was ready for them. They were never supposed to destroy such treasures.

'Now, with the benefit of hindsight, I think her reason for attempting to persuade me rather than just issuing a flat warning, stemmed from that guilt she felt over the destruction of that artefact.'

'Having a few conversations with you is a long way from being hunted down by her own friends,' I finally interjected, unable to restrain myself any further. 'Are you sure it's her they're looking for?'

'Yes, I'm sure, George,' he replied, with regret in his voice. 'You see, the order she belonged to is a strict religious branch of the historic Jesuit order, dating back to the seventeenth century. The Jesuits needed agents who were completely beyond suspicion, and who would ever suspect attractive young women of being the agents of an all-male military order? Even the modern Jesuit order know apparently nothing of its existence, let alone its goals.'

'And when you say "belonged", in the past tense, you mean she is no longer part of this organisation?'

'Very astute, George,' he replied. 'I had just been enjoying our discussions, and hadn't stopped to consider the risk she must be taking with her own people in talking to me. But eventually something in Selene's actions must've stirred a suspicion, and Mother Agostine or one of her henchwomen came to check up on Selene and observed us talking.

'It all happened quickly after that. They tried to send Selene off to some backwater location while they figured out what to do with her, but she'd decided long before then that her path was no longer the same as that followed by her order.

'She wouldn't or couldn't give me any of the details of what she was going to do, but she did give me the details of where our artefacts had been taken to in Rome, the buildings, the vaults, the possible ways in and the security arrangements.

'Finally, as we parted she encouraged me to lie low for a while as she could no longer predict what her sisters might choose to do, hence my retreat to Motya and subsequent stealthy arrival in Paris.

'She also gave me a rather tantalising offer to present to the rest of you, in the event that we chose to continue with our search.'

'An offer?' I voiced, unable to imagine what this could be.

'Yes, George,' Marlow responded, hesitating. 'Selene is still convinced the goal we seek is a dangerous one, which should be carefully considered and understood. But, if we are intent upon pursuing this goal she would like to accompany us, both to help us avoid further conflict with her former comrades in arms, and to continue her attempts to persuade us to leave this particular secret alone.'

I was already quite shocked by what my friend had been telling me during the course of the evening, but when he voiced this proposition I was almost too stunned to speak.

'I... I... don't know what to say, Rob,' I found myself stammering. 'Do you think she can be trusted?'

'Yes, for myself, I have no doubts,' he replied. 'If the conversations we had in Cairo were nothing but a ruse to obtain my confidence, then the morality of this organisation and of Selene personally would have to be nothing short of monstrous, and that I cannot believe.'

'I suppose in a way,' I replied. 'The conversation I overheard on the quayside does at least add some credence to the story. If she is truly being hunted by her own people, it at least suggests she isn't working with them anymore.'

A few other guests visited the lounge during the course of the evening while we talked, but for the most part we had the place to ourselves, so we sat before the glowing embers of the fire talking until quite late in the evening.

My mind was spinning with everything that had happened during the course of the day, and even more so following the revelation from Marlow that evening.

On the one hand it was reassuring to know that the Order, who I'd now learnt used the informal epithet of the Icarrii to refer to themselves, had been looking for Selene in Geneva rather than either myself or Marlow. On the other hand, the idea, and possible implications of Selene helping us, were just too great for me to absorb in such a short time.

We still had a significant and potentially risky journey ahead of us the following day, so once Marlow had shared everything he'd been keeping to himself, I thanked him for trusting me, and then we retired for the night, to get some rest before our journey the following day.

IN PLAIN SIGHT

DESPITE BEING DOG TIRED my mind refused to let me sleep for what seemed like hours, so while my legs felt much better the following morning, I had a dull headache that I knew wouldn't budge until I got some fresh air and exercise.

Having agreed the night before, that we stood out a lot less when we were travelling with the crowds of commuters, we'd decided to set off early while the streets would again be busy with people on their way to work. A decision I now lamented as I got ready for the day.

As for how we'd get to Annecy, we hadn't figured that out in any detail, so after a good breakfast at the hotel before checking out, we stopped off to telephone Jean from the post office before going in search of a bus or other means of travel.

It had felt slightly odd telephoning Jean, but we were connected without any problems and he answered the call quite promptly.

Using some code words we'd agreed upon in Fontainebleau, I quickly received confirmation from him that it was safe to travel the last stretch to the house, while I in return informed him I'd run into Marlow and that we'd be arriving together.

I didn't think it likely our adversaries would have the manpower to listen in on all the telephone calls being made across all of Europe, but we still made an effort to keep the conversation sounding normal, without using any of our real names or current locations, just in case. This would hopefully make it doubly difficult for anyone eavesdropping to spot that anything might be amiss.

Unfortunately, if there was a direct bus to Annecy it didn't leave from any of the bus stops we walked past, so in the hope of having better luck in the next town over, we hopped on a local bus that seemed to be heading in roughly the right direction.

The journey was a short one, only a couple of miles at most, and dropped us off early enough to still be surrounded by commuters in a large village by the name of Neydens. However, while small, it was clearly on one of the main transport routes to Annecy, and within ten minutes we'd not only found where to catch a bus, we'd fallen lucky again and managed to hop on one that was chock full of commuters on their way to work.

Most of the passengers weren't travelling all the way to Annecy, which resulted in the bus gradually emptying, and then filling again as we drew closer to our destination.

When we'd spoken to Jean, he'd guessed the bus would probably drop us off near to the train station, on the north-western side of the lake, not far from the Quay de la Tournette. From there we could apparently, find a boat to take us across Lake Annecy to Veyrier, where there was a small boating club dock on which people regularly disembarked.

Jean's guesswork was, as usual, uncannily good, and after getting off the bus, we simply strolled down the waterfront, arranged passage over to Veyrier, as though it were the most normal thing in the world. Half an hour later we stepped back ashore and strolled up the hill to find the house, only to be met by Peter and Harry who had decided to walk down and meet us.

I couldn't quite believe how relieved I felt to see my friends again. Though I was a little concerned not to see Androus straight away, until Harry informed us with a smile that Androus had picked up a minor injury on his journey over to Annecy, and was currently sat on a small pile of cushions waiting for the soreness to fade.

It was only a couple of minutes stroll to the house, but Harry felt he had to explain before we arrived, just to try and spare his friend's blushes.

Apparently after being dropped off by Jean, both Harry and Androus, who'd decided to travel together, had gone off to buy a couple of bicycles upon which they intended to ride to Annecy. This had proved all well and good for Harry, who had spent the last three months cycling and walking around the roads of New England in order to try and get his strength back. But for Androus, the sudden re-introduction to cycling, after not having been on a bicycle for nearly ten years, proved an altogether less comfortable experience, especially when they both got caught out in a rainstorm.

'We tried swapping bikes for a bit, once I realised he was struggling,' Harry explained. 'But by then I think he'd already reached the point at which no amount of padding on the saddle or newspaper down the trousers was going to help, so we just had to take it easy for a while. Doing a bit more walking, staying for an extra day in Chambery before trying to make the last step over to here.'

I really felt for Androus, and couldn't help but think of the time he'd also been forced to endure several days on horseback, when we'd made our way back through the Serengeti in order to recover the tablets hidden at the Singing Stones. We really would have to try and find a way to make this up to him at some point.

Being Androus of course, when we did reach the house, with the exception of the small pile of soft cushions he was propped up on, he gave no indication of the discomfort he was in.

As always, as soon as we were reunited, the conversation started to flow, and although it was still quite early in the day, it was clear we'd all had a slightly more tiring journey than any of us had anticipated, so without a word, we all decided we deserved at least one lazy day after our travels.

The house belonging to Jean's acquaintance was exceptionally comfortable and well furnished, with a lovely informal sitting room on the first floor that overlooked the pale shimmering blue of the lake.

Lake Annecy was nowhere near the size of Lake Geneva, but it was still a very significant body of water by most people's standards, and like all large bodies of water the sunlight reflecting from its surface seemed to lift the mood of the entire area, even when the sun was only partially visible through the cloud.

We settled down in this sitting room with some fresh coffee to share our respective tales of our journeys over to Annecy, starting with our usual mix of light-hearted discussion and joking.

Barring the issues Harry had already mentioned to us about the cycling, he and Androus had no significant other issues, nor had Jean when he'd driven over, but the same could not be said for Peter.

Jean had dropped him off in Nemours to the south of the forest of Fontainebleu, and to begin with he'd progressed well heading a little south and east toward the large town of Sens.

'I'd been quite enjoying the journey,' Peter explained. 'I walked between places for the most part, but had been given a lift part of the way, by a chap who was driving past me just as the heavens opened while I was in the middle nowhere, without a stick of cover for me to shelter under.

'He saved me a soaking, but in the process very nearly caused me to walk headlong into three young women that were cast in a very similar mould to Ms Autieri, Ms Sabbadini and Ms Galanis. In fact as chance would have it, it was only the allure of another patisserie that saved me.'

'Bravo,' interjected Jean, raising his coffee cup in salute.

'I must've walked into the bakery at exactly the same moment that the car belonging to our adversaries pulled up outside the hotel next door.' Peter continued, returning the salute with his own cup. 'It was only by chance that I happened to look in the mirror behind the counter and saw the young women decamp from their vehicle and head in different directions toward the three nearest hotels, including the one next to the bakery I was standing in.

'Well, I couldn't very well linger in the bakery indefinitely, so after paying for my purchase, I walked toward the exit desperately trying to think of some excuse to stay in the shop, when I suddenly remembered I was almost out of tobacco, so turned back to the proprietor behind the counter to ask if she might be able to direct me toward a local tobacconist.

'Fortunately for me, the nearest shop was closed temporarily so the directions to the next one took a few minutes for her to explain, by which time I noticed in the mirror again, those three women returning to their car.'

'How on earth did you proceed after discovering they were checking the hotels?' I asked, wondering how close I may have come to being discovered myself.

'Well, I was stumped at first,' Peter replied. 'So with no better idea I made my way to the tobacconist I'd been directed to, to re-stock my supply, after which I just kept on walking, keeping away from the bigger roads until I found a path that led through some light woodland, where I could sit down and think about what I might do next.

'I'd almost forgotten about the pastries I'd purchased, but after I'd been sat in thought for a minute or two I remembered them and, thinking I may as well make the most of a bad situation, I ate them. Well, I don't know whether French pastries are normally known to have a calming effect, but sitting there in a pleasant little woodland on a bright afternoon I realised that perhaps the situation wasn't quite so bad.

'Those three young women I'd seen may have been cut from the same elegant and poised mould as Selene, Miriam and Thea, but they were only spending a couple of minutes at most in each of the hotels, meaning they couldn't be searching all that thoroughly. They were probably just charming the owner with some story or other. But if that were the case all I'd have to do was disguise my identity a little, so that nobody would associate me with the description they might be using.

'Feeling a little more relaxed, I continued on through the woods for a while, and by the time I emerged onto a broad footpath, I'd decided to borrow the persona of a chap I'd run into while I was on a big engineering job over in Portugal. Thus, I became Frederick Erskine, a New Zealander of Scottish Highland descent. He was an eccentric character to talk to, with a passion for single malt whisky, and an accomplished structural engineer with a speciality in road bridges.

'With Frederick as my new travelling name and a ready-made background that I could adopt, I was confident I could carry the part when checking into hotels and guest houses.

'I was still vigilant of course, but I only had one other encounter with our adversaries, and that was just a couple of days ago when I was coming through Lyon.

'I'd hopped on a bus for the last stretch into the city, but before we'd arrived at the stop where everyone would get off, the bus came to a halt for a minute or two because of some delivery truck which was blocking the road, when who should I spot just about to get into another car but Thea and Miriam, with another one of their number instead of Selene.

'I could only have been twenty yards away from them, but the bus was packed to bursting and the centre of Lyon was crowded, so there was little chance of them spotting me, but this second near miss still sent a chill down my spine all the same.

'They must have already finished checking the hotels in Lyon, because as the congestion died down they got back into their car and headed off without stopping to check anywhere else further down the long market square.'

'That can only have been half a day or so before we arrived in Lyon ourselves,' Harry remarked.

'Yes indeed,' replied Jean, more thoughtfully. 'But I am more intrigued by the fact that Mademoiselle Autieri was no longer accompanying her former colleagues. But instead another had joined their number.'

I couldn't help but look at Marlow as Jean said this, unsure whether the things he'd told me were disclosed in some kind of confidence, but after a momentary hesitation, he confessed there were events he hadn't mentioned previously that may have a direct bearing upon that very fact.

After he'd explained what had happened in Cairo and had answered a few questions, we together explained the close call we'd also had with Miriam, Thea and their new third, as well as the snippets of conversation I'd overheard suggesting they might be paying as much if not more attention to tracking down Selene than they were to finding us.

'I take it you have some way of contacting Ms Autieri about her offer of assistance?' Harry asked quietly. 'In the unlikely event that we might decide to accept.'

'Yes, she had placed a small advertisement in Le Figaro pretending to be a buyer of antiquarian books, if we decided to accept her offer I would simply reply to the newspaper stating I had a collection and where I could be contacted.'

'Most ingenious my friend,' nodded Jean with approval.

'And you trust this is not an elaborate trap or ruse suggested by her employers?' he continued.

'I do, but that is not the same as suggesting I believe we should accept her offer,' Marlow replied.

'While I don't doubt Selene's integrity in this matter, or her intention to try and make up for the wanton destruction of the scroll, she made it perfectly clear she still felt we should take our search no further.'

'A very diplomatic answer, Robert,' Jean replied. 'However, perhaps as you have had longer than the rest of us to contemplate this question, would you consider giving us your opinion upon how we should in actuality respond.'

'Of course,' Marlow responded. 'To my mind we should not accept her offer.

'With or without Selene I believe we would find a way to continue our search. If the information she has provided about the location of the tablets proves accurate, then irrespective of whether we succeed in recovering them I would consider us even.'

'And if, as it appears, her own people are now

attempting to hunt her down because she chose to try and persuade you rather than to simply command you?' Jean asked, with a dangerous glimmer in his eye.

Marlow looked at him for a long moment before replying.

'Selene is a highly capable individual, as intelligent and independent as any of us here,' he began. 'So I do not for one moment think it likely that she will be found if she doesn't wish to be.

'But, despite her natural loyalties, her training and her upbringing by this strange order and Mother Agostine, I believe she has tried to do the right thing, the morally correct thing, and I don't think I could in good conscience stand by and watch someone being punished for acting in such a way.'

'Well said, Robert,' chipped in Androus from his small pile of cushions.

'Bravo indeed,' added Jean.

'I can't argue with you, Rob,' added Harry, with a gentle smile. 'But where does that leave us? If we take Selene up on her offer, we may well be asking her to put herself in greater jeopardy just to meet us. If we don't, we could be leaving her high and dry.'

Harry made an excellent point, and the more we tried to think through the options, the more elusive an answer it became. We considered various locations that might be more likely to be safe for both us and Selene to rendezvous, even though we had no way of knowing where she might be starting her journey from. Then we tried to think about the different ways we could respond to the newspaper advert, even trying to work out a way we could use the advert to lure Selene and those following her into the same place, so we could help the one and lay a trap for the others.

And then, as Jean came in with a fresh pot of coffee an idea came to me, and the more I thought about it the more I knew it had to be the answer. But that didn't mean I couldn't have a bit of fun with it along the way.

'You know I hadn't realised it was contagious,' I began, doing my best to channel the manner and posture of our most enigmatic Gascon friend.

Peter, who was sat opposite to me seemed to twig straight away that I was about to have a bit of a joke at Jean's expense.

'I beg your pardon, George, to what is it you refer?' Jean asked still looking fixedly at one of the maps we'd been examining on the coffee table.

'This Gascon sense of humour,' I replied, totally deadpan. 'I just feel it all of a sudden, it's like that first glass of something refreshing after a hot and bothersome day, it's quite energising.'

I could see the others cotton on to what I was doing then, and smiling to themselves, they all slowly sat back in their chairs to wait for the punchline.

'Yes, yes,' I continued, not giving Jean time to respond. 'Though I think perhaps exuberance would be a better word.'

'George, really you are making no sense,' Jean replied with a heavy accent of weariness to his voice. 'I am sure if you have something to add to our discussion it would be better for you to come straight to the point.'

This drew a very poorly disguised splutter from Harry who also failed to hide his smile behind his coffee cup, before Jean too finally caught on.

'Ah, you have perceived a solution to our dilemma, but you wish to provide us with the opportunity to figure it out for ourselves. Very noble of you my friend, very noble.' Jean now reposted to much mock outrage from everyone else.

'Alright George, you've made us wait long enough,' replied Marlow smiling. 'What's the plan?'

'It is of course simplicity itself,' I replied in my best impersonation of Jean, before reverting back to myself. 'We wish to retrieve the tablets that were taken from us, but we don't want to leave Selene out on a limb for trying to do the right thing, so we give our adversaries something better to think about!'

I didn't elaborate any further for a moment or two, I just let the idea sink in.

'Are you suggesting what I think you're suggesting?' replied Peter, slightly wide eyed.

'George, that is magnificent,' responded Jean, raising his coffee cup in salute. 'May I elaborate on your behalf?'

I nodded my approval, and Jean continued.

'Ah, but it is too perfect,' he began. 'We continue with our goal of reclaiming our lost possessions, but rather than attempting to complete the deed quietly and with our adversaries unaware of our little act of burglary, we reclaim the tablets in such a way that they cannot help but notice.

'We insult their security. . .

'We defy their authority. . .

'We ridicule their attempts to stop us. . .

'And in the process, we highlight that they have been so busy with their search for Mademoiselle Selene that they have allowed. No, encouraged this impudence to occur.'

It was all I could do not to applaud Jean's explanation, before I joined him in outlining the plan.

'At the very least we force them to divide their resources, and if we're lucky, they stop searching for Selene altogether and devote their attention wholly to finding us.'

Harry and Peter did actually offer up a very quiet round of applause to Jean and myself as we finished, while the others raised their coffee cups in toast.

The audacity of the idea had captivated and amused us all.

There would still be ample risks for us, but somehow now that we were talking about striking back at the Order in a way which challenged them to try and match themselves against us for a third time, we all seemed more comfortable with the proposal at hand.

It also in no small measure felt like we would be properly paying back Mother Agostine for the way she'd treated us in Kenya.

HONOUR AMONGST THEIVES

WITH OUR SPIRITS REVIVED and everyone feeling comfortable with the new goal, we got down to the business of figuring out how exactly we would break into the Vatican and recover that which had been taken from us.

Marlow began by sharing the information which Selene had given him.

'Firstly, you'll all be relieved to know we don't need to try and breach the walls of the modern-day Vatican City or start knocking holes into St Peter's Basilica,' he explained. 'The properties belonging to the Order of Icarus date from the sixteen-hundreds, when the Jesuit order was at its most powerful and most ambitious, and when the whole of Rome was governed by the church.

'The building we're interested in though is the Palazzo della Rovere, or more accurately the attached wings and courtyard that now lie behind it, and the secret catacombs which the Order has constructed below them.

'I know the area a little,' commented Androus. 'The building you refer to dates back to the thirteenth or fourteenth century, and now acts as the headquarters for the Order of the Holy Sepulchre, if I am not mistaken.'

'Precisely,' responded Marlow. 'Though the order that now occupies the Palace is more fully known as the Equestrian Order of the Holy Sepulchre of Jerusalem, with a mission to defend the Holy Sepulchre and other Holy Places within Jerusalem.'

'And you are about to tell us that the link back to Jerusalem is no mere coincidence?' Jean asked curiously.

'About that Selene offered no information,' Marlow conceded, before moving on. 'However, I can tell you that in the building attached to the rear of the Palace, is where the Jesuit Curia of Rome houses its main library, and at some point while these buildings were being constructed, it was discovered that they were sitting atop a natural labyrinth of tunnels and caves, which over time the Icarii expanded to form their headquarters.

'Today, with the modern Jesuit order being completely reformed, the scholars who work above ground in the library have no idea that beneath their feet sits a second archive of books and artefacts, laboratories, accommodation, even a gymnasium and training facilities.'

'It seems incredible,' commented Harry. 'How such a structure could have been constructed and continue to exist without anyone knowing.'

'Not to mention the dozens if not hundreds of people that must make their way down there every day without being noticed,' Peter observed, clearly wondering how we could stand any hope of making our way into such a place.

'Up until a hundred years ago you would both have been correct,' continued Marlow, replying to both comments. 'But the Order of Icarus has become a victim of its own success, and gradually, in pursuit of their goals they have succeeded in acquiring a huge stock of treasures which they have had to find space to accommodate, and in the process have had to convert more of their complex into shelving and storage.

'According to Selene, following the suppression of the Jesuit order in the 1770s the Icarii gradually moved their operations away from Rome in order to reduce the chances of detection while the mother church was at its most vigilant. As such, they relocated their training facilities, laboratories and many of the functions that required large numbers of personnel to other countries, where even if they were detected, nobody would understand or become suspicious. Consequently, the former headquarters is now staffed by a couple of dozen archivists and a small security team, with only the guards being present overnight.'

Marlow went on to outline what he'd been told about the different entrances into the complex, several of which were blocked-up these days, including one rarely used entrance just off the courtyard behind the Rovere Palace. It was retained purely as an emergency entrance or exit because its location made it completely impractical to block up without arousing the attention of the modern-day inhabitants of the palace above.

'The entrance is located at the back of a tool room just off the courtyard,' he continued. 'A small and completely innocuous looking room that doesn't even have a lock. Inside it, the grounds keeper who maintains the courtyard is allowed to keep a few basic tools, but unknown to him the back of the room contains a secret doorway, which has a simple but highly effective locking mechanism.

'If we can get into that courtyard once the library and the palace are closed for the evening, we should be able to use the secret entrance to get down into the Icarii vaults below, when there's practically nobody around. Selene has given me a crude map of the vaults and where the tablets and other items they took from us were lodged.

They're in a sub vault at the opposite end of the complex, so we'll have to be on our guard as we make our way there and back, but from what I understand the place is now a complete maze of shelving and storage boxes, so we should find plenty of cover if we need it.'

'I take it this courtyard at the back of the palace doesn't by any chance have just a small wall we can hop over?' Harry asked optimistically.

'Not unless you can hop over a twenty-five-foot-high stone and brick-built wall, with a set of iron-shod solid oak gates that are big enough to drive a coach and horses through,' replied Marlow with a smile.

'Suspected that might be the case,' replied Harry.

'And let us not forget we still have to make our journey to Rome,' commented Jean. 'As well as identify how we will get away from the city and the country once our little robbery is complete.'

Over the next few days we got down to work proper, splitting what we needed to do down into the three main jobs. Getting to Rome, getting into the courtyard and the secret vaults, and getting away from Rome with the tablets.

We thought about working on the different jobs separately, but with each step being potentially dependent upon the one before, we could end up solving one problem only to discover we'd made several others for ourselves in the process, so instead decided to work on them as a group one at a time.

Now that we suspected the Icarii were dividing their energies between searching for us and searching for their former colleague, the prospect of the trip south into Italy seemed a little less daunting. It would still be far from easy, but with each day we spent in Annecy we hoped the net that had been thrown around us would be getting ever more threadbare and ineffective.

The main checkpoints between countries would probably be the only places where we might still get tripped up, and even then if we timed our crossings for when the borders were busy with morning commuters and didn't all try to cross at the same time, we thought it likely we'd be able to slip through without attracting too much attention.

For the other end of the journey, in terms of where we'd go after Rome, hopefully with the tablets intact and once more in our possession, Androus suggested we might consider heading to Ankara in Turkey. It was somewhere the rest of us hadn't been before, but which Androus knew quite well on account of his family originating from near there. He still had friends in the city, including one with a hotel who our epigraphist was sure would be able to find rooms for us.

Travelling to Ankara could be done overland, but would be easier by boat as far as the Black Sea, and we knew the very man for the job in the form of our old friend Stephanos, who had helped us so much on our previous travels around the Mediterranean. It was possible the Icarii would be watching him of course, but it was difficult to keep tabs on where a boat went at the best of times. We reasoned that our adversaries, if they were there at all, would probably be keeping a watch over Stephanos' home port of Jaffa, on the off-chance we turned up there, but for obvious reasons they wouldn't be putting out to sea to follow him every time he made a commercial voyage or went somewhere in his boat.

The last piece of the puzzle was the thorny problem of the Jesuit library and how we were going to get into the courtyard.

Here we really struggled due to a lack of information. We knew there was a wall and gate at the back of the Palace, and we could see from the maps we'd managed to find that the building itself sat between the two roads of the Borgo Santo Spirito and the slightly larger Borgo Vecchio. But with all the demolition and construction work going on in Rome under the leadership of Benito Mussolini and his Fascist party, it was impossible to tell how accurate any of our maps still were.

We'd all seen the newsreels of the charismatic Italian leader talking about how he wanted to restore the Eternal City to its former glory. Demolishing much of the lower quality tenement housing that had been thrown up since the renaissance and opening the spaces around the great buildings and classical ruins so they could be more easily viewed.

What was clear from the maps, was that the Borgo

Vecchio as the main thoroughfare connecting St Peter's and the Castel Sant' Angelo, would always be busy. In contrast the Borgo Santo Spirito, which looked very much like a back road, could be comparatively quiet.

On the maps it ran parallel to the Borgo Vecchio, and straight past the courtyard at the back of the Rovere Palace, but it was clearly narrower in places, presumably where the type of buildings which Mussolini was removing, had prevented the road from being widened.

Whether these buildings still stood, leaving the Borgo Santo Spirito as a quiet street, it was impossible to guess.

We spent the best part of a day poring over the maps and trying to match them to the details which Marlow had been given, developing some ideas and possible approaches which we could refine once we got to Rome, but it quickly became clear we just didn't have enough detail to come up with even the vaguest of plans. What we really needed to do was reconnoitre the area first hand.

It was still time well spent. Since from the maps we were able to glean enough information to allow us to identify a number of hotels which might make a good base of operations, places that would give us ample opportunity to walk past the Palazzo della Rovere courtyard without raising suspicion. There was even one place located on the same street, that appeared to overlook the courtyard entrance, which would be invaluable if we could arrange at least one room at the front of the hotel.

Over the next few days we made our preparations, sending telegrams to Stephanos at the port in Jaffa, as well as the hotel in Ankara which Androus' relation owned, and selecting those belongings we wouldn't need until we reached Ankara to send-on ahead of us, so that we would attract less attention while travelling to Rome.

We needed to travel into Annecy itself to send the telegrams, and would have to travel in a second time to pick up the responses, which increased our chances of running into Miriam and Thea with their new third, or for that matter one of the other groups that Mother Agostine might have sent into the area.

There was no way to ensure we wouldn't run into our adversaries altogether, not without compromising our plans, so we adopted the same strategy we'd used before of splitting up into ones and twos and making our own way to and from the centre. Androus was understandably happy to allow any of us the use of his bicycle, as long as he didn't have to get back on it. Instead preferring to travel in the comfort of a boat back across the lake to the town.

Once in Annecy we each had our own missions. Jean took care of the telegrams, Marlow found a local travel agency to sort out our hotel bookings, Androus and I found the public library to review any newspapers and magazines which made any mention of the demolition or construction work currently taking place in Rome. Peter and Harry went hunting for provisions to last us a few days, and to see if they could find a bookshop selling larger scale or newer maps of the Eternal City.

On the days in between our trips into Annecy we reviewed all the additional information we could find, slowly building a better and more detailed understanding of what was happening in Rome and how it might impact on our own plans. We also tried to act like ordinary tourists visiting the area to enjoy the natural beauty of the place, which it has to be said, was considerable.

Walking up into the heavily wooded hills and mountains around the lake was a joy in the bright spring sunshine, which not only made the alpine countryside look lovely, but also made the clear waters of the lake glow with a rich blue that half reminded me of the lapis lazuli tablets we were going to so much trouble to recover.

The time passed in a delightful blend of activity and ease which made the days seem to flash by. Jean and Androus were wonders in the kitchen, cooking some delicious food which even seemed to satisfy the irrepressible appetite which the new slimmed down version of Harry had developed, complemented nicely by the pastries which Peter or I brought back with us whenever we found a new patisserie we'd not been into before, or when we passed one we'd enjoyed previously.

Towards the end of the week we travelled back into Annecy to follow up on our actions from our earlier visit and were rewarded with replies from both Stephanos and the Ankara Hotel. Even the travel agency which Marlow had contacted came back with a good list of hotels in the area of Rome we wanted, including the one which overlooked the courtyard we were so interested in.

We also managed to travel both into and out of the town again with no hint of the Icarii, which made us start to wonder whether our adversaries were still looking for us at all, or had now focused their entire attention upon hunting down their former comrade in arms.

Either way, with everything we'd been trying to arrange now having fallen into place it was fast approaching the time for us to make our own next move, and begin the journey to Rome.

It was too late to set off that day, once returned from Annecy, so we fell into our usual routine of 'helping' Jean to cook dinner.

This usually took the form of lounging around the kitchen with a glass of something, ready to jump at the chef's orders while simultaneously playing the ages old game of trying to be the last person put to work, by giving the impression of being the most willing and the least relaxed.

A fine-looking chicken was on the menu for the evening, to be served along with some lentils and assorted roasted vegetables, so there was the usual peeling, scrubbing and rinsing to be done along with some gentle fetching and carrying.

Jean was like a general marshalling his troops on the battlefield, and even Androus, whose injuries and general enthusiasm for good food, had spared him in the past, was this evening pressed into heroic service creating a fresh vegetable stock in which Jean could cook the lentils.

But as I absently peeled the potatoes I'd been asked to prepare, I couldn't help but notice Jean looking over from time to time as though about to say something but then stopping himself. I couldn't have said exactly what it was he was considering, but there was something about his expression when he did this that made me think there was a fresh topic he wanted to raise with us.

'It must be a thorny issue, Jean, for even you to hesitate,' I finally commented, while apparently intent upon the particularly knobbly potato in front of me.

'Ah, George, you have read my mind once again. What was it that gave me away this time?'

I responded with a shrug of appropriate vagueness by way of a response, hoping to encourage him to just get whatever it was he wanted to talk about off his chest.

'It matters not,' he replied, drying his hands on a cloth before turning to regard us all squarely. 'In actuality, there is a topic I have been trying to find the opportune moment to raise, but in delaying I have perhaps given myself the time to think too much about it.

'We are travelling to Rome, and in preparation we have researched and prepared a great deal, but I believe there is one additional topic which we should consider before our departure.

'Specifically,' he continued, after taking a breath. 'I have been wondering whether we should contact Luke while we are in the city he calls home.'

As soon as he said Luke's name, I knew he was right to have raised it, and couldn't quite believe it hadn't occurred to me or any of the others before now.

'You're not suggesting he might want to join us on our search again?' Harry asked, sounding as though he already knew the answer.

'No, my friend,' Jean replied, earnestly. 'Merely, that as a friend we should contact him before arriving in the city of his home, perhaps to arrange a meeting, but nothing more.'

'That would be a nice thing to do, Jean. Thank you for mentioning it,' Marlow replied.

It was a delicate subject, and the more we thought about it and discussed it the more delicate it seemed to become.

Oddly, none of us felt there was any doubt about whether Luke could be trusted with the truth of why we were in Rome. It might've taken him a while to realise that spying on us for the Icarii was wrong, but now he'd realised it, there was no way he would consider betraying us to them again.

Having said that, Luke had always been very clear that he felt the goal of our search, this search for the secret of everlasting life, was simply wrong, and not something we should be pursuing. This put us in the tricky situation of wanting to see him, without wanting to rub his face in the fact that we continued our search, and were in Rome specifically to obtain something that would further that search.

'I can't believe it didn't occur to me to look him up during the last year,' commented Peter. 'I could've invited him to Edinburgh or popped over to Rome to see him, but the thought never entered my head.'

'It was probably best that you kept the low profile you did, mon ami,' replied Jean, sympathetically. 'At the time there was no knowing how this Order of Icarus would take to you attempting to re-kindle your acquaintance with someone who had so clearly rejected their ideology.'

'So we have to leave it to Luke to decide how much he would like to know?' summed up Harry, questioningly.

We'd booked our rooms at the Hotel Artemisia in Rome for four days' time, with the intention of spending at least two days travelling to Rome via the coastal roads on the western side of Italy. They would be long days of being stuck in Jean's car, but we were still eager to start the journey.

In any event it was unlikely we'd be able to send a telegram and get a response from Luke in the time we would be remaining in Annecy, so instead we decided to simply write him a letter, suggesting a meeting at our hotel on the day we were due to arrive.

Jean dictated the letter to Androus while he continued to work on dinner, explaining in friendly terms that we would shortly be travelling to Rome and were planning to stay for a few days before moving on. No mention was made of our search, or where we were intending to head to next, just where we would be in a few days should he like to meet up, and that we would be travelling in the interim so had no return address.

There hadn't really been any tension before Jean raised the question of contacting Luke, but somehow, the simple act of attempting to rebuild our friendship with our former travelling companion, helped to put us more at ease about the circumstances which had led up to us going our separate ways.

DOUBTS

WITH THE LETTER TO LUKE POSTED, we spent the following day making all the last-minute arrangements we needed before setting off for Rome.

Harry and Androus made one final trip into Annecy to sell the bikes they'd bought for the trip over from Fontainebleau, while Jean wrote another letter arranging for his car to be picked up in Rome and driven back to Paris. He couldn't give any details about exactly where the car would be, just that he'd send another letter or telegram with instructions in due course.

I'd never much liked the time leading up to making a trip, and would always much rather be setting off than hanging around sorting out the details, but the time finally came and once again we all bundled into Jean's car with our remaining luggage.

We could've tried to navigate the more direct high roads to get from France over into Italy, but they were both exposed and isolated, so could be a bit unreliable, which unfortunately left only the more popular route to the south before cutting east to Turin.

Jean had some familiarity with the first part of the route, so he not only did the driving, he also gave us a running commentary on the attractions of the places we were driving past.

We set off very early and without breakfast, in order to get to the border with Italy at about the same time that it would be busy with commuters.

It promised to be another bright day with very little cloud in the sky, but there was a heavy dew upon the ground and a distinct chill in the air which made it feel more wintery than it looked. Once we got going though and the car had warmed up, watching the sun-drenched scenery glide by the windows soon made me forget the chilly start to the day.

'To the right my friends you will note the beautiful Bauges mountain range,' Jean pointed out, after about three quarters of an hour of driving. 'If we'd been here a little later in the year and perhaps under different circumstances I would've taken you hunting here, for slightly smaller game than that which we sought in Africa.'

This sparked the usual idle chatter amongst my friends as we travelled, but I found my mind wandering after a while and my thoughts turning again to the purpose which we had dedicated ourselves to. Here we were, travelling through France and shortly Italy at a pace that barely allowed us to notice the wonderful scenery, let alone enjoy it, and all in the name of trying to follow a set of directions laid down by some mythical figure who existed only in dreams.

For a moment it seemed the most foolish thing imaginable, and I found my mind dwelling upon some bitter and resentful thoughts, which it took me a good half hour to shake off.

In fairness we were beyond foolishness now, and deep down I knew what we sought was substantially more real than mere dreams. The tablets, the temple, the scroll, even Nelion were all very real, very tangible things, and that wasn't even counting the interest of a powerful organisation like the Icarii. In combination, these facts made it impossible to view our goal as anything other than something very real.

I still resented the loss of my carefree lifestyle for a moment, but when I cast my mind back to that shiftless, directionless state I was in, before I ever dreamed of setting off for Africa, and the mission I was now committed to, my situation quickly started to make sense again.

We travelled south-eastward around the Bauges to Albertville, then onto Aiton where we turned due east for a while toward Montgilbert, and then south again toward Modane and the Vanoise Massif mountain range.

I'd mostly shaken off my gloomy train of thought after the first hour of the trip, but as we started to climb higher into the mountains, on the way to Montgilbert, my attention was drawn towards the scenery, which wasn't so much gliding by the window anymore as crowding up against it. When we crested the top of the mountain pass and started to wind our way down the switchback road on the other side, the rocky sides of the road receded and I started to once more catch glimpses of a distant horizon.

Even framed by a car window this area of the world was breath-takingly beautiful, and the last vestiges of my melancholy were banished by the sheer majesty of the region through which we were passing.

Jean was either thinking the same, or saw something in my expression when he looked around.

'Ah, how I would like to introduce you to these mountains my friends, perhaps even attempt some skiing if the snow still persists, or simply visit the hot springs of Monetier over in the Guisane valley to our right.

'But perhaps this view of the valley below is not so terrible either?' he commented, looking over at me again.

Modane was the main route through the mountains from France into Italy, and hence the point at which we were hoping to cross over. Jean had travelled this way a few years ago and recalled the border being a fairly relaxed affair, much like the crossing into France from Geneva.

We'd set off early in order to try and get to this point while it would be busy with commuters, and our strategy seemed to once again pay off, as we not only found the border gate open but we were even waved through without having to stop.

A few minutes later and we were in Bardonecchia, where by way of a small celebration we stopped for breakfast and coffee.

We knew we weren't going to make it all the way to Rome on the first day, so we took our time, travelling first around the outskirts of the towns, then stopping off for the occasional break in a nice out of the way trattoria, coffee shop or hotel for the refreshments they offered, and more often than not also the opportunity to enjoy the spectacular mountain scenery which surrounded every town and village.

In this way we travelled from Bardonnechia almost due west to Turin, and then Alessandria, where we once again turned south toward our destination for the first day of Genoa.

Jean knew of a discreet hotel which he'd used before, no doubt with one or another of his acquaintances, and had managed to reserve us some rooms.

Even though we'd stopped off numerous times on the way to stretch our legs and get a bit of fresh air, it was still a long day of sitting in a car, so by the time we arrived in Genoa we were ready to stop.

Fortunately, our choice of destination was more than enough compensation for the long journey, so before we'd even made it to the reception desk the decision was made to drop the bags off and then get straight back outside to have a good stroll around the city before dinner.

It was still a while before the sunset, so after strolling down to a café on the waterfront which Jean suggested would make a good rendezvous point, we headed off in small groups to take in some of the city before meeting for dinner.

I wandered off in the same direction as Peter, through some intricately winding streets in the Caruggi district, where the stucco covered buildings on either side towered above our heads, and seemed to crowd in ever closer with each twist or turn of the streets.

The history of the place was palpable, and almost comic in the way it combined the ornately carved fine marble doorways and window surrounds in one building with the plainest or most weathered doors and shutters on another.

We walked at a slow pace while we shared our thoughts upon the different buildings we passed, although Peter being more knowledgeable about architecture than I, he was much better at spotting the features which signalled the genuinely ancient piles from the comparatively new seventeenth and eighteenth century impostors. A roof ridge going across the street was a sure sign of a modern impostor, while a sash window on another was just a modern addition to a genuine medieval original.

To me the distinctions were often too subtle, and several times I had to ask Peter to explain what he was talking about in simpler terms, but his knowledge reminded me of that which Harry and Androus had often shared on our various archaeological excavations.

The conversation between us had died down to a

sporadic comment after a while, and we walked in a comfortable silence for a few minutes before Peter suddenly piped up again.

'You're looking much more at ease with yourself than you were in the car this morning, George,' he commented, out of the blue.

'I didn't realise I'd been quite so obvious,' I replied a little defensively.

'Oh, if I hadn't had exactly the same thoughts passing through my mind at the time I don't think I'd have recognised what you were thinking.'

'You could tell what I was thinking?' I asked, more incredulous now than defensive.

'Absolutely,' Peter continued. 'You were looking at the many natural splendours of the mountains and valleys that lined our route, which Jean was so eloquently extolling the virtues of, and you were thinking we were all making a horrible mistake. Why should we run around trying to find some dusty old relic of a temple, no doubt located in some inhospitable backwater, when there were the delights of the Alps to discover, not to mention the more leisurely pleasures of a stroll through the French countryside and woodlands?'

I had to admit he was spot on, though in a strange way I was relieved it wasn't just me that had been having such doubts.

'Do you think any of the others still have similar thoughts?' I asked, hoping for some more reassurance.

'Honestly, George!' he replied, practically laughing at my question. 'You can be so perceptive sometimes, and as blind as a bat at others. I'm absolutely certain we've all had our doubts, even Rob has his moments, though possibly less frequently than the rest of us.'

'I hadn't realised,' I replied honestly. 'I thought I was just being a bit resentful of my own choices.'

'It's perfectly understandable and natural,' Peter replied, looking wistfully around at the ancient buildings that surrounded us. 'It reminds me of something one of my professors said, just after I'd finished my engineering studies at Durham. He was one of my favourite lecturers purely because he loved his subject and believed that engineering could and would change the world.

'Well, there was a big afternoon fete in the college grounds for all the undergraduates once the final set of exams were done, and I ran into this professor at the buffet table, so decided to tap his wisdom one last time by asking him for any parting wisdom before I went off to join the world of work.'

'The simplest and best advice I can give you, he said, is to be neither too brave nor too cautious in the kind of jobs you take on. Everything worth doing should seem completely overwhelming or impossible at some point. You'll think you've cracked the biggest problem at least once before an even more difficult and complex issue is discovered, and you'll question whether you have the energy and commitment to see the thing through to the end, right up to the point where it's suddenly all done.'

'And was he right?' I asked, feeling much cheered by this far from upbeat advice.

'Yes, but he did make it sound much easier than it actually is,' Peter replied, with a straight face.

I couldn't help but laugh out loud in response, the sound echoing off the narrow streets.

We continued chatting as we walked through the now fading light, with Peter talking about some of the more unusual engineering jobs he'd been involved in after he graduated, and before he'd come into enough money to allow him to take some time out to travel around Africa.

'It's odd looking back,' he commented in a slightly more subdued tone. 'While I was working all the hours in the day trying to get ahead, I knew I was doing increasingly difficult and challenging pieces of work, but I didn't realise until after I'd given it all up just how much I'd grown as a person in the process. How many skills and how much confidence I'd developed as a consequence of so often being almost overwhelmed.'

'Not to mention your considerable powers of self-control?' I joked, as his gaze lingered on the empty window of a tiny pasticceria we were passing.

'Oh, but George, wouldn't a few pastries be nice for our car journey tomorrow?'

It was all I could do not to burst out laughing again at Peter's increasing obsession with French and now Italian pastries, but it was time for us to be heading back in order to rendezvous with the others, outside the café that Jean had suggested.

It was a pleasant evening with good food at a pleasant ristorante overlooking the now dark waters of the Mediterranean. Both the conversation and the wine flowed freely, and we each enjoyed what we all knew could be our last carefree evening for some time.

The conversation roamed over a good many topics during the course of the evening, but not once did anyone mention our goals while in Rome, or the risks we were about to take in attempting to achieve them. Of Peter's burgeoning pastry addiction and Jean's mysterious 'close acquaintances' there was much good-natured humour. But in the end, it was the topic we spent the entire evening avoiding which told more clearly than anything else that Peter had been right.

ALL ROADS

WE ENTERED THE OUTSKIRTS of Rome just as its citizens were finishing work for the day and heading home through the diminishing late afternoon light.

We'd followed the coast roads all the way from Genoa, around the walled city of Lucca, then Pisa, Prombino and Grosseto before stopping off at Ostia to briefly rendezvous with Stephanos, who had arrived that same morning, before we headed on to Rome.

But while the day had started with another bright blue-bird sky. As we'd progressed south the clouds had started to appear and then multiply.

By the time we entered the city proper, the bright patches in the cloud were becoming fewer in number, between dark clouds that promised rain, and lots of it.

Whether it was the dark clouds hanging over us, or simply the knowledge that we had entered the heartlands of the Icarii, I don't know, but the mood in the car definitely changed as we made our way through the streets.

This was where the Order of Icarus had been born and the place where their power and influence would be at its greatest. For all our reasoning, we knew that being discovered by the Order here could place us in a very difficult situation.

As for the building work being carried out by Mussolini, I realised as we drove into the great city, how impossible it was to research such things through the newspapers, newsreels and magazines. The extent of works was simply enormous, and the tradespeople who had been employed to do the work were everywhere. Trucks and cars seemed more numerous than people in some areas, either moving between jobs or simply parked along roadsides that would normally not have a single vehicle in sight.

I thought we might just make it to the hotel before the rain started, but this time the crowded streets worked to our disadvantage, and the heavens opened while we were still winding our way through the Aventine area, in order to cross one of the bridges over the river.

When we finally made it to the hotel, Rome the Eternal City, famed for the way its pale marble buildings glowed in the ubiquitous golden sunlight, was a dark and dreary place comprised wholly of dull grey walls separated by inky waterlogged streets.

The overcast sky and constant downpour had simply drained the world of its colour, forcing those caught outside to scuttle along the pavements with faces turned toward the ground, brandishing anything that came to hand above their heads for shelter from the onslaught.

Even just getting into the hotel was a soggy affair as we hurried to unload the car. Thankfully the doormen were prepared with both sturdy umbrellas and extra hands to get our baggage into the foyer, but even so, we'd all had a good wetting by the time the job was done.

Harry unfortunately got the worst of it, as he'd been the one driving, and even though he'd managed to find a spot to park the car just down the road, he was positively soaked by the time he'd made the dash back to the hotel.

Thankfully, our rooms were prepared and ready for us, so our soggy arrival was forgotten as soon as we'd had the opportunity to change and dry out.

We'd all been given rooms at the front of the hotel as we'd requested, and they'd even managed to put us all on the same fourth floor level, which in ordinary conditions would've given us perfect views across the street, to the church of the Sancto Spirito on one side of the road and the library of the modern Jesuit order, our target, on the other.

Jean and Marlow had the best vantage points, as their rooms happened to be at the end of the hotel closest to the library, but we would all be able to see the courtyard wall, when the rain finally cleared, and the light improved.

There was still a little while before dinner, when we'd find out whether Luke was going to come and join us, so on a whim I decided to contact room service to see if they could provide me with some mint tea. Ever since tasting it for the first time in Jerusalem I'd loved the drink, with its heady aroma that never ceased to conjure up those first scorching hot days in the ancient city.

I'd neglected my journal since leaving Annecy, focusing instead on our plans for Rome, but I was feeling the need to straighten a few things out in my mind, which writing my journal often helped me to do.

There was a small bureau in my room with some complimentary hotel stationery and a few other odds and ends, placed between the two big windows that looked out over the rain-washed street below.

My tea arrived a few minutes later, but this being Italy, it was served with a small piece of exceptionally dark and deliciously bitter chocolate. As I settled down at the bureau with a china cup of the tea, the aroma of mint instantly worked its magic, and I immediately turned to a fresh page and began to write.

Our trip through the mountains and the crossing into Italy flowed from my pen, as did my recollection of the strange malaise which had gripped me on the way.

There was no sudden revelation as I sat and wrote, sipping the tea and occasionally glancing out upon the rain-clad gloom beyond the windows, but as often happened when I wrote, my mind began to wander and I found myself recalling the torrential rains we'd been caught in on our way back from the Singing Stones, after our encounter with Nelion, Lenana and Batian. Even now the memory still seemed unreal, but as I wrote and dreamed, my mind next wandered to the words which the three shaman had greeted us with, their meaning translated into English by my guide Mkize.

I recalled they'd talked of a path which we had taken the first steps upon, a path which had not been followed for many years. It was as they had talked about these things that we'd heard the soft rhythm of the drums again, and even now as my mind wandered amongst my memories, that second seductive heartbeat of the drums momentarily started to writhe and wrap itself around my mind before receding.

This idea of being on a pathway less trodden

seemed to be resonating with me for some reason, but I knew better than to force my mind to make the connection. Instead, I simply returned to my writing and the walk I'd had with Peter through the winding streets of Genoa, with its little Italian bakery and mismatched window frames.

And there the final piece of the problem gradually revealed itself to me. Why was the path less trodden? Naturally, because it was a more difficult path to follow, a path perhaps obscured by doubts, and blocked by necessary sacrifices, a path that had no guides to lead the way, and which to many people, would simply not be visible.

It seemed so obvious to me, and yet even as I brought my journal right up-to-date, I sensed it had already helped to resolve the conflict which had until that moment been nagging away at me.

I'd become lost in my memories as I wrote, but as I drank the last of the mint tea I realised the time was fast approaching when Luke would arrive, if he was going to join us for dinner. I couldn't say why, but I suspected he would show up, so I quickly got changed for dinner before heading downstairs to wait in the hotel bar.

The maître d'hôtel and reception staff already knew we were expecting a guest to join us for dinner, but after checking I was the first to come down, I asked the reception to direct Luke through to the bar upon his arrival, where I would wait for him.

The bar was an elegant space finished in the ubiquitous white marble and pale sandstone that graced so much of Rome's architecture. It was further accented with subdued lighting and a selection of comfortable chairs arranged around low tables. While in the centre of the room on a low platform, an ebony coloured grand piano stood in stark but refined contrast to the pale stonework.

There was a good selection of newspapers and magazines to choose from, including one in English, which amongst the usual political rumblings and speculation, had an article about yet another building project outside Rome under the leadership of Il Duce. Reading such articles was a habit now, so I settled into one of the chairs with the newspaper and a glass of bitter lemon from the bar, while I waited.

I'd chosen a table from where I could keep an eye on the foyer, and had been there scarcely a minute when Luke arrived and spotted me.

He looked very much like his old self, tanned and healthy as though he'd been keeping himself fit, with a genuine smile on his face.

'George, how nice to see you again,' he said. 'Please forgive me for being early, I had to take my chance between the rain showers.'

'Nice to see you as well, Luke,' I replied. 'I must admit I was hoping for a sunnier welcome to Rome, but I'm sure it will clear up before long.'

As the barman came over to see if Luke would like a drink, Jean and Harry arrived, and immediately embraced him as the long-lost friend he was.

Marlow appeared next, and in his own slightly quieter way seemed equally pleased to see Luke, followed a few minutes later by both Peter and Androus.

It was as friendly and light-hearted a reunion as any of us could've hoped for, but at the back of my mind I knew the real test would come later, when the conversation would inevitably turn to whether we were still engaged in the same endeavour.

We'd discussed this eventuality in some detail before contacting Luke, and had decided to just let the conversation take the course it would, and to trust our old friend to react as he wished.

Once everyone had arrived and the sensation of Harry's new slender profile had passed, we went through to take our table in the dining room, which I was pleased to note was discreetly placed at one end of the room, where we could talk without having to worry too much about being overheard.

The dining room was already busy by the time we took our table, no doubt in part due to the bad weather, and many of the hotel guests not wanting to venture out into the rain.

It was then that Luke decided to clear the air, and as much as possible to put us at our ease.

'I know it is perhaps difficult seeing me again, my friends, wondering whether you can mention the search which you are so clearly still pursuing.

'Rest assured, I am pleased to see you, and would very much like to hear everything which has happened to you since you released me from my tormented existence in Corinth. I would even like to hear what mysterious errand brings you to my home city in such inclement weather? If you wish to trust me with it of course.'

With that simple statement, what concerns we had, disappeared.

Over dinner, after sharing our own tale of what had happened since we'd parted ways, Luke told us a little about how he'd been filling his time in the last year, including, how he'd travelled to India to help recover the remains of Sofia, the young woman who had come to guide him during his visions at the Singing Stones, and who he hadn't known had died until that moment.

'I was unsure how I should even go about trying to find her without the help Miriam had promised on behalf of her order. But they must've decided against punishing me, because I got a letter from Selene a few weeks later, with the details of what they'd been able to find out, as well as the name of a local contact who could assist me once I got there.

'It was still an unpleasant business, but it needed to be done, and once her remains were returned to Rome and properly buried, I had another one of those dreams with the drums in which Sofia came to me to thank me for bringing her home.

'Since then I've decided to continue Sofia's work,

by joining a humanitarian mission, though to the Himalaya in the first instance.'

'Ah, you have found your own path to a life of meaning,' commented Jean. 'And in the name of a noble cause my friend.'

'I don't know whether I'll be any good at it, or how long they'll have me for, but I intend to give it my best.'

He wasn't due to head out for another couple of months, but had spent his time learning to speak and read a some of the local languages as well as some Hindi, and had also been brushing up on his basic medical skills.

'I wish now that my university studies had been in a more practical subject, like your study of engineering, Peter,' Luke continued. 'But the closest I came were a few optional courses in architectural design.

'Enough about me though. You are clearly in Rome for a reason. Do you feel like telling me what it is? I promise not to be offended if you'd rather keep it to yourselves.'

I couldn't help but look around the table to check we were still of the same mind to share our plans openly, and noticed that several of the others were doing exactly the same, but it was Marlow who spoke up, on our behalf.

'There is a building on the other side of this street, which we believe has a secret labyrinth of vaults hidden beneath it,' he explained, quietly. 'A complex which was for many years the secret headquarters for an organisation we now know by the name of the Order of Icarus. The same organisation which Selene, Miriam and Thea were working for when we last saw one another.'

In fairness Luke had been incredibly plainly spoken with us in order to lay our various concerns at rest, so I suppose it was only right that Marlow shouldn't tiptoe around the subject. At the same time, I couldn't help but smile at the slightly shocked expression which momentarily froze his features before he recovered.

'My friends, I am slightly taken aback at the idea, but I assure you the many rumours and legends about the remains of the historic city of Rome and other secret catacombs which supposedly lie beneath our feet are very much exaggerated, so whoever has told you this has I'm afraid led you slightly astray.'

'The information comes directly from one of those three young ladies who pursued us across the Mediterranean just over a year ago,' Marlow replied, patiently. 'And it was shared with me personally in order to make amends for the way the artefacts were stolen from us in Kenya.'

It was like watching a replay from a few moments earlier. The shock at what he'd just heard again momentarily freezing his expression.

'And, I take it Robert, that you are certain this information was not given in order to lure you into either wasting your time, or worse to get you into trouble with the authorities?'

'I have no doubt whatsoever,' replied Marlow simply.

'I find it very difficult to believe what you are saying could possibly be true, and yet if this information has come from one of those women and you are convinced it was shared with you in earnest, then I would be very intrigued to learn more about this organisation and to investigate the truth of this hidden labyrinth you mention.'

I couldn't help but notice Luke made no mention of helping us to gain entry to the vaults, nor did he talk of joining us for anything beyond our immediate goal, but there was still a part of me which felt, even a short-term reunion, would do much to improve how we thought about our friendship with one another.

The mood around the table became quickly quite buoyant at the prospect that Luke might join us as we tried to find the entrance into the Icarii vaults, and as we continued our meal we explained what little we knew and how we hoped to find a way to gain entrance to the courtyard, and from there the secret doorway down into the vaults themselves.

While Luke knew the city well and was familiar with both the library building and the adjoining palace, he had no idea how we might find our way into the courtyard without a ladder.

'You are fortunate this is a quiet road, but it is also quite well lit, unless you can arrange another downpour like we have had this evening.'

'What about the Jesuit Library or the building occupied by the Knights of the Holy Sepulchre,' speculated Harry. 'Are we likely to be able to get inside either of those?'

'The library, I'm not sure about. Perhaps with your credentials, Harry, or yours, Androus, you might have been able to arrange something with enough advanced notice, but I doubt you could just walk up to the front door and ask to look around without some form of introduction from a respected institution like your own library in Jerusalem.

'The Palazzo della Rovere on the other hand should be quite straight-forward,' Luke continued. 'It is considered one of the most elegant buildings in Rome and the artwork and murals inside are second to none. It is even said that in the past, kings have preferred to stay there than in the Vatican itself. It is quite common for visitors to the city to be granted access to view the interior.'

'I believe I remember a colleague recommending a visit to this building,' replied Androus, thoughtfully. 'There are different halls decorated with renaissance frescos if I recall correctly.'

'Precisely so,' responded Luke. 'The Hall of the Seasons, the Hall of the Prophets, and the Hall of the Demigods, though it has been years since I last visited. I will call in tomorrow to see if they might provide a guided tour for some friends of mine who have come to visit.'

'That would give the rest of us time to reconnoitre the library and its courtyard in the daylight,' commented Jean.

It wasn't much of a plan for our first day in Rome, but it was a lot more than we'd had that morning, and hopefully once we'd had a chance to look around we'd be able to start forming a plan of action.

We had a lot of catching up to do, so the conversation moved on fairly quickly. During our dinner and then later in the bar we reprised the topics we'd covered earlier on but in more detail.

Luke was particularly interested to hear about how we had finally been robbed of the various artefacts we'd discovered, although when we explained how Mother Agostine and her followers had achieved this under the threat to Harry's life he became quite angry.

For my part I was curious to hear more about the information which Miriam had promised him, in exchange for his help.

'It seemed so genuine when they first talked about it,' Luke explained, sadly, sitting back in his chair with his drink. 'When I discovered that Sophia had been killed I was filled with sorrow. The mission she was working for had managed to recover some of her blood-soaked belongings on one of the quiet trails back from a village she'd been visiting, but after three days of searching for her body, they'd had to concede there was no realistic way of finding her remains in order to afford her a proper burial.

'It was then that Miriam mentioned how the order she worked for had extensive connections through their own missions in India, and that she might be able to use those connections to investigate the matter further, perhaps even to arrange for some local volunteers to help search the area again.

'She seemed so sincere at the time, so genuine in her compassion, and to begin with there was no mention of me having to do anything in return. But of course they were very concerned about the search you had embarked upon through Africa, and over a few weeks I was gently persuaded that re-joining you would not only help to distract me while they made enquiries in India, it would also provide the opportunity for me to help you see sense, which would also help the Order in its Christian mission.

'It was when I informed them about your success in finding the scroll, and how you were using it to identify the location of other, even older, artefacts, that their expectations became more obvious, and they made it clear that if I didn't do what the Order wanted, then the efforts to find Sophia's remains wouldn't continue.

'I realise now how easily I was manipulated, but at the time I could see no way out, and was trapped until you discovered the truth and freed me.

'It was then that Miriam revealed her true nature. When the three of them returned to the hotel in Corinth I explained that you'd left, and how you'd clearly known what was going on for some time, which they were not happy to hear. Miriam in particular considered the failing to be entirely mine, and emphatically told me that even if they did discover the location of Sophia's remains, they would not be passing the information on to me.

'That was also the only time I ever saw the three of them disagree, with Selene not only reprimanding Miriam for her comments, but then openly apologising on her colleague's behalf.'

'It is interesting that Luke should say this about Mademoiselle Autieri,' commented Jean. 'Is it not my friends.'

We hadn't yet talked to Luke in any detail about Marlow's encounter with Selene in Cairo, nor had we mentioned our suspicion that she was even now being hunted by her former colleagues, because of the way in which she had tried to persuade Marlow to abandon the search.

It was all the more interesting to hear that Luke had also witnessed Selene expressing a divergent view to her colleagues in his dealings with her, and all this before she had openly confronted Mother Agostine over the destruction of the scroll.

Marlow again outlined how he'd found his way to

Cairo and had started researching anything and everything he could that might help in our search for the tablets. Then how Selene had arrived and attempted to persuade him that the path he was on should not be followed. And subsequently, during the course of several weeks of discussions, had acknowledged that her organisation had been wrong in the way it had treated us in Kenya.

By the time Marlow had finished describing his encounter with Selene, and then I'd taken my turn to describe what I'd overheard in Geneva, we'd talked our way to the small hours, which after a long day of travelling was enough to make even the ever-enthusiastic Harry feel tired.

It was still raining outside, so while we waited with Luke for his taxi, we agreed to meet again the following evening in order to report back on our first attempts at a reconnoitre of the library and palace.

With Luke in his car, the rest of us could finally turn in for the evening.

ILLUSIONS

ROME WAS STILL A WET, grey place when I woke up the following morning. Though the rain was by no means as heavy as it had been the previous afternoon and evening, it was still enough to make anyone who had to venture out in it thoroughly wet.

I'd dropped off to sleep almost as soon as my head hit the pillow the previous evening, but it had been a long day and late night, so although I woke up a good hour later than I would normally, I still felt I could've done with more sleep. Once awake though, it was rare for me to nod off again, so I got up, and was just about to start getting ready for the day, when I noticed a slip of paper had appeared under my door.

It was from Jean, informing me he'd woken early and was taking coffee in his room while he enjoyed a view of the piazza outside his window.

It was a carefully worded note, which would mean nothing to anyone outside our group, should it happen to go astray, while clearly informing the rest of us that the view from Jean's room did indeed provide a good vantage point upon the palace courtyard and adjoining Jesuit library.

I quickly completed my morning routine, and then walked down the corridor to Jean's suite to find out what we could see.

Harry and Peter had arrived before me, having clearly received exactly the same note as myself, along with a pot of tea and coffee which had been set on a small coffee table in the centre of the lounge which adjoined Jean's bedroom.

The others were standing, cups in hand, over by the big picture windows at the front of the room.

'Ah, George,' Jean said in welcome as he opened the door to let me in. 'You are just in time I think, the friars of our local Jesuit curia are about to open their library.'

I quickly entered and after availing myself of a fresh cup of good Italian coffee I joined the others at the window.

'It looks like someone has just entered the library through another door rather than through the courtyard,' commented Peter, as he scrutinised the place through a pair of small opera glasses. 'They seem to be just busying themselves getting the place ready for the day.'

Peter then handed the glasses to Jean, who I presume must've had the forethought to bring them with him from Paris, either that or to borrow them from the house in Annecy.

'We've seen the interior shutters on the ground floor opened up so far, and a thin trail of smoke start to rise out of one of the chimneys,' Peter continued. 'So we're speculating it's probably a caretaker rather than one of the academics.'

'Ah yes, the shutters are opening upstairs now,' observed Harry.

We continued to watch over the next few minutes as all the shutters were opened one at a time, and then smoke started to rise out of additional chimneys before eventually, the caretaker made an appearance in the courtyard for the first time.

We couldn't see as much of the courtyard's interior from Jean's room as we'd have liked, both because of several mature trees which were growing inside the courtyard, planted no doubt to provide some shade in the summer, but also because we were viewing the scene at an oblique angle. This meant we could only see the top of the steps leading down to the courtyard from the library, and a few yards of the library on either side.

It was clear from his repeated trips up and down the steps with a coal scuttle in each hand, that having set and started the fires in the various fireplaces throughout the building, the caretaker was now retrieving enough fuel to keep them all going for at least a few hours.

Only after we'd observed all these comings and goings did we finally see him descend the steps into the courtyard, and unlock the big gate onto the street.

'Curious indeed, is it not?' commented Jean, as he studied the movements of the caretaker through the opera glasses. 'This gentleman can clearly unlock the gates without needing to take any keys with him.'

It took my sleep deprived brain a few minutes to figure out what he was talking about, by which time Harry had also commented.

'And yet, now the gate is unlocked and ajar he seems to be carrying a set of heavy keys back into the library with him.

'Reminds me of something a local grocery store-keeper used to do when I was a youngster growing up in

New Hampshire. If it was a quiet day he'd often lock-up the front door of the shop while he went to work in the back, but he'd hang the keys up on a hook just inside the door where everyone could see them through the glass. All you had to do was knock on the door and wait for him to come and unlock it.

'Yet, as soon as he'd unlocked the door, those same keys went straight into his trouser pocket.'

We continued to watch in order to see what else we might learn, and over the next hour we saw first the librarians turning up for work, followed a few minutes later by the various academics and students.

It was a surprisingly busy place on a wet weekday morning, but we learned little else which might be of use to us. At one point another couple of visitors to the city walked into the courtyard through the open gate, presumably having mistaken the building for somewhere else, but after looking around for a moment or two and not seeing what they were expecting they turned around and left.

I was expecting to see someone appear from within the library to find out what they wanted, but the visitors came and went without being challenged.

'I think perhaps we have seen all we can for the moment,' commented Jean, putting his opera glasses down. 'Perhaps we should consider heading down for breakfast and letting the others join us there.'

We were all in agreement. Though Peter did suggest it might be worth returning in the afternoon to watch the same process again in reverse as the library was being closed, just to see if there was anything significantly different to what we had seen in the morning.

'It would also be good to see if your suspicions about the gate keys plays out,' continued Peter. 'If the caretaker does bring the keys out with him and then hangs them up inside the gate once he's locked up, it might be something we could use.'

Jean wrote another couple of notes for Marlow and

Androus, before we left his suite, but we'd no sooner stepped into the hallway when we saw them both walking along the corridor to come and join us.

We went down to breakfast as a group, and were shown through to the same table we'd had the previous evening for dinner.

The room was much quieter in the morning with just the guests of the hotel being present, so we could again talk relatively freely and bring Marlow and Androus up to speed on what we'd observed.

'So, if we can find a way to get somebody over the wall, we might well be able to just unlock the gate from the inside to let the rest of us in,' summarised Marlow.

'Either that,' replied Peter. 'Or we could try and get a copy of the key made. It looks like a big old lump of a lock so the key probably isn't all that sophisticated.

'If we could find a small workshop somewhere I could probably knock something up in a few hours from almost any old scrap that might be lying around.

'Perhaps Luke could help out with that,' I suggested. 'You could even pretend to be fixing something on Jean's car, just to make it seem a bit less suspicious to whoever owns the workshop.'

We'd already arranged to meet Luke for dinner that evening, so we could put the question to him then, and in the meantime devote our efforts to how we were going to get somebody over the wall in order to get the key.

Androus liked the idea of just wandering into the courtyard in the same way we'd seem two people do earlier on, and getting a bit more of a look at the interior that way. Odds were that nobody from the library would even notice, let alone have an objection, and at the very worst he'd just be asked to leave.

In the meanwhile the rest of us would do some of the usual tourist things so as not to attract any unwanted attention, and would then make our way back to the hotel via the streets immediately surrounding the library and

Palace Rovere, in order to have a thorough look around the place.

With Hadrian's mausoleum to the east of where we were staying and St Peter's Basilica to the west and countless other museums, art galleries and similar points of interest in the vicinity, it wouldn't be difficult to find any number of excuses to walk past every side of the Jesuit library and Rovere Palace at some point, but it all depended largely on the weather improving.

It was still wet outside by the time we finished breakfast, but the sky was definitely brightening, so we prepared to go out as normal, and by mid-morning the rain had stopped and we were able to head out onto the water slicked streets of Rome.

Androus, Peter and Harry headed off to look around the mausoleum or the Castel Sant Angelo as it was also called. While I headed in the opposite direction toward Saint Peter's Basilica with Jean and Marlow.

It seemed somehow wrong to be visiting the great old buildings of the Vatican merely to hide our scrutiny of the Rovere Palace and Jesuit library, but when it came to actually entering that great masterpiece of renaissance architecture which is St Peter's Basilica, it was difficult to be anything other than completely over awed by the scale and the magnificence of the place. Then of course there were the stunning artistic creations of Bernini, Michelangelo and the other great artists who had contributed works to its walls and open spaces.

For a long while we simply walked amongst those marble lined interiors, stopping every few feet to marvel at the wondrous frescos and sculptures which filled every alcove and corner. Eventually, we got to the point where we had seen so much we simply couldn't take anything else in.

'I think I could spend a lifetime studying the sculptures in this one building alone and I would still not be able to appreciate half their wonders,' Jean commented, wistfully, as we stood before the exquisite creation of

Michelangelo's Pietà, the sculpture depicting the dead body of Jesus lying across the lap of his mother Mary after the crucifixion.

I'd been so distracted by the beauty of the architecture and the artworks it contained that I hadn't really noticed how Jean and Marlow had been responding to them, but now after Jean's comment I turned my attention back to them both, and in particular to Marlow to see if he had also been similarly moved.

He too was gazing at the Pietà but there was something in his expression which I couldn't quite read, I thought at first it was sorrow, but then it seemed almost like disappointment.

Jean must have had the same thought, but a moment later he simply came out with it, and asked Marlow what he was thinking.

'You have been quite quiet while we've been here, Robert, I can't help but wonder what it is you see when you look upon these treasures?'

He didn't seem surprised to have been asked, but he hesitated as though struggling to find the right words with which to frame his thoughts while he continued to gaze upon the sculpture before him.

'It may sound harsh,' he finally replied. 'But while I can appreciate the skill it must've taken to create many of these objects, both in terms of the composition and the craft. I find the overtly clumsy sentiment to be at complete odds with those highly refined skills and expertise.'

'Surely you exaggerate, my friend,' replied Jean, clearly surprised.

'Perhaps I'm not explaining myself as well as I should,' Marlow conceded, frowning slightly as he tried again.

'When I look at this sculpture of Mary with her son's body,' he explained, 'I cannot help but marvel at the way in which this cold hard stone has been transformed into the soft and supple flesh of a human body. The skill is so great, it is impossible to imagine this pale flesh would not give beneath the touch of my hand, and yet… intellectually I know it is still the same cold, hard stone as the block from which it was carved.

'This I could marvel at with you for eternity, Jean, but then I look upon the impossibly young and tranquil face of the figure who is supposed to be Christ's mother, with an expression which I know is intended to be a mixture of quiet piety and sorrow, and here it seems the delicate hand which can transform bare stone into flesh has been paired with the heavy-handed sentiment of the newspaper front page.'

As Marlow described his thoughts and perceptions of Michelangelo's masterpiece I found I could almost agree with him until I looked back at the sculpture itself, when the simple beauty of it spoke to me, and his points seemed to lack all form of traction.

Jean, it has to be said was more definitive in his opinions.

'Robert,' he began, clearly exasperated, but smiling all the same. 'There are times when I swear your peculiar upbringing gives you such an outlandish perspective on things I barely know where to start arguing with you.'

'Surely that's just the same as admitting you can't find a flaw in my argument,' Marlow replied with an outrageously innocent expression on his face.

'No, it most assuredly is not,' Jean exploded in mock outrage. 'But you know full well we do not have sufficient time for me to explain this to you now.'

With that Jean, led us out of the basilica and back along the Borgo Vecchio to the Palazzo della Rovere.

It was such a simple comment made in passing I almost didn't pick up on the reference to Marlow's 'peculiar upbringing', but as we walked I tried to recall what I knew of his earlier life, and I couldn't quite figure out what Jean could be referring to.

I knew that Marlow had grown up in some remote

corner of Western Africa and hadn't really spent much time in England until it was time for him to go to Cambridge to complete his formal education. He didn't talk about this period in his life much, but he had previously mentioned that the formalities of university life had presented something of a challenge for him at first, as had the colder and wetter weather.

There was clearly something else though that Jean must've been alluding to which I wasn't aware of, so I made a mental note to raise it with him when the opportunity arose.

In the meantime we'd made our way back to the front of the Palace on the Borgo Vecchio, and were ambling around much like the many other tourists that filled the streets in the late afternoon. In the process we studied first one side of the building and then the other, before walking down the side street, that contained the Jesuit library and joined up with the road our hotel was on.

We studied the side of the library as we walked down the side street, but it was a fairly unremarkable building with a few small doorways at street level, below the main level of the windows. There was certainly no entrance suitable for the public or library users.

The rear of the building we'd already seen in some detail from Jean's room at the hotel, but now as we rounded the corner we were able to walk along the back of the building and past the open courtyard gate.

There were quite a few cars and vans parked on both sides of the street, including outside the courtyard, which obstructed the pavement in a slightly irritating way, but we managed to find a space between them big enough for the three of us to stand, just to one side of the gateway. Jean and Marlow filled and then lit their pipes, and then stayed to discuss the architecture of the church of Santa Spirito in Sassia on the opposite side of the street. There was much waving of arms and pointing with pipes as we talked, expressing our admiration for the attractive building that was set back slightly from the street.

In reality we were taking it in turns to look at the high wall which separated the courtyard from the street, and the gate in its centre which seemed to provide the main route of entry to the library.

Being stood right next to the wall and gate, also gave me the opportunity to study the street lights which would provide illumination to this part of the street after dark.

They were both old gas lights with decoratively moulded uprights and a big shepherds crook of a lamp at the top. More importantly though, they were both not only placed on the courtyard side of the street, the two nearest ones were also located to either side of the courtyard wall, just where it joined the buildings that formed the wings at the rear of the palace.

I'd been hoping the positioning of the street lights might not fully cover the courtyard wall and gate, but as I studied them now, with Jean and Marlow, it was clear to us that when they were both lit there would be no obvious shadows or shady areas we could use to hide whoever climbed the wall.

It was a bit disheartening to discover yet another difficulty for us to find a way around, but then I noticed the positioning of the street lights themselves was actually quite close to the courtyard wall, and on one side where the wall joined the library the street lamp was placed right in the corner between the courtyard wall and library wall, the ornate moulding of the upright providing several perfect footholds that would allow the streetlight itself to be used as a very convenient ladder.

I discreetly mentioned what I'd noticed to Jean and Marlow, who each agreed it looked like a good option.

With our reconnaissance completed, Jean and Marlow finished smoking and we wandered across the street to the hotel where we could join up with the others in Jean's rooms to observe the caretaker closing up the library, in the hope it would confirm our earlier observations.

Androus, Peter and Harry had already returned from their day of visiting Hadrian's mausoleum, and were waiting for us in the bar.

We stopped while they finished their drinks and then retired back to Jean's suite as a group, after first ordering a large pot of coffee to be sent up with a few sandwiches.

None of us knew what time the library stayed open until, so we took it in turns to keep an eye out while each group brought the others up-to-date.

I began by explaining about the placement of the street lamps and the possibility of using one of them as a ladder.

'So we need to wait for another torrential downpour like we had yesterday,' Harry commented, 'When it's so wet the lamp-lighters can't do their job, otherwise we're going to struggle.'

'We could try and create some kind of distraction,' offered Androus. 'As the stage magicians do, to prevent you from seeing how a trick is done.'

'Or we could hope that one of the local tradesmen might park their high-backed truck exactly where we want it, blocking the view of the lamp-post and wall at the same time,' Marlow commented from where he stood next to the window.

We all went over to the window, half expecting he was just pulling our legs, but there it was, a large glazier's van parked on the pavement like the cars had been earlier on, completely hiding the corner of the wall where the street lamp was located.

'Incredible,' commented Jean. 'We could not have arranged a more convenient and better concealment for our activities had we tried.'

Of course we had no way of knowing whether the vehicle had been parked up for the night or whether the tradesman had merely parked it there temporarily while doing a job.

'We could use your car to try and block it in,' suggested Peter, only half seriously.

'That could backfire on us quite badly if someone from the hotel noticed us going to move the car from further down the street in order to deliberately place it in front of that truck,' replied Harry. 'No, I think we just have to let the cards fall where they will on this occasion.'

We'd been caught off-guard by the unexpected opportunity presented by the truck, so we quickly tried to decide what our best course of action might be.

'Alright,' said Marlow, holding his hands up to ask for our patience.

'Presuming the truck doesn't move before it gets dark, we can probably use it to try and get someone into the courtyard, who can unlock the gate for everyone else.

'We could then make our attempt on the Icarii vaults tonight, and try to get in and out before dawn, unobserved and away from Rome before anyone realises anything is missing.'

'That sounds like an all or nothing proposal to me,' commented Jean. 'One mistake or piece of bad luck and we may not get a second chance.'

'Granted, that's a good point,' continued Marlow.

'Alternatively, we use the opportunity to prepare some more, figure out whether we could copy the key, and maybe reconnoitre of the secret entrance, but nothing more tonight.'

'But we don't know how we might go about making a copy of the key if Luke is unable to help us,' replied Jean, detailing the drawbacks to this option also.

'Well, that might be easier than we'd anticipated,' Peter commented, picking up a small haversack he'd brought with him. 'I had a bit of a wander around some of the antique shops in the area earlier on today while Androus and Harry went off to the mausoleum, and I managed to pick these up on the off-chance that one of them might be roughly the right size.'

With that he tipped out over a dozen old iron keys in various sizes and styles, along with a small selection of metal files, which he presumably intended to use to adapt them.

'Not only that, but I also managed to cobble this together, which I'm rather pleased with, if I do say so myself,' he said producing what for all the world looked like a medium sized tobacco tin from his jacket. 'Can you guess what it is?'

Jean opened the tin to reveal it was completely filled with a slightly sweet smelling pale yellow substance.

'Surely you have not managed to procure an explosive?' asked Jean, doubtfully.

'Is that your best guess?' Peter asked, clearly pleased that we hadn't immediately figured it out.

'Perhaps I should give you a demonstration?' he said picking up one of the keys and pressing it firmly into the filled tin to leave a perfect impression of the keys shape and size.

'Ah, Pierre, you have truly outdone yourself,' exclaimed Jean, examining the silhouette of the key impression in the tin. 'But what is this substance, it seems familiar but I cannot quite think what it is.'

'Well I have a some more of it here if you'd like to taste it?' Peter offered.

To say that Jean looked doubtful as he raised a crumb of the yellow substance to his lips would be a significant understatement, but the moment he tasted it his expression was transformed.

'Ah bravo! My friend. Of course, it is the almond paste or marzipan as I believe you call it in England.'

We all had to admit the genius of Peter's creation. It was so simple and yet so effective. He even showed us how he could erase all trace of the key's impression by simply pressing the marzipan back down into a perfectly flat surface with his thumbs. He had even found the time to use one of the small files he'd purchased to make a notch at one end of the tin so the key to be placed evenly in the marzipan for a more accurate impression.

Looking at the selection of keys, some of which must've been well over a hundred years old, I couldn't help but think that again, it should now be relatively simple to get one that was roughly the right size and then either file it down to fit, or if necessary add to the key with a bit of solder to make it larger.

We continued to talk through our options, but with the keys and the tin of marzipan we all agreed the more cautious approach to entering the vaults would give us the best of the limited opportunity we might have.

While we talked at least one of us continued to watch the street, and once again got the opportunity to carefully study the library caretaker as he performed his duties, this time closing rather than opening the library.

Sure enough he seemed to do exactly the opposite of what he'd done in the morning, starting with the locking of the gate shortly after the last of the librarians had finished work and left for the day. He came out of the library with a large key ring with the gate key on it, before returning empty handed once the gate was secured. We then watched as he went through the building closing the shutters and turning the lights off before he too seemed to leave via one of the small doorways on the far side of the building.

There was still no sign of the owner of the truck an hour later as the spring light started to fade and the lamp-lighter came along to light the street lights.

The problem of vehicles blocking access to some of the street lights must've been a relatively common occurrence, because the lamp-lighter didn't seem to give the street-light stuck behind the truck a second glance. He simply walked on to the next lamp on the street, presumably happy to finish his job earlier for the evening.

We'd agreed to meet Luke later on at a restaurant only a few minutes' walk away from our hotel, so we continued to study the street for as long as we could until it was time to get ready for dinner.

There were still a few people around on the streets by the time we left the hotel, but it was also much darker and as we left we walked past the parked glaziers van beneath its darkened street light. Even at that comparatively early hour of the evening it was already difficult to see the top of the wall where it jutted above the back of the van. A few hours later and I was confident the top of the wall would be shrouded in a perfect darkness.

Luke had suggested a trattoria just off the beaten track, where he assured us the food was very good, and which also had a number of small rooms where its guests could enjoy their meal away from the hustle and bustle of an open dining room.

He was already waiting for us by the time we reached the restaurant, having arrived there a few minutes early so he could have a chat with the proprietor, who was an old family friend.

We were shown through to our private dining room almost immediately. Luke had suggested we leave the selection of both the food and the wine entirely to the proprietor, who he assured us would serve us a truly memorable meal of the finest and freshest cuisine available, while also allowing us more time for conversation. This was clearly an arrangement quite familiar to the proprietor, who I believe, accepted it as a compliment upon not only the quality of his food, but also his judgment.

As soon as the wine was served we got straight down to business, and updated Luke on the outcome of our day's reconnaissance.

He was relieved to hear we'd had some luck, as he'd completely failed to get us a tour of the Rovere Palace, on account of several members of their staff currently being off work due to illness.

We explained about our observations of the caretaker and how he seemed to leave the courtyard key hanging up next to the gate overnight.

'Yes, this is most likely a precaution against fire,' he explained. 'The keys are probably left on a hook just inside the gate, so that in the event of a fire if anyone is trapped in the building they can still escape without having to first go searching for the keys to the gate. I understand it is a common practice in many monasteries and convents, where buildings will be inhabited overnight.'

'Perhaps, because the library is part of the Jesuit Curia they repeat the same practice out of habit even though the library will be empty,' Harry observed.

'Precisely,' replied Luke, as the restaurant waiting staff brought out the first course of our meal, some wonderfully flavoursome artichoke hearts and calamari served with a light lemon sauce.

For a moment the conversation lulled while we all enjoyed the delicious food before Harry brought our attention back to the topic at hand, by explaining about the placement of the street lights, and the glazier's truck which had prevented one of the street lights from being lit.

'This is also a common occurrence at the moment,' Luke informed us. 'On account of all the building works being carried out across the city. If the tradesman in question has found a spot where the road is wide enough for him to leave his vehicle without completely blocking the way, that also isn't too long a walk to where he is staying during the week, then his vehicle will probably return there each evening until the weekend.'

'Well, in this case it suits our purpose perfectly,' replied Harry. 'It provides the ideal opportunity for us to scale the wall in order to get an impression of the key.'

Peter had brought the tin of marzipan with him in the hope we might get to use it on our way back to the hotel, so he showed it to Luke now, who was equally as entranced with it as the rest of us had been.

'You are either a natural burglar or a budding pastry chef my friend,' Luke observed, not realising the barrage of comments and confessions on both mine and Peter's behalf, about career paths we only narrowly avoided.

It seemed like the natural time to ask Luke whether he might be able to help us in creating a duplicate key for the courtyard gate, assuming we could successfully get an impression. But we barely had to ask before he offered us access to the garage and small workshop attached to his family home.

'I won't pretend it's anything more than a couple of work benches with a few tools which are used to look after the car and to service the few bits of garden equipment we have, but its private and isn't used much, so you can pop over to use it whenever you like.'

We suggested the subterfuge of taking Jean's car over and opening the bonnet to make it look even more normal, which Luke liked.

With that we were all able to relax and enjoy the fine meal. Peter offered to be the one who would scale the wall, so he ate and drank more sparingly than he might normally have done, in order to make the climbing easier.

I was curious to hear a bit more about the work which Luke would be doing in the Himalaya once he joined his humanitarian mission, which he gladly expanded upon while at the same time giving us a few snippets of the Hindi and Himalayan languages he'd been learning.

After a truly delicious and enjoyable meal, we left the trattoria a few hours later to discover the sky had remained clear of cloud and a thin crescent of moon had risen above the rooftops.

'A burglar's moon,' Jean commented, as we made our way back to the hotel via the courtyard.

Peter separated from us when we reached the front of the Rovere Palace and walked down the other side street to the rest of us, while we strolled as an amiable group, providing what we hoped would be a gentle distraction for Peter, should anyone happen to come along.

We'd also agreed a signal which we could use to provide an alert if necessary.

I was pleased to see the glaziers truck was still exactly where it had been before, and that beneath the thin sliver of moon, which had now risen, the top of the wall behind the truck was completely invisible from the street.

There was no way of knowing how long Peter would take to climb the wall, find the key and climb back over the wall, but it seemed like we were stood in the piazza outside the hotel and the small church for an age before his familiar shape came strolling out of the darkness, looking for all the world like he'd just climbed over a filthy old wall.

We closed ranks around him quickly to conceal the state his clothes were in, just as two carabinieri officers doing their rounds came walking down the street.

'I knew the wall was a bit dirty, but I had no idea it was this bad,' Peter commented, as he did his best to brush off his clothes.

He still looked like he'd fallen in the gutter, even after he'd tried to brush the worst of it off, but fortunately the police officers didn't seem to spot anything untoward, and they continued on their rounds without bothering us.

'Probably best to try and get back to your room without being noticed by the hotel reception if you can,' advised Luke. 'Just in case you've left any kind of obvious marks on the wall where you climbed.'

We hadn't considered the fact that the wall might be filthy after it had been raining heavily for so long, let alone that the dirt might end up leaving some evidence of where we'd entered.

'Bring your clothes over with you when you come tomorrow, and I'll see if I can clean them up a bit while you work on the key.' Luke offered.

With that Luke took his leave and we bundled into the thankfully quiet reception as a group, with Peter hidden behind us as though still gripped in the depths of conversation about the wonderful meal we'd just had.

Jean collected our room keys for us, and we thankfully made it back to our rooms without encountering anyone.

A few minutes later, with Peter now changed, we congregated in Jean's room to take a look at the key imprint and discuss our next steps.

The impression was perfect, Peter had not only pressed it carefully into the marzipan, he'd also thought to press it in on both sides and at the end so we could more easily compare it with the selection of keys we already had.

It was clearly a large and simple looking key, which narrowed down our selection of possible matches, but a couple of the older keys were similar in size and Peter was confident he could make one of them work.

With the goal of the exercise looking like it might well pay off, we turned our attention to what had happened and how likely it was that someone would detect the wall had been scaled.

'I think we should get away with it,' Peter explained. 'The wall itself was easy enough to climb, especially with the lamp-post on this side and a conveniently placed tree on the other side of the courtyard wall.

'The difficulty was the terracotta tiles which run along the top of the wall. These were covered in lichen and moss and goodness knows what else, and I was obliged to straddle them to begin with in order to get on top of the wall, and then to carefully crawl along them to the tree where I could climb down on the other side.

'If it hadn't rained recently, it would probably have just been a bit dusty, but well you saw the effect of the rain.

'Anyway, the only place where there might be any trace of my climb is on top of the wall, which shouldn't be too visible to anyone.'

'Well, we didn't anticipate it, so we'll just have to hope for the best and deal with anything that might come up as best we can,' Marlow commented. 'Did you get the chance to take a look around inside the courtyard while you were over there?'

'I did better than that,' Peter replied. 'I had a quick

look inside the room where the gardening equipment is stored.

'It looks pretty much as you were told it would be, Robert, a bit cluttered with tools, but nothing that would stop us from getting to the back wall where you said the hidden doorway is supposed to be.'

'And the pattern of coloured stones in the brickwork?' Marlow asked, expectantly.

'Yes, that was there too, though I only lit my lighter for a moment just to be on the safe side.' Peter responded smiling.

This was another piece of good news, which corroborated the instructions Selene had given to Marlow and in the process gave me the distinct sensation that we were once again on the brink of taking a momentous decision.

We agreed the details for the following day, which would hopefully be our final preparations before we made our attempt on the Icarii vaults.

SHADOWS

I DREAMED OF AFRICA AGAIN THAT NIGHT, and found myself once more beneath the great overhanging rock face where we'd first met the three shaman. The fire had already burned low, and I was alone but for the youthful version of my father who was sitting on the other side of the fire, waiting patiently for me to wake up.

In the distance, I could hear the soft insinuating rhythm of the drums whispering their reassuring caress across the night air.

I wasn't in the mood for travel this time, preferring

instead to simply sit beneath that never-crashing wave of rock, and enjoy the warmth of the fire.

This was the start of it all, the point at which I'd stepped on the path we now followed, freely and without hesitation.

My father waited for the questions.

'Must I follow this path?' I finally asked. 'It is leading me to places and decisions I have doubts about.'

'The obligation is only to yourself,' he said simply, prodding the embers of the fire between us with a stick.

'But should I keep following it?' I asked, knowing it was an impossible question for anyone other than myself to answer.

'No, and… Yes,' he answered, with a sad smile.

'All things in life worth having come at a cost,' he continued, allowing his gaze to drift out over the valley. 'The most precious and worthwhile things in life, naturally, require the greatest effort and often also the greatest sacrifice.'

'But what if the cost is too high? What if the price is more than I want to pay?' I asked.

'What price would you put on a lifetime of regret?' he responded, still prodding at the fire. 'What would you pay to avoid it?

'Your friends cannot succeed without you, George, nor can you succeed without each of them. Abandon them and you doom them to failure. Stay on the path and you will surely pay a heavier price than you think imaginable.'

'But you cannot tell me what that price will be?'

'Not without sending you down a different path with a different price.'

Seeing that I was still uncertain, but had no further questions to ask, my father stood up and started to walk away, but on the very fringe of the firelight he paused, and turned back to me.

'Come, let me show you the valley,' he said simply before stepping into the darkness.

I followed not knowing why I was doing so.

We walked amongst the stars to the tempo of the idling drums for a while, before finally coming to a small kraal of the type common in Kenya.

I didn't recognise it as any of the villages I'd visited, but then from the darkness where I stood, I saw a second version of my father working with the villagers in the light of day, on his missionary work.

He was young, but already bronzed to the bone by the African sun, and clearly at ease in the village, where, in the passage of but a few heartbeats I saw him teaching both children and adults how to read and write, as well as how to do arithmetic, and other useful and practical things that could help to make their life easier. He helped cultivate plants, and taught how to erect a fence-post that can resist the pressure of a leaning cow.

In return, I saw him being taught Maasai skills, from the cattle crafting which those tall people had a strange affinity for, to bush-craft and hunting.

Years passed and I saw my farther thrive and grow beneath the African sun, but then, within a quickened heartbeat, I saw him meet my mother and their life as it began together. A life with my mother meant a life away from Africa for my father. Both paths came with a cost, which my father revealed to me now. A life as a missionary would mean sacrificing so much, a wife and family, support through life's trials and tribulations, a home. While a life with all these things would mean greater comfort, accepted responsibility, love, hopes, but also regret.

I guessed the rest of the details but my father showed them to me anyway. The sacrifices willingly made to spend his life with my mother, only for her death shortly after my birth to rob him of both the life he'd chosen, and the life he could have had back in Africa.

The knowledge he'd followed the wrong path.

Looking away from what my father had shown me, I glimpsed the two paths which now lay before me.

One was obscured and difficult to see, but it surely held threats and dangers that would test me to my limits, if not beyond.

The other way was clearer, an easy and comfortable path which would see me returning to Africa to continue retracing my father's footsteps.

In time this second path would see me exploring the Alps, I would visit elegant hotels and comfortable guest houses, and walk paths seldom trodden, but I would also spend my life thinking of the friends I'd abandoned as they journeyed away from the comfortable and pleasant into the unknown.

I had no more questions for my father as we walked quietly back to the dying fire beneath the rock face, but it seemed he had one final thought to share with me.

'My son, if you decide to continue following the path you are on, you must challenge and question everything. Doubt all that can be doubted, for while the other path has its costs, only the one you are on may lead to your destruction.'

The drums had faded and the sky on the horizon had paled. It was time to wake.

DAWN

THE HALF-HEARD DRUMS as I awoke were a familiar and now strangely comforting sound, so I rose with a less troubled head than I'd had in some time.

I was expecting to see another slip of paper beneath my door, but unlike the morning before I was already up and ready for the day before it arrived, so I was able to surprise Jean a moment after he delivered it, by opening my door and popping out into the hallway to join him, before he'd even reached the next doorway on the corridor.

Jean had again arranged for tea and coffee to be provided, so a few minutes later we were comfortably watching from his suite, when the library once more started to show the first signs of life.

All the shutters were open and trails of smoke were escaping through the chimneys as the caretaker descended to the courtyard for the first time to fill his coal scuttles, and then a few minutes later to open the courtyard gate.

Both Jean and I stood watching, breathlessly waiting for the caretaker to suddenly stop and notice something about the wall where Peter had clambered over it, but the man simply continued about his routine without so much as at glance at where Peter had climbed over.

It was the same when the owner of the glazier's van returned to drive his vehicle away for his day's work. As he manoeuvred the vehicle out into the street and exposed the outside wall next to the lamp-post. there were a couple of marks that might have been left by Peter's descent, but nothing as obvious as a footprint. In all honesty I wasn't even sure they hadn't been there before.

It looked like we'd gotten away with it for the moment, but we all knew we'd have to be more careful in the future.

Once everyone else had made their way to Jean's room, we sat down and discussed our plans for the day ahead.

Peter's task was already well defined. He'd be taking Jean's car over to Luke's home to use his garage to work on the copy of the courtyard key.

The rest of us had a few things we'd need to pick up, which we now divided up amongst us, with Jean acting as the quartermaster.

'Well, the time is almost upon us, my friends. This

evening with luck we will all have the dubious honour of adding burglary to our résumés,' he joked. 'But first, we will need to find our way into the vaults below the courtyard, and for that, according to Selene's instructions, we will need nothing more complex than a long and slender bladed knife, which when inserted between the correct stones will lift a series of hidden latches.

'Now while simple, we know this mechanism is old, and in all probability has not been used for a great many years, so I would suggest we acquire at least two such blades, probably of the long and slender poignard variety that would have been common at the time of the vault's construction.

'If you can find some, it would also be helpful to have a small tin of oil, preferably one with a long nozzle, that we can use to lubricate the mechanism through the gaps in the stonework.'

Peter was sure he'd seen a couple of knives, of the correct type, in one of the antique shops he'd visited the day before, which Harry and Androus offered to pick up in exchange for some directions. He wasn't so sure about the oil, but suggested a sewing machine shop might be a good place to try.

'We will also need some torches or lamps,' continued Jean, checking off the items on his list. 'As well as perhaps a raincoat each to help keep our clothes free of any incriminating dirt or dust.'

It was a sensible precaution and with all the rain which had recently fallen, it would also be entirely natural for anyone out for the evening to be wearing some kind of protection against the elements.

'Finally, it is perhaps time for us to discuss our firearms.'

I was slightly shocked at Jean raising this last point, but I listened to what he had to say.

'We know our adversaries are trained and ruthless individuals, but on this occasion we are anticipating the vault to be staffed only very lightly. As such, our aim is to enter it, retrieve the artefacts stolen from us and exit, without our presence having been immediately detected. Even if we are leaving a message on our way out for Mother Agostine to discover later. Consequently, I believe there is no reason for us, as civilised men, to take guns with us.'

'I couldn't agree with you more, Jean,' I ventured, without hesitation. 'If Peter can make a serviceable copy of the courtyard key we can always come back another day if we encounter difficulties.'

Marlow hesitated for a moment before he answered.

'I agree with you, Jean, but your point, George, about being able to bide our time and return another day is well made,' he answered, earnestly. 'I would never be able to forgive myself if any of you were to be seriously hurt in the pursuit of these artefacts or our larger goal. So, if we have the choice, a more cautious approach will for me always be the more reasonable course.'

I saw now that Jean was right to raise this as a topic, even though we were all in complete agreement. After our last confrontation with them in Africa it would be very easy for us to justify uncivilised conduct even when we were in the heart of one of the great cities of the civilised world.

We came to the final question of how we should approach entering the courtyard that evening. We could pop out for a meal again, but we could hardly take the bags with us without appearing odd.

We briefly considered obtaining some wrapping paper and boxes and adopting the pretence of taking presents out with us for somebody's birthday, but that would hardly allow us to bring the same parcels back into the hotel with us, and we couldn't use the same ploy more than once without definitely arousing some suspicion.

'We could use the car again,' Peter suggested. 'If I can get the key to the courtyard completed in good time, I'll be returning by mid-afternoon, when the streets have fewer parked cars on them. I could leave Jean's car just next to the library where it would be convenient for us to pick up the extra tools and equipment once it was sufficiently dark. We could then drop them off in the car, along with the artefacts, on the way out if all goes to plan, before walking back over to the hotel, looking just as we did when we left.'

'Sounds good,' Harry agreed. 'But make sure you leave enough space for that glazier's van to pull in again. If we could get that in more or less the same place then getting in and out of the courtyard unobserved would be much easier.'

Of course we had no way of knowing whether the tradesman in question would oblige us in this way, but we might get lucky.

With the jobs divided up between us, we headed down for a hearty breakfast before heading out into the bustling streets of Rome to buy what we'd need for our first burglary.

It was unlikely anyone would get suspicious at the purchase of half a dozen pocket torches, or a small tin of oil, but as we had a day to prepare and enough of us to spread the tasks out, there was no need to take any unnecessary risks.

At Peter's suggestion, I also picked up a small screwdriver and pair of wire cutters, in case we needed to cut the power to a light or stop a switch from working. As for the torch and raincoat they were easy to pick up so I got one set for me and another for Peter. I also found a new hat, which I thought went rather well with my raincoat, and a medium sized canvas and leather shoulder bag, a little larger than the one I'd used on the journey over from Fontainebleau to Annecy, and which was also big enough to carry all my new acquisitions.

Finally, I browsed through some antique shops I stumbled across, for a long slender dagger under the pretence of wanting something to use as a letter opener, and found a couple that might do in the event that Harry and

Androus didn't manage to get the ones which Peter had spotted.

I still had nearly two hours to kill by the time I'd bought everything I needed, so I found a café with a nice view down the Borgo Vecchio toward St Peter's, where I could loiter and maybe scribble a few notes for inclusion in my journal later on that evening.

We'd all agreed to stay away from the hotel until mid-afternoon in order to maintain our image as tourists. After all, what self-respecting tourist would travel all the way to Rome only to spend their time in a hotel?

I'd found a sunny spot near the front window and was just sipping a strong coffee, when I saw Miriam walking down the street, followed by one of those strangely docile male servants.

There was no mistaking the confidence in her walk, or the tumble of long auburn hair that surrounded her features like a living flame.

She was still a way off, and I instinctively started to scan the street for any sign of her two compatriots, but she seemed to be by herself.

It wasn't likely she'd see me even if she walked all the way down the street, but the fact I'd walked exactly the same route which she now followed, with Jean and Marlow just yesterday, made my heart flutter.

She wasn't looking at any of the shops as she passed. Instead her gaze roved restlessly across the people in the street, like the predatory gaze of a lioness. A moment later she reached her destination, a small bookshop which she instantly entered with her servant.

I still had a good half hour to kill before I'd need to set off back to the hotel, and there was a part of me which wanted nothing more than to leave the café and head away from Miriam as quickly as I could. However, there was another part of me which knew that if Miriam were here, then the more we knew about it the better.

Thankful again for my new hat, which I hoped

disguised me, I swallowed the last of my coffee and walked down the street toward the bookshop.

As I drew closer I was sure my heart was beating loud enough for other people in the street to hear it, but I pushed on, endeavouring to look as much like a relaxed sight-seer as I possibly could.

Once I got to the shop, I looked in through the window as though perusing the books on display, but the sun was in just the wrong place and I couldn't see in past the reflections. So, pulling the brim of my hat down a little further, I ventured inside

It was a quiet shop comprised of two medium sized rooms, with thousands of books arranged on shelves which lined every wall, alcove and recess. Just inside the door was an elderly Italian gentleman in a neatly pressed suit and tie that seemed to envelop him.

He greeted me now in English and asked if there was anything he could assist me with, which I struggled for a moment to think of a suitable reply to.

'How on earth did you know I was an Englishman?' I floundered.

Clearly accustomed to such puzzlement, he simply shrugged and with a small smile explained that Rome received a great many visitors from England.

This gave me a few precious moments to think of a book which I could be looking for.

'Erm, I was wondering whether you might have any books on the history of Rome,' I asked. 'The Renaissance period in particular, when I believe a lot of the art on display in St Peter's was commissioned?'

'Of course, signor,' the owner conceded, moving away from his desk. 'You would prefer something in English?'

After indicating that I would, the owner took me into the back room, and showed me two separate alcoves, one containing books relating to the city's history, the other more specifically on its artworks.

As soon as I set foot in the back room, I spotted the only other doorway leading from the shop, through which Miriam must have exited. It was at the back of another alcove between the two I'd been directed to, and had a sign on it, which even my poor Italian was good enough to tell me said 'Private – no entry'.

Thanking the proprietor, I started looking along the shelves he had pointed out, while he returned to this desk.

As soon as he was back at his desk, I stopped for a moment to consider what I was doing, and to let my racing heart calm do.

The odds of Miriam being in Rome for a reason unrelated to our own seemed remote to say the least. And if she wasn't here searching the hotels like she and her counterparts had been doing in both France and Switzerland, then what else could she be up to?

Selecting a book with a picture of the Rovere Palace on the front, I shuffled around to the other alcove which the shopkeeper had pointed out to me, and feigned interest in some of the books there also. Thankfully, he showed no interest in my movements.

I quickly selected another book about the works of Michelangelo contained in St Peter's Basilica, and then, pretending to be undecided between the two, I stepped back out of the alcove. I'd already spotted a chair in the middle alcove, near the doorway, but I pretended to spot it for the first time, before moving over to sit down on it and make myself comfortable while I scrutinised the books in more detail.

It creaked loudly under me, as I went through the motions of reading for a minute or two in case the proprietor wished to check up on me, and then I quietly moved over to see if I could hear anything through the door.

But I couldn't hear a thing.

I checked on the proprietor again, by making a small show of putting one of the books back before returning to the chair, but he seemed intent on his own reading. Feeling bolder I moved back over to the door and inched it open. There was light on the other side, but more importantly I could just make out the voice of Miriam as she talked heatedly with someone.

They were talking in Italian, so once again I was left desperately trying to make out enough words to get the gist of what they were talking about.

I quickly jotted some notes in the back of the book on the Rovere Palace, with some phonetic spellings of the words I didn't recognise or wasn't sure about, and then when the conversation seemed to be coming to an end, I put my pencil away, and moved back around to the first alcove in case Miriam or her servant suddenly appeared.

I must have been quiet for too long, because when I shuffled out of the middle alcove, book in hand, the proprietor was walking over, presumably to check on me.

'Is everything alright, signor?' he asked innocently

'Yes, I think so,' I tried to reply nonchalantly, despite my heart hammering in my chest again.

'I think I'll just take this one today. A friend of mine is going to try and arrange a visit to this very place,' I said tapping the picture of the Rovere on the cover.

I was sure Miriam would be appearing through the door at the back of the shop at any second, so I either needed to get back into one of the alcoves, or try to pay for the book and get out of the shop before she spotted me.

'There is another slightly more extensive volume if the Rovere is of particular interest?' he said, ushering me back into the far alcove, just as I heard the door in the middle alcove swing open, and bang against the wall.

I didn't dare look up at the noise, for fear that Miriam might somehow catch a glimpse of my face. But I think my caution was uncalled-for, as for whatever reason, Miriam whisked out of the place with barely a civil word to the proprietor.

My heart was still racing a minute or two later when I finally plucked up the courage to return to the front desk.

There was no sign of Miriam or her servant through the front window, so I thanked the shop owner for his help, and paid for the book I'd made the notes in. Then, once again pulling the brim of my hat down I left.

I could just make out Miriam and her servant in the distance, walking down the road toward St Peter's as I left the shop, but after pushing my luck as much as I had, I decided against following her any further and turned on my heel to make my way back to the hotel.

SUBTERFUGE

B Y THE TIME I'D DROPPED MY THINGS off in my hotel, and then made my way along the corridor to Jean's room, my heart rate had just about returned to normal, so I was able to enter the room and take a seat beside Jean's coffee table without giving any indication of the ordeal I'd just put myself through.

Even so, Jean's keen eyes must have noticed something, because he commented on it straight-away.

'Are you alright, George, you look a little… pale,' he said simply.

'I've just seen Miriam,' I replied as nonchalantly as I could manage while reaching for the coffee pot.

Well, it was like an electric shock had been passed through everybody's chairs. From everyone being relaxed and engaged in the usual chit-chat amongst themselves while they waited for the last person to arrive, they all went very quiet and focused their attention on me.

I quickly explained about how I'd finished picking up all the things I needed earlier than expected, so had taken shelter in a coffee shop to kill a bit of time before heading back to the hotel. Then, while there, how I'd spied Miriam walking down the Borgo Vecchio before going into a bookshop.

'I knew she had to be in Rome for a reason, and odds are good that reason had something to do with us, so I walked down to the shop she had gone into to see if I could find anything out.'

'And to think I once thought Robert was the most reckless one amongst us,' Jean commented. 'George, you are truly fearless.'

'I assure you, Jean, I felt anything but fearless at the time,' I replied.

I went on to describe the layout of the shop and my subterfuge of looking for a book which allowed me to listen at the doorway through which I could hear Miriam talking.

'Well as you all know my command of the Italian language is rather poor, so I only managed to catch a few words, which I scribbled in the back of a book I was pretending to read.'

With that I opened the book I'd bought and attempted to read out the phonetic transcription of what I'd heard.

'It was something like . . . Andare . . . camera della verita . . . . edi cancellare tutti rifuti, then something like svuoto . . . and . . . entro la mezzanotte.'

Everyone was silent for a moment before Jean asked to see what I'd written down.

'And how much of what was said do you think you heard, George?' He finally asked without looking up from my notes.

'Half, perhaps three quarters of what Miriam was saying. But I couldn't make out a single word of the response she received, though the tone of it made me think she was talking to one of those servants that seem to follow these women around and he was pleading with her about something.'

'Well, from the words you did catch, it sounds like

she was telling the poor fellow to go to somewhere called the Chamber of Truth and to perhaps have something done or cleaned up by midnight.' Jean explained.

'Could that be the name of the room where they keep all the artefacts?' Peter asked. 'And when they talk about having it cleaned up by midnight, could they be talking about moving everything stored there?'

'I don't think so,' replied Marlow, still clearly trying to figure it out. 'From what Selene told me about the size of the vaults it would take years to completely clear them of all the artefacts stored there.'

'Perhaps it is just a housekeeping measure, and nothing to do with us after all,' suggested Harry, hopefully.

'With luck we could be in and out well before midnight,' pointed out Peter.

'This is true,' Jean agreed. 'But if what they are doing results in our adversaries realising the artefacts are missing immediately after we have taken them, this could cause us significant problems.'

'In that case,' Harry suggested. 'Perhaps we should consider getting the artefacts out of there and then trying to find out exactly what it is they are doing at midnight. Even if it proves completely unrelated to our goals it might give us more insight into our adversaries.'

'To think,' I replied. 'Just a few moments ago I was being called reckless for following Miriam into a shop! Now you suggest we should willingly wait around in the vaults, the heart of their operations, just to find out what they're up to, even if we can get the artefacts out beforehand?'

'Enthusiasm, mon ami, it can be contagious!' Jean joked.

'It's a fair point, George,' chipped in Marlow. 'But we shouldn't forget that the Order has kept watch on all of us over the past year, so even if they're distracted by Selene or some other factor at present, sooner or later their attention will fall back upon us. And when it does, we would be better off knowing as much about the Order of Icarus and what it's capable of as we can.'

I hadn't been entirely serious in my mockery of them for thinking of me as being reckless, but I hadn't been entirely joking either. Now, I had to concede to Marlow's point, that the more we knew about this secretive religious order the better.

'I'm glad you agree,' Marlow replied. 'Because I was actually thinking you would be the ideal candidate to stay behind and spy on Miriam and her friends. As you have a natural talent for it!'

I nearly spat the mouthful of coffee I'd just swallowed across the room as he said this, much to everyone else's amusement, before I realised he was joking.

Of course, we knew even getting into the former Icarii stronghold could still present us with problems enough, so with the light entertainment out of the way for the afternoon we settled down to discuss our final preparations.

Peter had managed to park Jean's car exactly where we wanted it on the corner of the street straight outside the Jesuit library, so we had some moving of equipment and clothing to do to begin with.

Androus and Harry had managed to pick up the two old and not-quite matching poignards, whilst Peter had done an amazing job of copying the key, though he insisted it was more down to luck in finding a very similar old key in one of the antique shops than any great skill on his behalf.

We'd all obtained suitably dark coloured overcoats to help keep our evening clothes clean and also to make it easier for us to blend into the shadows. Peter had been busy working on the key, so I'd picked one for him, which I now gave to him.

Between us we'd also sorted out an electric torch each and an assortment of other tools which might come in handy.

We checked everything off on the list of what we might need, and then packed it up into a couple of the larger haversacks we had. In addition, Androus had prepared a couple of smaller bags for the artefacts we hoped to recover. These he had stuffed with scarves and other bits of soft cloth to protect the tablets and prevent them from making any noise.

There was no subtle way to get the bags out to the car, so we just went with the casual approach. Jean and Peter simply walked out to the car with the bags while amiably chatting about something or other, popping them into the passenger foot well of the car, and then opening the bonnet as though to show Jean something, before closing it all back up and strolling back without the bags.

As though on cue, just as they were both heading back across the street the glazier's van returned and parked up once more in front of the courtyard gates, directly behind Jean's car.

Peter had parked the car just below the streetlight this time so the van was further along, blocking the view of the gate itself. It meant the lamp-lighter might be able to do his job properly, but if the key worked it wouldn't matter if the street-lights were both illuminated, as this time, if anyone saw us they probably wouldn't think twice about it because we obviously had a key.

With everything set, there was very little left for us to do other than wait for darkness to fall.

We still planned to have a meal first, because the street wouldn't quieten down until past eight o'clock, so Luke had made a pre-theatre table reservation in one of his other favourite restaurants, which would allow us to be back in position at the appointed time.

We continued to watch the street as the clock slowly crawled around to the library closing time, after which the patrons and library staff once again disappeared, followed a few minutes later by the caretaker locking the gate and closing the shutters. Suddenly, the time seemed to start passing more quickly, and within what seemed moments we were stepping out of the hotel with Luke, just in time to see the lamp-lighter doing his rounds.

Without any warning, Luke peeled off from the rest of us to go and talk to the lamp-lighter, just as the fellow was approaching the lamp above Jean's car. I couldn't hear what he said, but I could see Luke pointing back at Jean before pressing something into the hand of street-lighter, who walked on leaving the light unlit.

Seeing the question in our eyes, Luke explained.

'I merely asked the fellow to be especially careful, because the car in question belonged to a friend of mine, who had only just had it repaired after a slate had fallen from a nearby building and smashed his windscreen. We Italians as you know are a superstitious bunch, and have a saying that ill fortune often arrives in threes.'

'But why would that concern the lamp-lighter?' I asked not seeing the connection.

'Well,' explained Luke with a smile. 'If something had fallen off the lamp and damaged Jean's car while we were watching, it would have to be reported, and a supervisor would have to come and inspect the scene. All the while the poor chap's dinner would be waiting for him at home.'

'Ah, the elegance of it,' murmured Harry. 'You have missed your calling as a diplomat, Luke.'

While Luke had distracted us for a short while, time once again seemed to bound forward and it felt like we'd no sooner sat down to dinner than darkness proper had descended and we were heading back to the now shadowy courtyard.

Over dinner we'd discussed how to best approach getting into the courtyard, and Peter had suggested he walk on ahead to unlock the gate. This would avoid us hanging around suspiciously, if there was a problem with the key. We would then follow in pairs a few meters apart. Luke and Jean would go last, and would provide a distraction if need be, though what they would do we hadn't decided upon.

INTO THE DEPTHS

PETER WAS NOWHERE IN SIGHT, which was either a good thing or something had gone wrong and he'd been unable to signal us.

Marlow and I were the first two to follow Peter from the restaurant, but we'd perhaps hung back a bit too far, so we hoped he'd just moved through into the courtyard before we'd rounded the corner.

'You know, George,' commented Marlow with the hint of a smile on his face. 'I think there might be more to this burglary business than meets the eye. There always seems to be something we haven't thought of.'

'I know what you mean, Rob,' I replied in a similar tone. 'I hadn't realised just how hard working our criminal classes are.'

A moment later and the smile was wiped off my face, as two Carabinieri appeared a couple of streets away and started heading toward us.

We were supposed to be the ones who retrieved the bags from the car on our way into the courtyard, but as soon as I saw the two policemen, I had visions of not even being able to complete that bit of the job without being arrested.

Marlow was clearly made of sterner stuff, as he just continued on in the same jovial manner.

'Oh, you have to give these Italian policemen their due,' he commented, still smiling. 'They're so good they're on to us before we've even done anything wrong.'

I had to laugh at his manner, which relaxed me, and was even able to mutter something in response as we approached the officers. Apparently the humour helped to hide our guilt, because we were still joking with one another as we passed the policemen with polite nods on both sides.

Marlow stopped shortly afterward to light his pipe, and give the two officers time to walk on, before we went over to the car.

While the Carabinieri didn't seem in any great rush, they only walked down the street to the next junction before turning off, so we were able to walk over to the car without having to worry what they might think.

My heart was still thundering as we made our way along between the wall and the car, which was now in deep shadow, retrieved the bags and then casually walked up to the gate, opened it and stepped inside.

The courtyard was as I'd expected. A large cobblestone area, shaded by several handsome looking trees, which were still coming into leaf, but even with the light canopy they already had, they still created an impressively shade below the one working street light, especially toward the back of the courtyard.

Peter was nowhere in sight, but there was a glimmer of light coming from behind one of the doors leading off the courtyard. Presumably the gardeners tool store.

We weren't likely to be seen in the courtyard, but we moved further back toward the door from which we could see the faint light.

Quickly slipping inside we found Peter had balanced his torch on a small shelf, and was using the light it cast to clear the garden tools away from the back wall with its patterned brickwork.

As soon as the door closed behind us we fished the daggers and the oil out of our bags and got on with counting the bricks.

The slender crevices we were looking for were exactly where Selene had said they would be, though to me they looked more like natural cracks or gaps in the bricks and mortar, until we tried one with a knife and discovered the innocuous looking blemish was well over eight inches deep.

'Alright,' Marlow began, taking his poignard to the first hole. 'We're supposed to insert the blade into each hole, one after the other in a clockwise direction, starting at twelve o'clock.'

The knife went straight in at twelve o'clock with barely a sound, then again at two o'clock, five o'clock, seven o'clock, eleven o'clock and finally back at twelve.

Nothing obvious happened, and we all stood back waiting.

'Should we try pushing?' Peter asked, before putting his shoulder to it with no effect.

'Feels a lot like pushing at a brick wall,' he observed.

'Do you think we were supposed to take the knife out of the last slot?' Marlow asked, looking at the knife still sticking out of the twelve o'clock position where he'd left it.

'Worth a go,' suggested Peter, just as Harry and Androus appeared through the door.

'Any problems?' I asked them, once they'd closed the door behind them, only to receive a nod from Androus in response.

As we watched, Marlow retrieved the knife from the slot and motioned for Peter to give the wall another push with his shoulder, which he did and very nearly fell down the hidden staircase behind the wall, as it silently swung away more easily than he'd expected.

The entire back wall of the tool room had simply swung backwards on some kind of massive hinge, to reveal a three-foot-wide spiral staircase which descended to the left.

'That's a rather well engineered door,' Peter observed, dusting his shoulder off, before shining a torch down the staircase.

'The steps seem in good order,' he observed, putting his weight on the first one.

It took me a minute to realise we were about to descend into a secret place, the presence of which most people in the city above would have no suspicion even existed.

A moment later and Jean and Luke arrived, quickly shutting the door behind them before turning to discover we'd already opened the secret doorway.

It wasn't often I could so easily tell what was going through my friends' minds, especially Jean's, but now as they both stood at the back of the overcrowded room, I knew they had both been expecting it to take longer to open the hidden door, if we managed it at all.

'Incroyable!' was all Jean said.

'Well, the street outside is still quiet, the gate to the street is locked, and it appears the secret door which I admit to being sceptical about the existence of, has not only been found, it has already been opened,' observed Luke.

'Wait until you see what's around the corner,' Peter said, coming back up the stairs. 'Looks like we've got to navigate a bit of Roman archaeology before we get to the vaults.'

We'd all spent enough time by now in the room that acted as a garden store, so, one after another we followed Peter down the spiral staircase into what looked like part of a Roman house.

It was a medium sized space with a fairly elaborate, if damaged, mosaic on the floor. The plainly decorated stucco covered walls were a terracotta colour up to waist height, and then a cream or stone colour above, topped by a simple barrel shaped ceiling.

There were various pieces of pottery stacked in the corners of the room, some broken, some still completely intact, along with other items that could've been made of wood or metal.

The entire room was covered in a thick layer of dust, with the exception of a slightly less dusty pathway across the middle of the room, which led to another doorway and set of steps.

'I haven't scouted out the steps at the far end of the

room yet,' Peter whispered. 'Might be best to keep our voices down for a minute or two while I take a look.'

It was a good point and while we spread out around the room, when we did speak to one another we did so very quietly.

Androus and Harry were in their element, and after casting their torch beams around the room for a moment, they went over to a corner where the mosaic wasn't covered up with debris.

'A wolf with a small boy playing between its legs,' Harry observed quietly. 'Perhaps a reference to the mythical founders of Rome, but it seems unusual to depict either Romulus or Remus without the other.'

'I was thinking exactly the same,' replied Androus. 'But there's something odd about this infant. Is there a brush or cloth which we could use to remove some of the dust?'

I was stood nearby, and had just spotted a small brush amongst the pots. Picking it up I passed it over and then watched what they were uncovering.

Androus took the brush and carefully dusted off the mosaic of the figures in the corner, before standing up again so we could all see.

'A female infant with longer curly hair,' he explained, intrigued.

'Could it be a reference to the wolf cults and the Harpy Sorani this far south?' Harry asked.

'Well they are one of the few chthonic cults we know about, and we are located just above what to the Romans might well have looked like an entrance to the underworld…' Androus speculated.

I think they'd have happily continued with their academic speculation, completely forgetful of the reason we were stood in this subterranean room, had it not been for Peter reappearing at the top of the next set of steps.

He still spoke quietly, but was no longer whispering as we gathering around.

'The steps led down another forty or fifty feet below the level of this chamber, and come out at a large iron gate. No locks, but it's probably best if we oil up the hinges before attempting to open it. From what I can see through the bars of the gate, it opens out into a largish store room or archive that's filled floor to ceiling with crates and cardboard boxes. Couldn't see anyone moving around down there.'

It all matched Selene's instructions, with the exception of the Roman room we now stood in, which she'd not mentioned.

Before we descended down the second set of steps we all took a moment to put our overcoats on, and fasten them to the neck in order to hide the white of our dinner-shirts.

As we descended the second set of steps toward the iron gate which Peter had mentioned, I noticed the steps were more crudely fashioned and seemed worn, while those on the spiral staircase were still regular and in pristine condition. The course of this second set of steps was also quite erratic, twisting first one way then another, at times descending steeply and then being level. I tried to keep track of where we might be in relation to the buildings on the surface, but after a couple of minutes I'd lost all sense of direction.

I was following Harry and Androus this time, with Jean, Marlow and Luke bringing up the rear. As we walked I could hear the two historians quietly commenting on the different features they observed along the way. Some paved flooring in one section of the tunnel, a deliberately carved oil lamp niche in another, some traces of ochre paint here and there. I honestly don't think they could help themselves when they were surrounded by the remains from antiquity.

Soon the corridor started to spread out and become more finely hewn, with higher ceilings and well finished walls. A few steps further on and we reached the gate which Peter had mentioned. It was over nine feet tall, and constructed from thick iron bars riveted together with massive two-inch-wide rivets, looking more like something from a mediaeval castle. It was crudely made but doubtless a very effective barrier if it had to be barred for any reason.

On our side of the gate the corridor was relatively straight for a good fifty or sixty feet, with very little cover for us to hide behind if we'd needed it, but it would also be quite dark if it weren't for our torches.

As soon as we'd all arrived Peter came in close to us, and again started to whisper.

'I can't imagine there's any way this gate isn't going to squeal loud enough to alert everyone in this place if we don't get some oil onto those hinges before we try and open it,' he pointed out.

'Now we've got the time to do it properly, so I'll put a bit of oil on the top of the hinges, which will soak down eventually, but if the rest of you can manage to lift the gate just a fraction and then hold it for a few seconds I'll get some oil on the base of the hinge also.'

The gate was wide enough for three of us to get a hold of it and lift at the same time.

Jean, Marlow and Luke did the honours, while both myself and Androus kept our torches shining on the hinges so that Peter could see what he was doing.

Then Peter oiled the top of the hinges, and when the others were ready he got into a position where he could get the oil onto the bottom of the hinges as soon as the gate was lifted.

The three of them then took the strain, and on a count of three just managed to inch the heavy gate up on its hinges for a couple of seconds before they had to it let back down.

There was a dull thud as the gate went back down, but nothing loud enough to be heard beyond the corridor.

Jean, Marlow and Luke stepped away to get their breath back after their exertions.

Peter had managed to get some oil on both hinges,

though had obviously been a bit rushed with the second.

As soon as everyone had recovered, Peter unfastened the simple chain that held the gate shut and carefully pushed it open.

It still wasn't silent by any measure, but by moving the gate slowly it was quiet enough. Eventually the gap was wide enough for a person to get through, which was all we needed.

Turning most of the flashlights off now, we one by one slipped through the gap into the store room on the other side.

As soon as they were through, Peter and Jean began to scout the room while the rest of us waited.

Both men shielded the light from their torches with their fingers while they explored, so that within a few yards it was impossible to see where either of them were. Occasionally we would catch a glimpse of light, from one or the other, when they needed to see something more clearly, but it was only ever momentary, and we couldn't be sure where they were until they returned to where we were waiting.

'It is a most curious place this vault of the Icarii,' Jean informed us in a low voice. 'The room is irregularly shaped and from what I can tell was once a natural cave which has been enlarged.'

'I'd agree,' commented Peter. 'Though whether it was one cave originally or several it's impossible to tell, but there are clearly large areas where the walls and floor show signs of having been worked, while there are other sections which look completely natural.'

'Can you tell what it is they've stored in here?' Harry asked.

'From what I can see, this room is mostly a research archive,' explained Jean. 'Made up of newspaper clippings and academic publications that suggest unusual theories about the origins of humankind or lost civilisations. There's a big section on early church history and excavations in the

Holy Land.

'I also found a disturbingly large section of files on politicians, including detailed biographies, interests, known habits and predilections.

'Fortunately, most of the files seem to be relating to political figures from thirty plus years ago, so I'm guessing this is all the older archived data which doesn't need to be consulted very often.'

'It was the same with the documents I looked at,' confirmed Peter. 'The vast majority of it was at least thirty years old.'

'And what about exits?' asked Marlow.

'Only one,' replied Jean. 'At the far end of the room, there's an ordinary looking doorway which leads on to a corridor lit by old electric bulkhead lights, not particularly bright, but good enough to allow us to dispense with the flash lights. The corridor also appears to be lined with a great many boxes and shelves, which may be enough to provide us with some cover should we need it.'

'Well, Selene's instructions were to leave the room and head southwards down the corridor, and then to take the fourth corridor on the left, at which point the room we're after should be the last one on the right,' Marlow added.

The main difficulty with the instructions, was a complete lack of scale. Selene had told Marlow only that the place was very large and sprawling, because it followed a natural cavern complex, but cave systems could stretch on for miles if not tens of miles, so we were hoping that Selene's idea of very large was considerably smaller than that.

We fell into a stalking pattern as we stepped into the corridor, a long strung-out line like we'd used in Africa, when following the trail of an animal. Each person close enough to the one in front to support them, but not so close they'd add to any slight noise they might make.

Peter had taken the lead again, and we quietly

followed him down the gently sloping corridor, passing a number of doors leading into other rooms, as well as the occasional side passage or set of steps leading off to the sides.

After about a hundred yards, the corridor ended at a wide set of steps down to another, broader corridor, that appeared to run directly below the one we were in.

Ahead of us Peter hesitated at the bottom of the steps before quietly coming back up them and indicating we should back up a fraction, away from the top of the steps.

'The corridor below seems like a larger version of this one,' he whispered. 'But fifty yards or so back from the steps there's a desk with a guard.

'Now the steps are wide and solid, so as long as we keep those between us and the guard he won't be able to see us, and further on, the corridor bends, at which point we'll be out of sight.'

Peter would again go first, but then find a shadowy spot from where he could watch the guard, in order to give us a signal if we'd attracted his attention.

Stepping softly was at least something we all knew how to do, even if most of our experience was from the African bush.

We followed Peter one by one with Jean the last to join us. He was still careful, but barely needed to try when it came to walking quietly, even in a pair of dress shoes. Something I couldn't help but smile slightly at the sight of, wondering if this was a skill his female acquaintances valued for some reason.

He caught the smile on my face and raised an intrigued eyebrow in response, which I knew meant it was something he'd want to ask me about later on. Assuming we managed to find what we wanted and get out undetected.

We moved around the corner without anyone attracting the guard's attention, and almost immediately came to the second and then the third junction on our left. There was some activity coming from the second corridor though, so we all hid while Peter investigated.

He was almost at the left-hand corridor when suddenly we saw him step close into the wall and crouch down behind one of the stacks of boxes which seemed to litter every corridor in this place.

We all did likewise and a heartbeat later two more guards walked around the corner wheeling an empty sack trolley each, and turning away from us but in the direction we wanted to go.

I wasn't sure what we were going to do for a moment, but as soon as the guards had moved a short way ahead of us, Peter simply stood up out of his hiding place and started to follow them, hugging the shadows and stepping into cover whenever possible.

The corridor continued to twist and turn, so there were times when we could move quicker, catching up to the guards almost, only to drop back a moment later until they went out of sight again.

Eventually they turned into the fourth corridor on our left, the same corridor we were after, but no sooner had they turned off than they seemed to disappear again into an opening which looked as though it led out into a larger space.

Peter followed them to see where they'd gone, but then came scuttling back almost immediately, motioning for us all to hide further along the corridor we'd just turned off.

Sure enough, seconds behind him another two guards came walking along with two sack trolleys, this time weighed down with boxes and tea chests overflowing with documents.

While the guards were all of the same rather docile looking type, these were definitely not the same two we'd just followed. They did however retrace the same route the first two guards had used to get here.

Peter moved again before these two guards were even fully out of sight. Quickly stepping over to the side corridor they'd emerged from, and then again ducking into the anonymous room.

I was curious to find out what was going on, but Peter seemed eager to get back into the room before updating us.

We watched as he slowly made his way to the threshold, and then pressed himself against the wall before looking around the corner. He stayed rooted to the spot for a good two minutes before quietly retracing his steps towards where we were waiting.

Silently he motioned us into the side corridor, and past the entrance to the room the men had come out of, before leading us through an ordinary looking door and up some steps.

The steps ended in a small anteroom and door. This Peter carefully opened before motioning us through, indicating we should stay low and quiet.

We'd stepped out onto a theatre style balcony, that overlooked a small cavern of a singularly curious design.

The walls of the cavern were in deep shadow, but it appeared to be a roughly circular space about thirty yards across. In its centre was a large sunken area with a sandy looking base and steep walls that could almost have passed for a very deep swimming pool.

Around the edges of this waterless 'pool' stood six low marble plinths, and then behind these the room was unfurnished aside from several doorways, again six in number, and each one closed off with heavy looking wooden doors.

I could make neither head nor tail of the purpose of the room, but this wasn't made any the easier by the stacks of crates and boxes which seemed to fill almost every spare inch of it.

Labouring to load these boxes onto their sack trolleys we could see the two men we'd just followed, as well as another six, with stepladders, who seemed to be engaged in moving boxes from the pool and centre of the room out to the walls, even if that meant blocking most of the entrances and stacking the boxes dangerously high.

We watched for another few minutes trying to make sense of what we were seeing before Jean finally indicated we should move.

The first two men we'd followed down the corridor with the empty trolleys had now left with a full load and been replaced by those we'd watched depart, so it seemed like a safe bet that we'd have another few minutes to get back down the stairs and out of sight before either pair returned or departed the room again.

We needed somewhere to discuss what we'd seen, but it would have to be a distance away from this odd room.

The directions we had from Selene led us further down this side corridor, through another large storage room and then down another set of steps and short corridor to the room we were the tablets had been stored.

We looked in on a couple of side rooms on the way, and were just shy of the room where our artefacts were supposed to be stored when we discovered an office, which still had a few desks and chairs in it that weren't completely covered by boxes and crates.

There were no windows in the room, so we risked switching one of the table lamps on for a bit of extra light, and to save our torches.

'I don't much like the look of that room, my friends,' Jean began, seriously. 'I cannot say for sure why, but it looks as though it is intended to keep something or somebody captive.'

'I thought the same,' commented Harry. 'All that ironwork hanging from the ceiling, I don't know what it was for, but it had a distinctly mediaeval cast to it.'

'It certainly appears to have some kind of ceremonial function,' Androus agreed. 'Perhaps a religious test of some sort.'

'I can't help but wonder if it could be related to the fragment of Miriam's conversation which I overheard at the bookshop,' I ventured.

'I agree, George,' replied Jean. 'Which would make it the Chamber of Truth would it not?'

'If it is the same thing you overheard, George,' Marlow said. 'Then I believe Miriam's instructions were for those men to have the room ready for midnight?'

'That gives us barely an hour and a half to find the tablets and get into a position where we've got a good view of the proceedings,' Marlow continued, with a dangerous glint in his eye.

It was a risk we all knew we didn't need to take, but at the same time, knowing so little about the Icarii meant every scrap of additional intelligence was valuable. It was Jean who again provided the rationale which decided us.

'I know what Robert is suggesting is not part of the plan we had in coming here, and the temptation is to think only of today, to strike this blow against our enemy in a way which they may not even notice for several days.

'But equally, this could be a significant opportunity we have stumbled across, which may enable us to strike back at them in other ways, or even avoid a trap which they have been carefully laying for us.

'Perhaps though, it is possible for us to follow Peter's fine and frequent example,' he continued, with that familiar mirthful gleam in his eye. 'We could have our cakes and eat them!'

'Of course!' Harry said, almost laughing at the pleasure of it. 'We find the tablets and take them back to the car, and then even if we're detected we can still make a run for it, in the full knowledge that we've already gotten away with the loot!'

There was no denying the elegance of it as a solution, even if I didn't cherish the idea of having to run for my life through the warren of tunnels.

In any event we had to concentrate on our primary aim of finding the tablets, so with a revised plan, we turned the light off and checked the corridor outside before making our way to the room where Selene had indicated the tablets would be stored.

I was already impressed by the scale of the Icarii complex, which had existed for several hundred years in secret beneath one of the most populous European cities, but the archive room we now entered took my breath away.

It was simply colossal, the like of which I'd never imagined let alone seen, big enough to fit St Peter's Basilica inside. It must have been over three hundred feet high in the centre, more than that wide, and easily six hundred feet long.

The floor of this cavern was covered in wooden shelving over thirty feet tall, accessible only via tall wheeled-ladders which were placed in the aisles between the countless lines of shelves.

I couldn't begin to estimate how many boxes, chests, cases, folders, crates and books were contained in that one room alone. It was no wonder the Order had chosen to relocate all of the operational activities elsewhere, rather than moving the myriad items they had archived here.

Before we'd come into this room I'd considered an hour and a half to be plenty of time to locate the items belonging to us, but looking at the size of the place, I realised with dismay that we could spend a month searching and still not find what we were after.

Fortunately, Androus was less easily overawed, and after looking at the row upon row of shelving with the rest of us for a moment, he simply turned on his heel and walked over to a desk just inside the entrance door, where Jean had stayed to keep a lookout.

There were a couple of very ordinary looking bookshelves behind the desk, which I don't think I'd even noticed in contrast to the gigantic stacks of shelving which filled the rest of the cavern. But to Androus they were the obvious place to look for what he was after.

'Ah yes, here we are,' he said, as much to himself as anyone else. 'Last year's ledger. January, February, March, April, "Cuneiform tablets – recovered from unknown source, nineteen pieces with associated notes." They even kept my notes from the look of it. Row twelve, section fifty-four, racks six and seven.

'Rather a basic cataloguing system by modern standards, but it should be sufficient to get us in the general area.'

With that he walked off to the clearly marked Row Twelve, just as though he were making his way around his own library archives back in Jerusalem.

Like the rest of us Harry was a bit overwhelmed at the scale of the archive we now found ourselves in, but he dashed after his friend trying his level best to keep up with Androus' continuing dialogue.

'It is always the way with these independent museums and libraries. They're set up by those with more enthusiasm than knowledge of effective classification,' he muttered.

'I mean, "Cuneiform tablets", would you not from such a brief description expect to find a collection of the traditional baked clay tablets that are so numerously extant in the cuneiform languages, rather than the considerably more majestic carved lapis creations we now see before us?'

There they were, stacked one on top of the other the blue and gold of the stone shimmering in the light from our torches.

Androus had led us straight to them, no detours or mistakes, straight to the exact shelf.

Fortunately, the shelf in question was located at eye level, so we could not only see the tablets, we could start retrieving them immediately, carefully wrapping each one in a piece of cloth before placing them in one of the bags which we'd brought along expressly for the purpose.

There seemed no order or theme to the rest of the items shelved in this location, and on the shelves below I could see some occult writings from an infamous Victorian spiritualist, while above there were ceramics of an obviously classical origin.

'Androus,' I found myself saying before I'd really thought it through. 'Do you suppose the tablets which they beat us to in Crete might also be stored here?'

'It would be a simple matter to check,' replied our epigraphist, as he led us back to the desk.

'Would it be the end of February or start of March when they were on the island?' Androus asked none of us in particular.

'I believe it was the very end of February when they found the tablets,' Luke offered. 'But it would've been the start of March at the earliest before they arrived here in Rome.'

'Ah yes, here we are,' confirmed Androus, with his finger on the ledger. 'March the tenth, again the ledger simply reads, "Cuneiform tablets", recovered from pre-classical Cretan hermitage, nine pieces.'

He didn't waste time reading aloud the location details, he just led us straight to the relevant shelf, though this time we had to bring one of the ladders along in order to retrieve them.

It was the same mishmash of items surrounding them again, Egyptian papyri, large carved stones that featured unmistakably Norse imagery.

We quickly secured these tablets as well, again wrapping them carefully before placing them in a separate canvass bag, so we wouldn't confuse them with the first set.

It was so tempting to look at some of the other treasures which this mysterious order had squirrelled away down here, but Jean had a more mischievous plan in mind.

'Am I correct in thinking it would be immeasurably more difficult for our adversaries to discover these artefacts are missing if the entries in that ledger were to be damaged or to go missing?' he asked with a feigned note of innocence in his voice.

'Immeasurably more difficult would be a complete understatement,' confirmed Androus. 'With neither any form of cross reference, nor apparently any trace of systematic shelving, these items might never be missed.'

It still took a minute for the penny to drop, before Androus suddenly realised what Jean was suggesting.

'Oh, oh yes. Yes of course, if we were to simply extract the relevant pages, perhaps even make it look like a page had simply come loose, and create a page of fake entries to really mislead them.'

'Could it be done quickly,' Jean asked, clearly concerned that the time we had before midnight was running out.

As though in response, Androus took his pocket knife out and expertly extracted the pages which mentioned the tablets, gave Harry one to copy while he did the other himself. Keeping all the other entries the same, but completely changing the location details for the tablets to somewhere he just copied from another page in the ledger, he then reinserted those two copies of the original page in the relevant places before returning the ledger to where he'd found it.

Five minutes later and we were once more threading our way through the maze of tunnels and corridors back the way we'd come.

It was difficult negotiating the corridor down which the guards were transporting their trolleys full of boxes to a different storage area, but we managed to slip past them again and in no time were back up the stairs and in the Roman room where we could relax and finalise our plans.

Some of us would head back to the hotel with the tablets, while the rest would once again head down into the vaults in order to eavesdrop on whatever was about to happen in that strange ceremonial chamber.

TRIAL

I COULD SEE ABSOLUTELY NOTHING in the inky blackness of the strange cavern, which we believed the Order called the Chamber of Truth.

But from my position between the towering piles of crates and files, I knew that once the lights were back on I'd be able to see a reasonable part of the room, including whatever was about to happen in the deeply sunken area which dominated the centre of the floor.

Jean was to my right at about shoulder height, perched on top of an old portmanteau.

Marlow and Luke were on the other side of the room, similarly hidden away amongst another huge pile of files, books and artefacts.

We'd been waiting in our positions for about half an hour, and I was beginning to lament not having taken an extra few minutes to find a larger space in which to hide, but at the time we hadn't known how long we'd have before someone might turn up, so we'd all just ducked in amongst the boxes and found a spot that would do.

I thought I'd struck it lucky when I found a space behind a packing crate containing some carved classical busts loosely packed in straw. The sides of the crate were made of widely spaced slats that allowed me to see through to the centre of the room, once the straw was pushed out of the way.

A couple of similar crates had been placed on top of it, which would make a deep shadow of my hiding place no matter how brightly lit the chamber became.

Jean, while more comfortable had a more restricted

view through what looked like a map cabinet. Roll upon roll of maps jammed lengthways into a backless cabinet allowed him to see through the centre of each parchment, several of which he'd also removed to improve his view.

The others I suspected were stuck in very similar positions, but once they'd disappeared into the stacks I'd lost sight of them.

We'd seen Harry, Androus and Peter up to the courtyard next to the Jesuit library, which was exactly as we'd left it, and even managed to get them out of the gate without attracting any attention.

Peter had given us the key he'd fashioned as we closed the gate behind him, so we'd be able to lock up on our way out after witnessing whatever it was we were about to see. Then it was time for the rest of us to return to the vaults below.

I saw the luminous hands on Jean's wristwatch move in the dark as he looked at the time, before he whispered to me that it was now just turning midnight.

As though in response one of the doors into the chamber opened and a guard entered to light several heavily shaded gas lamps which hung from the ceiling in the centre of the room. This created a stark cone of light around the pit, but left the rest of the room in deep shadow.

The guard then retreated, closing the door behind him.

Not being able to see the edges of the chamber was unexpected, and I couldn't help but remember there was a balcony on the far side which remained invisible to us. On the plus side it meant we were completely hidden in the shadows.

We sat there quietly for a few more minutes with no further sign of anything happening. Then two of the doors suddenly opened and six cloaked figures, three robed in black and three in brown, all with hoods drawn forward over their faces, walked into the room. The three on our side of the room in the black cloaks were accompanied by two elaborately clad guards, each wearing a blackened version of the armour worn by the Swiss guard in the Vatican, and bearing an unsheathed great-sword, point down in their hands.

The cloaked figures walked to the centre and then in unison stepped up onto the six marble plinths which overlooked the pit. Meanwhile the two guards stood behind the black cloaked figures on our side of the room, the tips of their swords now resting lightly upon the ground.

'Thank you all for attending this solemn occasion,' one of the figures on our side of the room began in English. 'It is with a heavy heart that we are gathered here today to pass judgment upon one of our own number who has been accused of betraying her sacred vows.

'Who now names the accused?'

'I Agostine of Padua, name the accused as Sister Selene of Florence,' responded one of the brown cloaked figures on the other side of the room in a familiar voice.

'Sister Selene of Florence? My predecessors own protégé. This is who you accuse?' asked the black cloaked figure more sternly.

'That is correct, Reverend Mother.'

'Superior Agostine, I am now even more troubled than before at your call for a judgment. Not only has this chamber been unused in nearly one hundred years, but now you wish us to pass judgment upon a sister who has for several years been considered one of our most promising operatives?'

'That is correct, Reverend Mother.'

'As you will,' replied the more senior figure with a trace of hesitation. 'But this chamber will demand unequivocal evidence from you, to justify this accusation and the severe penalty which would attach to a guilty verdict in this place.'

'Yes, Reverend Mother. I understand and stand ready to provide that evidence.'

With this the figure which mother Agostine had

addressed only as Reverend Mother turned her head to each of the other two black clad figures on either side of her, who seemed to signal their satisfaction or willingness to proceed by simply nodding their hooded heads.

'Very well,' the senior woman finally said. 'Bring forth the accused.'

I started at these words, having assumed that the judgement upon Selene was going to be carried out in her absence. At the black cloaked figure's words the two elaborately clad guards walked to the side of the room to lay their swords down on a long wooden table, and then retrieved an iron ladder which had been hanging from the wall. They then lowered one end of this ladder into the pit before climbing down and moving to a small iron gate at its end. This they unlocked before passing through and out of our view.

The chamber remained quiet while the guards brought out the prisoner.

Jean placed his hand on my shoulder as we waited and carefully leaned across to whisper in my ear, telling me there was nothing we could do unless Selene's life appeared to be in grave danger.

I made a deliberate effort to brace myself for the ordeal ahead, though I was sure the betrayal of which Mother Agostine spoke, must relate to the way in which Selene had attempted to persuade Marlow not to pursue his search any further while he was in Cairo.

A couple of minutes later the guards reappeared with Selene manacled and chained between them. She was barefoot, and wearing only a long white shift.

I could also see bruising on Selene's arms and a fading bruise on her face, which suggested she hadn't been captured without a fight.

Despite the restraints her posture remained upright and defiant, and as she walked between the guards she looked around the pit and up at the figures standing on their plinths with no trace of fear in her eyes.

As they reached the centre of the pit the guards uncovered first one iron ring buried in the sand, and then another, which they then proceeded to fasten Selene's chains to, one at a time, before removing the manacles that held her hands together.

There was something about the way these two powerfully built men carefully re-chained Selene that made me think they were wary of their prisoner, manacles or not.

'Sister Selene of Florence, you have been brought here today to this the ancient Chamber of Truth to answer one of the most serious accusations that can be made within our order. Namely, that you have knowingly and willingly betrayed our order and in so doing have broken your sacred vows.

'How do you respond to this charge?'

For a moment I thought Selene was going to refuse to answer as she looked first from the speaker to the figures in the brown robes, but then in a clear voice she answered.

'I neither recognise nor choose to respond to the anonymous charges made by those who fear to show their faces.'

'This is the traditional form of judgement performed in this chamber,' snapped Mother Agostine, from her side of the room. 'As well you know, Sister Selene.'

Selene didn't even turn to face Mother Agostine as she said this. She simply stood facing the more senior speaker in the black robe.

'I am no more an admirer of these theatrics than you, Selene. Will you answer the charge if we dispense with these outdated tokens of a former age?'

'I will, Reverend Mother.'

'Then we will proceed with this matter in the light,' the senior speaker said, before carefully removing her hood and cloak and allowing it to fall to the ground, closely followed by all the other five figures.

Without the cloaks, we could see now that Mother Agostine was flanked on one side by Miriam, and on the other, by the Arabic looking woman that had travelled with Miriam and Thea in Geneva.

Across the pit from these three figures who had been wearing the brown cloaks, I could now see the figures who had been wearing black. In the centre stood a slender older woman of medium height with shoulder length white hair, cut in a fashionable style. To either side of her were women of a roughly similar age, with equally strong and confident postures. They all wore expensively tailored clothes.

'Thank you, Reverend Mother,' said Selene, without pause. 'In response to your question and the charges levelled against me I admit to defying the misguided instructions of Mother Agostine and of leaving the Order. But I deny utterly the charge of betraying our holy order or the sacred mission to which it was entrusted nearly four hundred years ago.'

'Your response concerns me in several ways, my child,' the Reverend Mother replied. 'Firstly, because you choose to draw a distinction between the defiance of your superior's instructions and the betrayal of our order. But also secondly, because you openly admit to leaving the order, an act which you know full well from your vows is not possible.

'Mother Agostine, do you have any response you wish to make to the defendant's statement?'

'Only that I interpret Sister Selene's statement as a confession of guilt.' Mother Agostine replied coldly.

'Very well, we will have to deal with these matters individually, beginning with your defiance of Mother Agostine's instructions.

We sat through Mother Agostine giving her account of how she had personally warned off a group of 'adventurers' who had stumbled upon some ancient artefacts after being seduced by a native African cult, and how she had subsequently dispatched operatives to monitor the members of that group to ensure they didn't return to the search for more artefacts.

'I recall your report on this episode, Superior Agostine, and was perturbed then as I am now, that even after managing to turn one of their number, events still somehow deteriorated to the point where you were forced to confront this group both openly and in person.'

'It was indeed regrettable Reverend Mother, but the composition of the group proved unusually… capable. We also became aware of their activities only after they had already achieved a degree of success, by which point there was only limited time to identify the usual personal, political, societal and familial weaknesses which could be exploited to influence the group, or if need be destroy its cohesion.'

These last comments were delivered by Mother Agostine, and received by the room so casually, I felt quite shocked.

But the more senior woman was now speaking again.

'I see,' she said, simply. 'Sister Selene, do you confirm and accept your accuser's version of accounts so far?'

'No, Reverend Mother, the account is incomplete,' Selene responded, again without turning to face Agostine.

'In what way, child?'

'Superior Agostine neglects to mention that in the process of confronting this group, she chose to violate her own sacred vows by deliberately destroying an ancient and unique artefact rather than returning it to this vault, as we are all sworn to do.'

'Is this true, Agostine?' The Reverend Mother asked bluntly, neglecting even to use the other woman's title.

'It was necessary,' broke in Miriam passionately, in Mother Agostine's defence. 'They'd beaten us, and needed to be taught a lesson.'

'Hush, Miriam!' Agostine responded sternly.

'Introduce yourself, child,' the Reverend Mother said coldly. 'And then explain to me what you meant by that statement.'

Miriam introduced herself as Miriam of Palermo, and then recounted what had happened in Corinth, where after rebuffing the legal challenge to have the artefacts confiscated, we had revealed our knowledge of both Luke as a spy amongst us, and of the three Icarii operatives who he'd been working for.

'These amateurs played with us, feeding us false information through our informant, causing us to expend our resources in order to stay ahead of them, only to discover it was a deliberate bluff to blind-side us while they went off to find the artefacts they sought.

'We needed to not only stop them, but to discourage them from ever attempting to oppose our wishes again.'

'I will ask you again, Superior Agostine,' The Reverend Mother said with a cold deliberation. 'Did you order the destruction of a unique artefact in order to teach this group a lesson?'

'I did, Reverend Mother, and I would do the same again.' Mother Agostine responded defiantly.

'That is a serious breach of both our code and the purview of our mission,' the more senior woman responded, clearly displeased at what she was hearing. 'But we will deal with that matter separately.

'Are there any other inaccuracies in Mother Agostine's account to this point, which you wish to make us aware of, Sister Selene?' The Reverend Mother asked.

'No, Reverend Mother,' was Selene's simple reply.

'Very well then, we shall proceed,' the senior woman replied.

'Superior Agostine, you have described how you warned this group off. Please tell us what happened next.'

'Yes, Reverend Mother,' Agostine responded.

This is where the description became more interesting for us, because while we'd suspected the Icarii were keeping an eye on us, we had no idea when it started or how it was done.

Mother Agostine proceeded to describe how we had each been allowed to go our own way, but how she'd deployed a team of operatives to watch us, and gather additional information that could be used for potential leverage in the future.

We had apparently all led exceptionally quiet lives, with the exception of Harry and Marlow. Harry, it appeared had started to brush up on his pre-Babylonian history and had also tried to learn whatever he could about early cuneiform writing, while convalescing from his broken shoulder and subsequent bout of malaria.

The Order had managed to intercept or significantly hinder most of his efforts, without raising his suspicions.

Marlow was another matter.

'Him we lost track of altogether for a while,' she explained, very matter-of-factly. 'We knew he was raised in West Africa by his adoptive parents who were working there as missionaries, and that he'd apparently come close to going completely native in his teens, spending days at first and then weeks away from home in the jungle, as much a wild creature as a civilised human being, before being sent back to England to bring him back in line.

'We knew he'd reappear eventually though, so in addition to sending out the usual notices to our satellite sites, I also dispatched the team that had the greatest familiarity with him to monitor the main centres of activity across north Africa.

'As expected he showed up in Cairo three months later, like his colleague, attempting to further his knowledge in subjects related to the activity the group had been warned not to pursue.'

'And how did you respond to this information?' The Reverend Mother asked.

'I dispatched the closest senior operative, Sister Selene, to monitor his activities and report back on whether a more permanent intervention was merited,' Mother

Agostine responded with complete equanimity.

'And this is when you allege Sister Selene betrayed the Order?' the more senior woman asked.

'It is, Reverend Mother,' Agostine continued. 'Sister Selene had been in position for over a month, and had reported nothing but a lack of progress with the authorities in Cairo, who as you know, have a history of being uncooperative with both the Order and the mother church.

'But she also seemed reluctant to confirm the need for any further sanctions against the individual, despite having no evidence to suggest he was or could be diverted from resuming his prior activities.

'Eventually, after nearly six weeks of inadequate progress I engaged Sister Haleena of Kos,' she said, indicating the Egyptian looking woman on the other side of her. 'Who I instructed to travel to Cairo and investigate how Sister Selene was proceeding with her instructions.

'What I learned was that instead of monitoring the subject, she was seen to be freely consorting with him in public cafés and restaurants.'

'I see,' replied the Reverend Mother sternly. 'And how did you choose to act upon receiving this shocking information?'

'Naturally, I was seriously concerned, so I ordered Sister Selene's second, Miriam of Palermo and her third, Thea of Turin, to attend her in Cairo. However, as it would take several days for them to arrive, I also instructed Sister Haleena to make her presence known to Sister Selene and to convey the instruction that she was to sequester herself and have no further contact with the subject of her operation, until I arrived in Cairo.'

'And how did Sister Selene respond to these instructions?'

'She responded by incapacitating Haleena and then warning the subject of her investigation to flee the city, which he did, resulting in the Order again losing track of him, and his whereabouts, which are still unknown.'

'I cannot begin to express how shocking and disappointing these allegations are to hear,' the Reverend Mother replied. 'As such my child, I must urge you to think carefully before you answer the following questions, and to answer them fully and frankly so that this court may judge you fairly and accurately.

'Sister Selene, do you accept this version of accounts described my Superior Agostine?'

'I do not,' Selene replied.

'Do you deny consorting with the subject of your operations?'

'I did not consort with him. I engaged him openly in an attempt to dissuade him from continuing any further search for the artefacts he had been seeking.'

'Sister Selene, I should not need to remind you how the Order operates and how important secrecy is to our mission. I accept your motives may have been well intentioned, but surely you must accept that for even a first-class operative such as yourself, the decision to engage the subject of your operation was your superior's alone.'

'Yes, Reverend Mother,' was Selene's simple reply

'Then why did you make the decision to pursue this reckless course of action, knowing it would be against the wishes of your superior?'

'Because I found myself in a position of conflict. I could not obey my superior without breaking my vows, and I could not keep my vows without defying my superior.

'I could not condone the destruction of that precious artefact, an artefact like so many others which I have vowed to preserve and safeguard, until such a time as those more learned than ourselves have decided what should be done with it.

'Furthermore, I found I could not in good conscience consider killing one of those men who found that artefact purely to make up for my own superior's earlier failings. Accordingly, the only way I could find of doing that which was in keeping with our mission and my vows, was to go outside our normal method of operation, and to reason with this man, and persuade him to follow his current course no further.'

It was a genuine and impassioned statement from Selene, but I could tell it was falling on deaf ears when it came to the Reverend Mother.

'And what did you do when you received the order from your Superior to sequester yourself and have no further contact with this man?'

'I chose to leave this order to which I have devoted my life, and to make amends for superior Agostine's actions, by warning the subject of my operation of our intentions to kill him.'

'And in the process you also incapacitated your fellow Sister who was sent to deliver these instructions to you.'

'Sister Haleena attempted to do more than merely deliver the superiors instructions. She attempted to enforce them,' Selene responded, defiantly. 'A mistake for which I could've chosen to take her life.'

'Nevertheless, Sister Selene, your responses during this judgement are concerning, I have no choice but to find the allegations made against you by superior Agostine to be justified. This Chamber finds you guilty of betraying the Order to which you have pledged your service, and of undermining the sacred mission to which this order is dedicated.

'Are my Second and Third in agreement with this judgement?'

With this the Reverend Mother looked first to her colleague on her left, who instantly nodded her agreement, and then to the woman on her right, who also nodded without hesitation.

'Thank you, Reverend Mothers. The decision of the Chamber is unanimous.

'As all present must be aware, there is only one sentence for a unanimous verdict within this Chamber and that sentence is death. This sentence will be carried out at midnight tomorrow, at which time, Selene Autieri, you will be brought back to this chamber and exposed to the mercy of the Tiber. May God have mercy on your soul.

'If the condemned wishes to make a final statement, you may do so now, but do not waste your time requesting clemency for I tell you now, none shall be given.'

Selene hesitated for a moment and bowed her head for the first time during the proceedings, almost as though in resignation to her fate, but when she raised her eyes again to look upon the three Reverend Mothers who had condemned her, I saw an almost inhuman calm in her eyes, the kind of unwavering stillness few people would be able to return.

For a moment, I thought I saw the most senior of the Reverend Mothers waver beneath that gaze, before steeling herself to confront it.

It was only then that Selene finally spoke.

'I reject the findings of this chamber and denounce you who have sat in judgement upon me without hearing the words which I have spoken, and I decry the warped and twisted thing which you have made our once noble order into. May God have mercy on your souls.'

Those who had passed their judgment upon Selene bridled at these comments before signalling to the guards to convey her back to whatever dungeon or cell they had fetched her from.

As soon as the guards had returned and locked the sturdy iron gate which led from the pit where Selene had been standing, they once more climbed the ladder and reclaimed their swords before following the two groups of women as they departed the chamber. A few minutes afterward another guard appeared to douse the gas lights, once again plunging us into darkness.

After waiting another few minutes just to be on the safe side, we switched our flash-lights on and emerged from our hiding places, before gathering together beside one of the large doorways.

I could see in everyone's eyes we had all been appalled at what we had witnessed, but it was Marlow who voiced what we were all thinking.

'My friends, I know Selene has been a member of the secretive order which has worked so hard to thwart our plans, but we cannot allow this barbarism to take place,' he said simply. 'We must return here before tomorrow night to prevent this sentence from being carried out.'

'Ordinarily, Robert,' Jean replied. 'I would use this moment to remind you that in so doing we will be placing ourselves squarely beneath the gaze of our adversaries, who will surely move heaven and earth to find us and punish us for this deed. But, on this occasion, I am in full agreement with you, and we will deal with the consequences as best we can.'

'Is there no possibility of rescuing her now from wherever it is she has been locked up?' I asked rather hopefully.

'We have neither the tools, the expertise or the weaponry needed to break her out of a locked and perhaps guarded cell,' Jean replied. 'This gateway alone which leads from the pit into the cells has two substantial locks on it and appears to be constructed of the stoutest iron bars.

'Far better and more reliable to let her captors release her for us,' Jean concluded. 'Irrespective of the cost to ourselves.'

'We have a lot to do before tomorrow night,' Marlow observed. 'It's time to go.'

JUDGMENT

IT WAS NEARLY THREE O'CLOCK in the morning when we made it back to our hotel, closing the secret doorway from the tool room and then locking the courtyard gate on our way out.

Luke went his own way once we were back on the street, but only after first arranging to join us for breakfast the following morning.

The others were still awake and waiting for us in Jean's suite.

Not knowing how long we'd be, Harry and Peter had taken the opportunity to get some sleep in the comfortable armchairs, while Androus kept watch over the street for any sign of trouble around the building, or for us as we left the courtyard.

He'd seen us walking back toward the hotel and had prepared a glass of brandy for each of us before rousing the others, who were still rubbing their eyes and looking half asleep when we arrived.

They could tell it wasn't good news from our expressions the moment we set foot in the room, so we quickly sat down, and between us, described the trial we'd witnessed and the draconian sentence which had been passed.

But it was late, and despite the extent of the work we needed to do before nightfall the following day, we all needed some rest.

As always it was Jean who suggested the path of reason.

'I know we all wish to help Ms Autieri and prevent

this terrible sentence from being carried out,' he began. 'But tomorrow we must be at our best, not just during the day while we make our preparations, but tomorrow night when we confront this terrible organisation in its stronghold.

'With that in mind I suggest we re-convene in the morning. I will place a note beneath your doors as soon as I am awake and we will take matters from there.

We all knew he was right, so after downing our drinks, we quietly made our way to our rooms, for what I was anticipating would be a restless night all round.

I was exhausted, but didn't honestly think I would manage to get any sleep that night, until I woke up the following morning having slept a deep and dreamless sleep right the way through to nine o'clock.

The note from Jean was already present beneath my door, so I quickly freshened up and dressed before making my way to his suite.

Marlow, Luke and Harry were already there, but the others had yet to arrive, so I didn't feel too bad about my tardiness.

Jean had also asked the hotel's room service to bring a breakfast table up to his suite. This had already arrived to replace his coffee table and chairs, but breakfast had not yet been served.

'Good morning, George,' he welcomed me as he opened the door. 'Have you slept a little?'

I admitted I'd slept straight through, much to my surprise.

'Ah, the natural soldier,' Jean commented, before going on to explain, after seeing my look of puzzlement. 'One of the skills it is most difficult for soldiers to acquire is that of sleeping before a battle.

'The anticipation of combat is enough to keep most people and new recruits especially, awake, even though sleep will restore their strength, refresh their senses and enliven their minds.'

Pleasantries aside, we sat down and started making

plans for the day and night ahead.

'The way I see it,' Marlow explained. 'The ideal time for us to make our move is when the guards descend into the pit to retrieve Selene. They will have put their swords down in order to go and fetch her, leaving the others, who don't appear to be carrying weapons, undefended.'

'Yes, but what do we do once we've got them at gunpoint?' Harry asked.

'We could force them all down into the pit and through the gate into the cells,' I suggested. 'Lock it after them and they'd be stuck there until they're found.'

'No, we have no idea whether this prison has another entrance or exit,' replied Jean, thoughtfully. 'In fact it would be almost unimaginable for it not to have a more practical entrance than the one we have seen in the Chamber.'

'How about if we get them to lock the gate and give us the keys,' I said, thinking out loud. 'As soon as we pull up the ladder they'd be trapped in the pit, which was obviously designed to be difficult for prisoners to climb out of.'

'Yes, that might work,' replied Marlow. 'They could still shout in order to try and attract attention, but we only saw one other guard come into the room and the walls of that chamber are very thick.'

'What if we were to bring the other guard into the chamber and force him to join the others in the pit?' suggested Luke.

'Good,' commented Jean, thinking it through. 'We don't know how long the execution would be expected to take, but I cannot imagine anyone would think the situation amiss if the judges and their guards didn't show up for half an hour to an hour, which should give us more than enough time to get out of the complex.

'Of course, freeing Ms Autieri from the vaults is one thing. But getting us all away from Rome and Italy is quite another.'

He was right of course. Buying enough time to get out of the Icarii complex was the easy part. We did, after all have the advantage of surprise on our side, but as soon as we freed Selene that advantage would be gone. And once Agostine and the Reverend Mothers were free of the pit they would no doubt bring the entire capacity of their organisation to bear in finding us.

But how long it would take the Order to respond, and what forms their response might take, we just didn't know.

Androus and Peter joined us as we were deliberating this issue, at which point Jean called the hotel's room service to arrange for breakfast to be served.

During the course of the morning we worked through the various problems, breaking them down into more manageable pieces before coming up with solutions.

We would obviously need to let the hotel know we were leaving, and of course come up with some plausible reason for our early morning departure, but it didn't take us long to figure that bit out.

Luke could be standing-by with Jean's car to take us to the coast where Stephanos was waiting, but there was no way we'd get eight of us into one car, as it had been a squash with six.

That meant a couple of us would have to go on ahead, but as we also needed to move our luggage, and more importantly, the tablets, on to Stephanos' boat, why not kill two birds with one stone? We'd check-out in the early evening under the pretext of having been invited to go and stay with a friend of ours for a few days. At which point Luke, Androus and Peter would transport our belongings to the boat in Ostia, while the rest of us killed time somewhere before breaking back into the Icarii complex. This would give Luke time to return to Rome in Jean's car, arriving shortly before midnight, in good time to rendezvous with the rest of us as we emerged from the courtyard.

Luke could then drive us back to the coast where

we would say our goodbyes, before driving himself back to Rome. He would then hide the car in his garage until Jean's valet arrived from Paris to collect it.

'It sounds too easy,' Harry suggested. 'We need to consider what Agostine and the Order will be doing once they're free.'

'That's easier said than done,' I suggested. 'This is the Order's home territory, where they're going to have influence pretty much everywhere that would be useful.'

'Perhaps, George, perhaps,' commented Jean. 'But there are also some things we must remember.

'Rome is also the place where this Order wishes to keep strictly to the shadows, because this is their safe harbour, the place to which they wish to be able to return in times of trouble.'

'And,' added Harry, waving a piece of toast. 'The bulk of their operatives will be stationed outside Rome and even outside Italy, because that's where the focus of their mission needs them to be. You don't need to work too hard to protect the mother church in arguably the most Christian country on the planet.

'Alright,' suggested Marlow, trying to distil what we were all saying. 'So they won't have that many people they can draw on, and they can't act too conspicuously, but they'll probably be able to mobilise the authorities under some pretext to get them to look for us.'

'Contacting the Carabinieri to report you for anti-government activities would be the easiest way to get the authorities involved in the hunt,' suggested Luke. 'Over recent years Mussolini's government has become increasingly heavy handed at dealing with those who oppose the current regime, whether foreigners or Italians.'

'If they can persuade the police to put up road-blocks, or perhaps close all the ports and airports,' Harry speculated. 'How long is the journey likely to take at that time of night?'

'I would suggest two hours,' replied Luke. 'Perhaps

longer, considering we will have to drive through much of the city before we get to the open road, and to travel at speed would attract a great deal of attention.'

'I don't think they're going to be able to react quickly enough,' ventured Marlow. 'Say we only get half an hour head start, which is probably realistic. It will take ten or fifteen minutes to get out of the vaults and then straight into the car.

'Even if they have the presence of mind to start calling their contacts straight away, at that time of night it's going to take a while to get hold of people and for those people to act.'

'I agree,' replied Luke. 'If they wish to keep a low profile they will not wish to be waking up the General Intendent of Police in the small hours of the morning, not without having a convincing cover story to give them, which itself will take time to arrange.'

We talked through the various options from a number of different angles, and discussed a couple of possible contingency routes out of the city in case things didn't go our way. We even considered how we might lay a false trail to try and make our adversaries think we had headed across Italy to the Adriatic coast, and then on to Montenegro or Albania, but eventually we decided to keep our plan simple.

Not overthinking things made the arrangements relatively easy to make. We only needed to pack our things and check out of the hotel, before transporting everything we didn't require for the evening to Stephanos' boat.

The final arrangements involved what we'd need to take into the vaults. We'd have to take our guns with us this time, though none of us felt particularly comfortable with the idea, as well as the poignards and other equipment we'd taken the night before.

It was the timing that caused us the greatest problems. We'd have to check-out of the hotel in the early evening to give Luke time to drive to the coast and back before midnight, which left the rest of us needing to kill some time in the centre of the city with a bag full of dangerous weapons and equipment, until it was dark enough to make our entrance into the courtyard.

Luke suggested another bistro worth trying, which again had a reputation for discretion. He also suggested that the idea we'd had a couple of days ago, of disguising our weapons and other equipment in a gift box would be an ideal solution to our dilemma. It would after all seem perfectly natural to take a wrapped gift with us for an early evening meal, as everyone would assume we were meeting the intended recipient later in the evening.

'Half a case of champagne would be the ideal sized box.' Jean suggested, with a mischievous twinkle in his eye. 'We might even pick up a few glasses to go with it and leave both the wine and the glasses in the car, as a disguise in case we need to pass ourselves off as party goers on the way to some late-night revelry.'

It was a ridiculous idea, to try and keep a low profile by disguising ourselves as a car load of high-lifers on our way to a party. As I thought it through though, I had to admit if we managed to get out of the vaults in one piece it might be nice to have something to drink irrespective of whether we needed it for a disguise.

After agreeing to pick up the champagne, and going over the details of our plan once more, we realised that our preparations for getting Selene out of the Icarii complex and then all of us out of Rome was complete.

What would happen once we got to the boat was another question. Would Agostine or the Reverend Mothers be able to mobilise the Italian navy to pursue us, or even the Regia Aeronautica to search the land and sea. We just didn't know. All we could realistically do was avoid making any obvious mistakes like going back to somewhere that the Order knew we'd already been, and where they could send an operative to keep a lookout for us.

By the time we'd finished making our plans it was

midday, and while we'd had to get the work done, we were all now in need of a break.

Luke suggested we should get out into the fresh air, to stretch our legs and revive our minds, before we came back to the hotel to pack and then check-out.

It was a glorious spring day with clear blue skies, so he suggested we head over to a restaurant he knew which had a rooftop terrace overlooking the botanic gardens.

I hesitated at the idea of walking around the city streets any more than we had to, now that we knew Mother Agostine, Miriam and probably Thea were also in the vicinity, but guessing what I was thinking Luke attempted to reassure me.

'I can offer you no guarantees, George,' he explained. 'It is a slightly longer walk, but we can take the back-streets to reduce our chance of running into any of Selene's former colleagues.'

For a moment all I could think about was the unnecessary gamble we would be taking. If we were somehow spotted walking the streets of Rome I had absolutely no idea how the Icarii would react, whether they'd attempt to move against us, or ignore us for the moment while they focussed on the more pressing matter of Selene, or any of a dozen other options I hadn't thought of.

They all gave me a moment, and gradually my perspective started to return. This was Rome, one of the largest and most populous cities in the world. Even if we wanted to run into our adversaries, we might walk the streets for weeks without ever coming across them.

Nobody questioned me about my doubts, probably because the same thoughts had already crossed their minds, but after our long session of trying to out-think our opponents, I'd lost sight of the reality of our situation. Namely, that the Order didn't even suspect we were here in Rome, and even if they were still looking for us, they weren't doing so here, where they had far more significant matters to attend to.

While I reproached myself for my foolishness, I indicated that I was ready to go, so we set off, away from the Vatican and the Jesuit library, through an area of the city we hadn't visited yet, to a stunning bistro overlooking the lush green of the Orto Botanico.

It was a good half-hour walk to our destination, and by the time we arrived the fresh air and exercise had worked its magic, and I was feeling myself once more.

We enjoyed a lovely meal there, made all the better by the warm weather, which allowed us to sit outside in the sunshine, but this was also our last real opportunity to speak to Luke and to say our goodbyes. If all went well, we'd still have the car journey together, and a few minutes at the port. But there were no guarantees from this point on, so we took the time now, while we had it, to talk once more as friends.

He gave us the address of the mission he'd be working at in the Himalaya, and taught us how to address a letter in the local script so it would stand the best chance of reaching him. In return we asked him more about the work he'd be doing and how long he was thinking of devoting his life to it.

The work he explained would be varied, but teaching would form a significant part, as would helping to rebuild the local school house. How long he'd stay, he was unsure about, saying only that he was thinking of a year initially, beyond that he hadn't planned.

We all admired Luke for what he'd decided to do, and for the peace which his decision had clearly brought him, so had no difficulty in wishing him well in his new vocation.

Time, however, seemed to race past as we sat there in the warm sunshine enjoying our time as a group once more. There was a part of me which couldn't help but compare Luke's decision to devote his life to such a meaningful goal, with the decision the rest of us had made.

He had simply chosen to help those less fortunate

than himself, in contrast, we had chosen to pit ourselves against a powerful and dangerous enemy, that considered the killing of private citizens to be simply the most practical solution in some circumstances.

Granted, we also had the lofty goal of finding the secret of everlasting life, though we had yet to decide between us whether such a thing was for the public good, or a disastrous burden from which society might never recover.

I resisted the temptation to dwell upon the choices we'd made. As all too quickly it would be time to return to our hotel, and then once more down into the Icarii stronghold.

JUSTICE

WE'D CROSSED OUR RUBICON. There had been a moment in the last few days when we'd reached the point of no return, and while I sat in the darkness of the Chamber of Truth, deep within the vaults of the Icarii, waiting for our enemy to return, I was trying to figure out where that line had been.

After easily entering the courtyard again using the key which Peter had created. We'd opened the secret door at the back of the tool room as though we'd been using it all our lives, before making our way down into the complex below.

Presumably, with no more boxes or crates to move, the guards were busying themselves with their normal duties, so we'd been able to wind our way to the chamber without delay, using just a little caution to make sure we didn't encounter a patrol.

As a consequence, we had arrived at the chamber over two hours early, which gave us time to make our preparations, moving a few things around, to make our hiding places more comfortable, and the cover we would be hiding behind, easier to get past when we needed to make our move.

This still left well over an hour before we were expecting anyone to turn up in the Chamber, which gave me plenty of time to reflect on how we'd come to this point.

Since the dream I'd had a few days ago with my father, I'd been feeling more at ease with the course we'd chosen to follow. But, perhaps as a consequence of talking to Luke about his choices, and then finding myself in this almost unimaginable position, deep within a secret labyrinth controlled by people with an all too mercenary mentality, I felt the old doubts creeping in once again around the edges of my mind.

I was sure it was when we'd witnessed the perverse trial of Selene. That was the point at which we could no longer morally choose to walk away, the point at which we were committed to going back and confronting our adversaries head on.

The irony of the situation made me smile into the darkness, as I once again ran my hands over my familiar Enfield revolver.

Here we were, about to confront the Icarii to save Selene's life, but in retaliation the Icarii would surely expend every resource available to hunt us down. We in return would work twice as hard to decipher the tablets and find our way to the first great temple, and the secret which above all else the Icarii didn't want us to find.

'Something amuses you, my friend,' Jean whispered through the darkness beside me.

'How on earth did you know that I was smiling?' I replied, just as one of the doors to the chamber opened and a guard entered. Without even looking around, he lit the gas lights over the pit and the six marble pedestals which surrounded it, before leaving the way he had come.

Once more the narrow cone of light illuminated the pit in the centre of the chamber, leaving the rest, including our hiding places, steeped in the deepest shadow.

Things happened quickly then.

The six cloaked figures entered the room, the three in the black robes flanked by the sword-wielding ceremonial guard, who took up position nearest to where Jean and I were hiding. The other three in the brown taking up their positions on the far side of the pit nearest to Marlow and Harry.

We had no idea how they intended to execute Selene, so we were all poised to step out of the shadows at a moment's notice even though we hoped that Selene would be brought out first.

Once they were all in position on the low marble plinths, they began by pushing back their hoods to reveal their faces.

It was the same six people who had passed judgement the previous day, and the same Reverend Mother who began the proceedings.

'We have gathered here this evening to ensure the sentence of death handed down to Selene Autieri is dutifully carried out,' she began. 'However, as this sentence is so final in its nature, I feel it only appropriate that the verdict of this chamber should be validated a second time by those present before it is carried out.

'To this end, I wish to again ask you all if you are happy with the verdict of this chamber, and also with the sentence of death, which a unanimous verdict in this chamber traditionally carries.

'Agostine of Padua, as the accuser, are you content with both the verdict of this chamber and the sentence which will be carried out?'

'I am,' replied Mother Agostine quite simply, as though talking about nothing of any great significance.

'Thank you,' replied the Reverend Mother before

moving on to Miriam and Haleena, who both also signalled their satisfaction with the verdict and sentence.

The Reverend Mother next addressed herself to the black robed woman on her left, her 'Third' as she referred to her.

'Are you also content with the verdict and the sentence?'

'I am content with the verdict,' came the woman's reply. 'But I view the sentence as a harsh punishment for the crime, and only agree to it because I see no practical alternative which wouldn't err equally toward leniency.'

'It is a fine distinction you draw, Third, but it is a reasonable one,' replied the Reverend Mother before turning to her second.

'I am in agreement with Third,' replied the woman referred to as Second. 'For a less accomplished and less knowledgeable operative a more lenient sentence may have been possible, but for our former sister, Selene of Florence, who has not only distinguished herself by her service, but who was widely considered to be a likely candidate to lead this order in the future, a more lenient sentence would be no sentence at all, and if she were still intent upon leaving us it would surely only be a matter of time before she was successful.'

The Reverend Mother nodded her head thoughtfully in response to these words, and then once more addressed the room.

'It is agreed. Both the verdict and the sentence remain uncontested. Let the prisoner be brought forth for the sentence to be carried out.'

At this the guards, as they had done the previous day, first placed their swords on a nearby table before proceeding to lower the iron ladder down into the pit before climbing down it themselves.

One of them unlocked the iron gate to the cells where Selene was held, through which they both proceeded and then returned a few minutes later with her again manacled and chained between them.

Her posture was defiant, shoulders back and spine ramrod straight even though she knew her death was surely only a few minutes away. Her eyes also were unchanged, the dark stillness still glittered in those orbs.

While her bearing and expression remained unchanged though, her time in the cells had clearly started to take its toll in other ways, with both the long shift she was wearing and her hair now looking sadly dishevelled.

Time slowed to a honeyed crawl as they brought her to the centre of the pit and began the process of chaining her to the ring set into the floor.

This was the moment we'd been waiting for. The guard with the key had relocked the gate to the cells, and all three of them had started to move to the first ring set into the floor.

As a shadow I stepped out from behind the boxes I'd been hiding behind, the reassuringly heavy weight of my pistol in hand, as I quietly walked over to stand behind the three Reverend Mothers, in much the same position that their guards had adopted.

Jean did likewise, and through the gloom I could just make out the shadowy outlines of Marlow and Harry on the other side of the room doing the same.

'That won't be necessary,' Marlow calmly stated from the shadows, closely followed by the sound of his gun being cocked.

'Who dares disturb the sanctity of…' Mother Agostine demanded as she turned on her plinth to see Marlow pointing his Webley directly at her. 'You! You cannot be in this place.'

'On the contrary, Mother Agostine,' replied Jean from beside me, causing the Reverend Mothers on our side of the pit to spin around at the sound from behind them. 'With such ineffective security measures in place beneath that nice little bookshop on the Borgo Vecchio, which Miriam led us to yesterday, we not only can be here, but it would be wrong of us not to interpret such negligence as anything but an invitation.'

Jean was ad-libbing, but I realised fairly quickly that he was taking the opportunity to sow a bit of discord amongst our adversaries.

'Agostine, who are these men?' demanded the Reverend Mother, practically incandescent with rage.

'I'm afraid your questions for Superior Agostine are going to have to wait until after you've climbed down into the pit, Reverend Mother,' Marlow broke in, without taking his gun off Agostine. 'Now! If you wouldn't mind.'

'And if we do mind?' The Reverend Mother asked, regaining some of her composure. 'You do not look like the kind of men who would find it easy to kill six defenceless women.'

'Defenceless women are you?' asked Jean, with an amused tone to his voice. 'The same defenceless women who so casually discussed the murder of my friend over there, simply because he would not forsake the goal that as a free man he has every right to pursue. The same defenceless women who also bemoaned the lack of information which had inhibited their ability to blackmail us into giving up our search, or which they could use to destroy our friendships.

'Madame,' Jean continued, his words pronounced now with an icy cordiality, as he too cocked his pistol. 'You are anything but defenceless, and I would be doing humanity a great favour in pulling this trigger.'

I hoped the words Jean was speaking were just a pretence, for in truth the Reverend Mother had divined the one weakness in our strategy, that unlike our adversaries we were still bound by the expectations of a civilised society.

But while she had played an excellent card, Jean's bluff clearly convinced her.

'As you will, M'sieur, we will play this game for the moment.

'Release the prisoner,' she commanded, speaking to

the guards in the pit.

I couldn't see either the guards or Selene from my current vantage point, so I moved along to the end of the room which offered a better angle of sight, while simultaneously keeping my pistol trained on the cloaked figures.

The guards were doing as they were told, and as soon as I saw that Selene was free of her manacles and chains it was time to make sure they couldn't easily follow us.

'Ms Autieri,' I began. 'Before you climb out of the pit, would you mind relieving the gentleman who has just unchained you of his keys, and then chain both him and his colleague to the ring mounted in the floor?

'Much obliged.'

'You cannot imagine we will allow you to get away with this affront,' seethed Mother Agostine as Selene did exactly as requested.

'Yes, madame,' I found myself saying with more than a trace of the frosty tone that Jean had employed.

'That is exactly what I imagine, unless you think we'd be better off dealing with you more harshly now while we have the chance?'

It was a villainous comment on my behalf, which I would normally have been none too proud of, but on this occasion I decided to follow Jean's lead in order to encourage these mercenary women to play along with us for the moment.

With Selene out of the pit, it was Jean's turn to exercise his menacing charm once more.

'Ladies, please after you,' he said simply nodding his head toward the ladder.

With faces like thunder the Reverend Mothers descended the iron ladder one after another into the pit, after which it was the turn of Mother Agostine, Miriam and Haleena, but not before Selene had insisted the Miriam first remove her boots, trousers and blouse and throw them over the pit to her.

The fury on Miriam's face made me think it was a step too far, and that she was going to call our bluff rather than face such indignity, but Selene knowing her all too well, crushed any idea of defiance before Miriam could voice it.

'I won't tell you again, my Second, or do you perhaps doubt my ability to deal with you harshly, after you have just sentenced me to death by drowning.'

That quenched the fire which had been building behind Miriam's eyes, and while she was still clearly seething she did as she had been told and slipped off her boots, trousers and blouse for her former colleague.

As soon as the other three women had climbed down into the pit Selene stepped away from the light for a moment to get changed into Miriam's clothes and boots.

With everyone in the pit, the tension in the room dropped a notch, and now Marlow and Harry stepped out through the door to the chamber to find the guard who had been responsible for lighting the gas lamps.

They returned a minute later with a rather surprised and pale looking fellow, who'd clearly been caught completely by surprise.

After checking him for weapons, he too climbed down into the pit before we pulled the ladder back up and moved it off to the side.

'Very good, you have us captive in our own facility,' the Reverend Mother taunted us. 'But what will you do now gentlemen? It is only a matter of time before we will be free to pursue you.'

'Well, perhaps I can help them with that,' replied Selene stepping back out of the shadows, looking much more like her old self, albeit in Miriam's clothes.

As she spoke she walked over to a shadowy corner of the room, which I hadn't paid much attention to previously, where she pulled a lever.

A moment later and a large iron portcullis started to rattle down from the ceiling, over the gas lights and down to form an iron grate across the top of the pit.

'My child,' spoke the Reverend Mother now with an edge of concern in her voice. 'Do not do anything you may come to regret later on.'

'I am no longer your child, Jessica, you have made that very clear. But why are you so concerned? Is it perhaps that you think I may choose to show these gentlemen what it is to be exposed to the mercy of the Tiber?'

At this Selene walked back over to the corner where she'd pulled the lever to lower the grate, and then pulled another lever which didn't seem to do anything for a moment.

'Ms Autieri,' Jean said simply. 'I hope you have not done anything hasty.'

'M'sieur de Gris,' she replied, looking down through the bars of the grate. 'The mercy of the Tiber is anything but hasty. Behold the water as it begins to flow in through the sluices.'

As she pointed into the pit, I noticed several smaller grates around the edge, which now started to let a steady stream of water flow into the pit.

'This pit is connected directly to the river Tiber,' Selene explained. 'As you will see it fills the pit only slowly. Anything from ten minutes to an hour depending on how far the sluices at the other end of the pit are opened.

'A merciful Reverend Mother might have ordered the drainage sluices to remain closed so that the prisoner might drown in only a few minutes. A less charitable Chamber may open the sluices sufficiently once the water was up to the prisoner's mouth so that they are forced to struggle for breath for hours before their strength failed.

'Would you have been a merciful Reverend Mother, Jessica?' Selene asked looking down at the woman in the pit who was the First amongst the black cloaked women.

The water was past waist level on the inhabitants of the pit now, and the Reverend Mother simply glowered up through the bars at Selene without saying a word.

As the water rose higher still and Selene didn't do anything to stop it I began to get concerned that she was actually intending to drown her inquisitors.

Jean, perhaps thinking the same, spoke up.

'Ms Autieri, I'm afraid it is time for us to leave this place.

She nodded almost imperceptibly, and then as the water reached the necks of those in the pit she returned to the levers in the corner and pulled a third lever, which seemed to result in the water level no longer rising.

'Both sluices are now fully open so the water will rise no higher, but the cold waters of the Tiber will continue to flow through the pit, making their stay an unpleasant one.'

With that she turned to us, indicating she was ready to leave.

We made our way back through the labyrinth of tunnels toward the secret entrance. At one point Selene was clearly expecting us to turn off in order to make our way out via the bookshop entrance, until Jean explained his attempted misdirection.

The route was a familiar one for us by now, although we still had to be wary of any guards who might be patrolling the corridors.

Within a few minutes we'd reached the Roman cellar, and then back to the tool storage room and finally out into the courtyard, closing all the gates and doors on the way as we did so, hoping as much as possible to hide the route we'd used.

Only the gate to the courtyard remained for us to make our way out of. Placing our various guns, knives and other pieces of equipment back into the gift wrapped champagne box and re-fastening the gift wrapping, we carefully inched open the courtyard gate after unlocking it to find that Jean's car was parked directly outside in the space it had vacated earlier, when Luke had driven Peter and Androus to the coast. The engine was running and the lights were on, and Luke was standing in the full glare of the beams enjoying his pipe as casually as anything. Looking for all the world like a man patiently waiting for his friends to arrive before heading home for the evening.

To us the pipe smoking was the all clear sign, telling us it was safe to emerge.

Jean went first, slipping out through the gate with the gift-wrapped box and walking up to Luke, who pretended not to notice him until he stepped around the side of the car.

They greeted one another, and began to chat, Luke continuing to smoke while Jean took his own pipe out and did much the same looking down the street the other way.

Harry and Selene went next, sticking to the shadows and sliding straight into the back seat of the waiting car. Marlow followed a few moments later, doing the same. After one final check that the coast was still clear I went last, locking the courtyard gate on my way out and pocketing the key which Peter had fashioned as I did so, before joining the others in the back of the car.

A moment later and both Jean and Luke dispensed with their pipes before taking their seats in the front of the car and gently driving away.

The light inside the car was quite dim, as only the passing street lamps provided us with any light, but as we drove away from the Icarii complex and wound our way through the centre of Rome toward Ostia, where Stephanos' boat was moored, I thought I saw Selene slump slightly with relief, before pulling herself back together again a minute later.

'I am indebted to you, gentlemen,' she finally said, looking at each of us. 'Though I fear you have imperilled yourselves more than you realise in helping me.'

'Madame,' replied Jean gracefully. 'After sitting through your trial, I assure you we have few illusions of what your former colleagues are capable of. As for being indebted to us, preventing such an evil deed is something I think we would struggle not to oppose, no matter where we found it and who it affected.

'But we can debate such things later on if you wish. For the moment I would first like to check you have not been too adversely affected by your ordeal. We have some bread, cheese and a little fruit with us, should you be in need of some food.'

The gratitude in Selene's eyes spoke for her when Jean said this, and she accepted some of all we had to offer with thanks.

Harry found and opened one of the bottles of champagne for the rest of us, though Selene also accepted some, once she'd eaten something, and then as we drove, Marlow explained where we were headed, and how we intended to sail southwards around the tip of Italy and Greece, before heading over to Istanbul and the Black Sea.

'You are of course welcome to travel with us, or to go your own way at any point,' he explained. 'Though we would greatly appreciate your assistance in avoiding your colleagues until we get clear of the Italian mainland.'

'Thank you,' she replied simply. 'Passage away from these shores would suit me very well for the moment, but if I may make a suggestion.

'While the new Turkish Republic is one nation where the Order has very little influence, it still has operatives in a great many places, even if they have not yet attained positions of power. The eastern Mediterranean and east Africa are considered to be two of the most likely destinations for your group, so they are two localities where the Order will surely concentrate their resources to find you.

'If you wish to avoid attention in both the short and medium term you may be better to head for the French Riviera, perhaps Monaco, Nice or Marseilles, where the number of boats coming and going is much greater, making them all but impossible to keep track of. These locations also have a great many foreigners who will be visiting, even this early in the season, and a significant number of boats available for charter, should you wish to obscure your trail further.'

We hadn't even considered finding somewhere else to lie low, let alone switching boats so soon after we'd boarded one, but Selene's suggestions all made a great deal of sense.

'In the spirit of full disclosure,' she continued, with a slight smile on her face as she indicated the one set of borrowed clothes she was wearing. 'Mooring in such a place for a few days would also give me the opportunity to pick up some much-needed essentials.'

The more we talked about it, the more it made sense. We would simply telegraph the hotel to where we'd forwarded our things, to inform them we'd be delayed by a week or two, and then as Selene had suggested we'd lay low for a while, hopefully learning as much as we could about the Order from her while we did so.

In the meantime, as we made our way through the outskirts of the city and into the open countryside, we asked Selene about how her erstwhile colleagues would react and what they might be capable of when they did.

'It will all depend upon when the guard is due to be relieved from his post outside the chamber,' she explained. 'With luck his shift will be at least two hours long and will coincide with the patrols which are also performed every two hours.

'Even with the guard outside missing they would be very reluctant to enter the Chamber while it's in session, so will probably just report back to the most senior guard initially, and then check again in another hour.

'If there's still no sign of him they would convey their concerns to the Trinity of sisters overseeing the complex. The sisters will then enter the complex and convene outside the chamber. If there's still no sign of the guard or the occupants of the chamber, then their First will probably make her way up onto the balcony to check on the situation.

'From that point, it would only take moments to free everyone from the pit and raise the alarm.

'In the worst-case scenario, we've got just over an hour before the alarm goes out. Most likely it will be two to three hours.'

'And in terms of the actions they would be likely to take at that time?' asked Jean from the front seat, before explaining our concern about road-blocks.

'Checkpoints will certainly appear on the major arterial roads by dawn tomorrow,' Selene replied. 'But probably not before then. It's the port which will be the danger. It is very easy for us to issue an alert to all port authorities and border crossings in Italy, listing all of you as persons of interest in some crime or another, which is of course easily fabricated once the alert has been sent out.

'Even if we are unlucky, we should still get to the boat. It's getting away from the port and into international waters without being pursued by the coast-guard which will be the difficult part. Having said that, if the boat you've chartered is just one of the many yachts available for hire, it will not be easy for the authorities to be sure they have the right people, so they will probably err on the side of caution.'

Fortunately, Luke had already driven out to the boat this evening and was happy to confirm that everything had seemed normal, with no unusual interest being paid to him, Androus or Peter when they'd arrived. And that Stephanos who'd had his boat docked at the port for several days had also reported nothing out of the ordinary.

'Not Stephanos Alexandrakis?' Selene asked, looking more concerned. 'The boat owner you used before, to carry you to Corinth.'

'Yes, it is the same man and the same boat,' confirmed Harry.

'It was a mistake for you to use this same contact,' Selene asserted. 'This was such an effective form of transport for you last time, the Order researched Mr

Alexandrakis and have been watching his boat on the off chance you hired him again. I would be surprised if notice of his arrival hasn't already been reported to the Order.

'We must move quickly if we are to get away from the mainland before an instruction to seize the boat is issued by the authorities.'

It was such an obvious flaw in our plans when Selene pointed it out, and wouldn't have been such a big risk if we'd kept Stephanos's stay to a shorter duration, but by asking him to moor up and wait, we'd given the authorities more than enough time to cross reference the identity of his boat and report back through their formal channels.

With Peter and Androus already at the port, along with the tablets and our belongings, we couldn't even change our plans now that we realised our mistake. All we could do was hope we'd get to the port and under sail before the port authorities or coast guard were told to detain us.

We were just over half-way to the coast when Selene pointed out our mistake, which made for a pensive last hour of driving, but eventually we reached our destination.

It was just three o'clock when Luke drove us along the quayside, switching the headlights off to make our approach less obvious.

Silently we unloaded the car and made our way to Stephanos's boat, where Androus and Peter were watching out for us.

Stephanos had started to untie his boat even before we were aboard, which gave us precious little time to thank Luke for his help and say goodbye, before we were slipping away from the mooring and out into the inky night time waters of the Tyrrhenean Sea.

The space inside the boat was too small for us all to fit inside, but there were seats at the back behind the tiller, so we all managed to find somewhere out of Stephanos's way.

Once he'd successfully navigated away from the marina and into open waters, we explained to him about our change of plans and how we now wanted to head towards the French Riviera.

'We would also like to leave Italian waters as soon as possible,' added Jean. 'And to avoid re-entering them if possible between here and the French coast.'

Stephanos, ever discreet, didn't ask why we needed to do these things. He explained our quickest and best route was to sail to Corsica, as this was officially the property of France, including the waters around the southern end of the island in the gap between Corsica and Sardinia.

It was only after this that Androus and Peter confirmed our worst fears, namely that someone from the harbour-master's office had been out to the boat earlier, asking Stephanos where he'd sailed from and where he was heading next.

Understanding our concern, Stephanos explained it would take at least three hours for us to reach international waters, and up to twelve hours for us to reach the safety of French waters around Corsica.

In the mean-time, with a smile that I was sure had disarmed many a port official, he explained there were one or two small compartments aboard his vessel which 'were very rarely discovered' by anyone searching, where we could hide anything of especial value. There was even space enough for one of us to hide in, provided we weren't claustrophobic.

It was a wise precaution, so we carefully stashed the tablets and the research papers, and agreed amongst ourselves to offer Selene the hiding space, as she was both smaller than the rest of us and potentially at the greatest risk should we be caught.

We also reasoned that we could credibly claim to have posted the artefacts to safety and that Selene had chosen not to travel with us, should we need an explanation, both of which would be believable.

Having hidden the tablets and worked out how to quickly get Selene into the hiding place, we settled back to await our fate over the next few hours.

TIME AND TIDE

I'D NEVER SAILED through the darkness before. I remembered when we'd been using the boat to search the Gulf of Corinth, we'd departed in the morning before the sun had risen, and occasionally not returned until after it had set. But at three o'clock in the morning, in the open ocean it was pitch black. What starlight there was, made the sky seem bright in contrast to the inky water, as we headed out into the Tyrrhenian Sea, the light from the coast quickly fading behind us.

Stephanos appeared as relaxed and at home in the engulfing blackness as he did in the daylight. Space was limited below decks, so after I'd gotten changed out of my evening wear and put on a warm coat, I chose to sit in the stern with Jean and Marlow. From where we sat, Stephanos was a shadow against the darkness as he steered us through the night.

He was happy for us to be there, but sailing at night demanded his full attention, so we were permitted to stay on the condition we allowed him to do his job, without distraction, and certainly without creating any unnecessary light that would interfere with his night vision. Even lighting our pipes had to be done carefully, and I understood why, after helping Jean to shield his lighter, both from the wind and Stephanos.

Even though his lighter produced what I'd previously considered only a weak light, being a petrol flame, it took my eyes a good thirty minutes to readjust after looking at it, during which time I could see absolutely nothing. My night vision did eventually return, so that I could again make out the pin pricks of light from the stars and shadowy outlines of the boat against the water.

We talked quietly amongst ourselves every now and again to pass the time, keeping our voices down. There was no point raising the topic we were all thinking about, of whether the navy or the coastguard would be after us yet, and if so how would they go about finding us?

It was only when we'd been sailing for an hour, and saw the running lights of another boat far off in the distance, that I realised Stephanos hadn't switched his own boat lights on. Not that we would be able to see much of the stern or mast lights from where we were, but the red and green port and starboard lights should have been at least partly visible to us.

It was obviously a deliberate move on Stephanos' part to help us avoid the authorities, something he'd done without needing to be asked, and which explained why he was now so intent upon what he was doing. In the darkness of the small hours we'd be completely invisible to any other vessel until they were right on top of us, so Stephanos alone had to take responsibility for avoiding a collision.

This knowledge both calmed and alarmed me, so I thought it best to keep it to myself.

In time, the other boat we'd seen in the distance disappeared from view, so we sailed on with only the stars for company.

Eventually after what seemed an age, but could only have been three hours or so, a pale line started to appear on the horizon heralding the dawn. Followed shortly afterward by Stephanos informing us we had reached international waters, and were about half way to the Corsican coast.

This meant we were still vulnerable to being stopped or detained by the Italian authorities, but we were making better time than expected, so it wouldn't be long before the French waters around Corsica, and safety would be coming into sight.

Despite the brightening horizon we were still sailing through inky blackness, and without any of the boat's lights switched on we would still be difficult to spot, so I couldn't help but think our odds were improving.

It was almost as though Jean were once again reading my mind in the darkness.

'The moment of truth,' he observed from his seat beside me. 'Will our adversaries be able to use their influence to have a boat watching for our approach?'

'Surely you don't think it likely they could anticipate us so completely?' I asked.

'Alas, my friend, I think exactly that,' Jean replied, with a tone of regret in his voice. 'The more I consider Ms Autieri's words, the more foolish I believe we have been.

'If they are, as we suspect, aware of our intention to use this boat to make good our escape, then the only question remaining is, in what direction have we sailed? And there are clearly only three directions available to us, so I am sure it is not beyond the wit of Mother Agostine and the Reverend Mothers to come to the same conclusion.'

'When you put it like that,' I admitted. 'Our chances seem slim.'

'No, George, that is perhaps to overstate things,' Jean retorted, very matter-of-factly.

'The darkness is our greatest ally without doubt, but there are many ways and places where the information about Stephanos's boat could be delayed in reaching the right ears.

'No, our chances are perhaps even, the remaining darkness and gloom of the pre-dawn may yet allow us to get close enough to Corsica to be safe, but it will be close.'

The next two hours, were I think, two of the slowest I have ever known.

We barely talked, instead scouring the horizon and the sea to either side of us for any sign of another vessel.

The horizon grew paler and paler as we sailed. To the point where after another hour I could no longer see how we could remain hidden from anyone.

'Do not be fooled, my friend,' Jean commented, after hearing me mutter something about how light it had become.

'Your eyes have adjusted now to the darkness, but I assure you, until the sun finally breaks over the horizon behind us it will still be very difficult for anyone to see us.'

I trusted Jean in these matters, so felt momentarily reassured, but a few minutes later Marlow spotted the running lights of another boat to our port side.

It was a long way off, but it had appeared from the direction of the Sardinian mainland, exactly where we'd expect a navy or coastguard vessel to be coming from.

If it hadn't been for the running lights I don't think we'd have seen it, which again Jean pointed out meant they could not see us yet.

As if the sign of another boat wasn't bad enough, moments later we heard the distant drone of a small aircraft, which we then spotted, flying in a back and forth search pattern several miles behind us.

It could all have been completely innocent of course, and neither the boat nor the aircraft had anything to do with the Icarii, but a glance to Jean and Marlow told me that none of us thought it likely.

Oddly enough I felt almost relieved now that we'd finally sighted our adversaries, and I don't think it was because of the distance which still separated them from us, though that certainly helped. It was as much to do with finally knowing where they were and the anticipation being over.

We still stood a chance of making it to French waters.

While powerless to do anything about how soon they spotted us, we could at least keep an eye on the boat and the plane, both of which seemed to be steadily closing upon us, the plane flying its search pattern, up and down the Italian coast, mile after mile before turning and flying back the other way, each time I thought it might spot us and change its course, but each time it continued its pattern.

Meanwhile the boat over to our port side, seemed to be drawing steadily closer, but much more slowly than I'd expected, until eventually when it had closed enough for us to see its port and starboard lights, we realised it was a boat very similar to Stephanos's, which was sailing an almost parallel course to our own, toward Corsica.

Stephanos had checked the boat several times through his binoculars, but had said nothing to us until it closed, but eventually after scrutinising it again he turned and handed the binoculars to Jean and pointed over at the other craft.

'Can you see the flag which flies from the mast of that boat?' he asked simply.

Perplexed, Jean took the glasses and scrutinised the other vessel which mirrored our course.

'Yes, it appears to be a simple black or dark coloured pennant,' Jean replied, uncertainly.

'That is correct, M'sieur,' Stephanos replied, smiling as he briefly turned toward us. 'It is also the signal I asked my cousin to use if he was able to join us on our excursion to Corsica.'

It took a moment for what Stephanos was saying to sink in.

'You mean you asked your cousin to sail his boat over to the islands at exactly the same time we were also sailing that way?' asked Jean, now with the glimmer of a smile on his face.

'And have you asked your cousin to do anything else on this journey, other than simply accompany us?'

'Well my cousin is a very nervous person by nature,' Stephanos replied, still smiling. 'So it is not possible for me to ask him to do much else. If we were to encounter the navy or the coastguard, he would almost certainly loose his nerve and attempt to avoid them.'

'And yet that is exactly the kind of behaviour which

can attract the attention of the authorities,' Jean replied, chuckling quietly.

'I have pointed this out to him on many occasions,' responded Stephanos. 'But he seems incapable of changing.'

With these last comments Stephanos also leaned over and switched his boats running lights on, which I found perplexing as it would soon be light enough not to need them anyway. But then the penny dropped and I realised that Stephanos had once again come to our aid without us needing to even ask him.

I borrowed the binoculars from Jean in order to take a closer look at the other boat, which was still a good half mile from us, in order to confirm my suspicions.

The boat belonging to Stephanos' cousin wasn't identical to the boat we were on, but it was certainly similar enough to confuse anyone from a distance.

As if to illustrate the point, a few minutes later the plane finally spotted us, and abandoning its search pattern, it flew overhead and immediately started to circle our boats, presumably radioing its findings back to the authorities, before finally flying off back toward the Italian mainland.

It took the coastguard ship longer than I expected to appear over the horizon in front of us. Whether it had been sat at anchor somewhere just outside the French waters around Corsica we had no way of knowing, but it was clearly a powerful and fast vessel, and when it did finally come into view it started to close the distance with us quite rapidly.

We were still a good half hour's sail from French waters so there was no way we could avoid them if they chose to come after us rather than Stephanos' cousin, but here his cousin came to our aid.

He waited until the coastguard vessel would definitely have seen us both, and then he immediately changed tack in order to sail away from them, acting in an unmistakably guilty fashion in the eyes of the authorities, who a moment later must have decided the vessel which continued to placidly sail straight toward them must be the honest party, and the vessel attempting to get away was their quarry.

The strategy was simple but brilliant. Fortunately we were close enough to French waters for the coastguard to have to make a decision, because they wouldn't be able to get near enough to either vessel to read the name on the hull without allowing the other to reach French waters.

BLUFF

WE KEPT OUR HEADS DOWN on Stephanos' boat while we watched the coastguard vessel accelerate over to Stephanos' cousin, knowing that at any moment it could turn back and still have time to catch us. It was a tense few minutes, with every second that passed increasing our chances of escape.

The captain of the coastguard vessel must have decided it was pure coincidence which had brought two similar looking boats into his path, and that the craft he was after could only be the one which was trying to avoid him.

Even with the binoculars, it was difficult to make out the two vessels by the time Stephanos' cousin finally furled his sails and heaved-to, by which time the Corsican mainland and its French waters were just ahead of us.

It seemed an age before the coastguard realised their mistake, and they were barely more than a speck on the horizon, when they separated from the other boat and turned back toward us.

Despite the distance, they still had a powerful boat, and if they'd had just a few minutes more they might still have been able to head us off, but just as they got close enough for us to see the figures moving around on deck, they slowed and altered course.

Stephanos was his usual imperturbable self, sailing onward for a few more minutes toward the coast before slowly turning the helm toward the south and the narrow strait of water which separated Corsica from Sardinia.

The coastguard vessel continued to shadow us for a while as we headed along the coast, but when Stephanos reduced his sail and we started to make our way through Corsica's waters more slowly, they lost interest and moved off at greater speed.

The dawn continued to brighten for a little while longer, and then suddenly the sun crested the Italian mainland behind us, filling the day with pale golden light which transformed the sea from an inky darkness, to the iridescent azure blues which this part of the Mediterranean was rightly famous for.

Within another hour we'd reached the southern tip of Corsica, sailing between the small islands of Ile Piana and Cavallo, then westward to the Cape of Pertusato with its attractive lighthouse perched atop the cliffs.

With the risk of being caught and taken back to the Italian mainland now behind us, the nervous energy which had been keeping us all going, started to dissipate, and before I knew it I'd dozed off.

When I spoke to Jean and Marlow later on they confirmed that shortly after I'd fallen asleep, they'd both done likewise, after first checking with Stephanos that he didn't need someone to keep him company, as he must've also been feeling quite tired.

When I woke up it was to find that Harry had come up from the cabin and was helping Stephanos with the sails as we approached the port of Calvi at the very north of the island. Apparently, I'd slept my way through most of the morning and had only woken up now, just before noon because of the movement on deck.

Jean was still sleeping soundly in his chair beside

me, as was Marlow on the other side of the tiller, so I gently roused them both before turning my attention back to the boat, and whether there was anything I could be doing to help.

Docking and mooring always seemed to take longer than I expected, and as Stephanos sailed his boat into the small marina and the berth he'd been directed to by the port authorities, time once again seemed to slow as we glided over the placid waters.

Despite involving a longer voyage, Stephanos had recommended Calvi to us because it was a good-sized port, with a wide selection of hotels and restaurants, that would allow us to relax for a few days, before we headed over to the mainland.

It might have been tempting to sail straight on to one of the large ports along the Cote d'Azure, rather than staying over on Corsica, but we were all tired, including Stephanos, though he didn't show it. And the more we considered it the more we thought a day or two in Calvi would make it more difficult for the Order to trace us.

Calvi itself was an elegant and bustling port, which encircled the western end of a wide bay that looked northwards toward the French Riviera, that famous strip of coastline stretching from Cannes and Nice right the way up to Monte-Carlo and Genoa, the last of which we'd visited on our way to Rome.

While less well known than its cousins on the French Riviera, Calvi shared many of their charms, including the azure water, and stylishly modern marina, and while smaller than its mainland cousins, it also boasted the attractive remnants of the mediaeval and Napoleonic fortresses.

Unlike the mainland which attracted just as many visitors by car and train, Calvi was clearly dominated by the boating and sailing classes, as evidenced by the harbour full of sleek yachts, and the wide-open promenade, which still contained a mixture of expensive hotels and restaurants, just along the way from the altogether more practical sailing tack suppliers.

Behind the town, to the south, rose-up an impressively rocky mountain-range, which could've given the place a rather foreboding and dark air, if the craggy backdrop hadn't been bathed in golden sunshine.

As we didn't need to unload everything from the boat, it was a relatively quick and painless process to find a hotel, by which time, having missed breakfast and lunch, we were all ready for something to eat.

Jean had previously sailed to Corsica from Monaco with the 'close acquaintance' whose house we'd stayed at in Annecy, and as ever, he recalled a pleasant bistro just above the old city ramparts, with a sheltered terrace that looked across the marina toward the mountains.

But, hungry though we all were, Jean was sensitive to the fact that Selene may have some even more pressing requirements that she'd prefer to address before sitting down to lunch. So, after he'd furnished her with some money we split up to explore the town before rendezvousing an hour later at the bistro.

To say that Selene was grateful for Jean's consideration would be an understatement, but while she kept her thanks to a few words, her expression showed immense relief.

She was still looking rather tired and dishevelled after her imprisonment in the Icarii prison, and I was half expecting her to opt for a bath and the opportunity to freshen up at the hotel, rather than joining us for lunch. But I was of course forgetting she was also a trained soldier, so when the need arose she could be ready quickly.

An hour later and after the rest of us had ambled around the streets for a while, in my case with Jean as my guide, we rendezvoused at the bistro, where a much refreshed and almost unrecognisable Selene arrived in a light summer dress.

'Ah, Ms Autieri, you look much more like your

usual self,' Harry commented, as soon as she joined us at our table.

'Thank you, Mr Sutherland,' she replied graciously. 'I feel much better for the chance to freshen up and put on some clean clothes.'

'We must also offer our thanks again for your warning about the boat and the suggestion we head in the opposite direction to our original plan,' Jean added. 'If we'd sailed south, it is difficult to imagine how we could have avoided the coastguard before getting to safe waters.'

'Well I must admit to also serving my own interests in offering you that advice,' Selene replied, smiling. 'I am, as I'm sure you can imagine, none too keen to see my former colleagues again anytime soon.'

I'd forgotten that Harry, Selene, Peter and Androus would have had no inkling of the drama we'd had with the coastguard off the coast of Corsica, until Jean said this, and Harry looked at him questioningly.

Realising our mistake, we quickly ordered something for lunch, and then as we waited for it to be served, we filled them all in on the close encounter we'd had with the coastguard vessel and the help we'd received from Stephanos' cousin in leading the authorities astray.

Selene was clearly not surprised by anything we were explaining, and I couldn't help but wonder if there was any other advice or guidance she might offer about what the Order would do next to try and find us.

'I cannot say exactly what my former colleagues will do,' she explained. 'As my presence with your group will doubtless cause them to alter their standard operating procedures, but I can tell you how the Order would normally respond, in fact how we responded when you escaped us in Corinth.'

As our food arrived we all agreed that this would be a valuable insight, but before she began, both Jean and Marlow felt the need to clarify our position.

'Before you begin, Selene,' Marlow began. 'I feel we

should first be clear, that we hold you under no obligation to us for freeing you from the circumstance we found you in. We did what we did because it was the right thing to do, and if you now, or at any point in the future, wish to go your own way, you are entirely free to do so.'

'Absolutely,' chimed in Jean. 'Though forgive me, Robert, we must be equally clear, that you are also welcome to travel with us as far as you wish, irrespective of what your conscience or your former loyalties dictate.'

'Thank you, Robert, M'sieur de Gris . . .'

'Please, Ms Autieri, to my friends I am simply Jean.'

'Thank you, Jean,' Selene continued. 'But I assure you all, I have seriously considered what you have done for me, and how I must repay that debt.'

'Selene…' Jean attempted to interrupt her, only for her to politely raise her hand to stop him before continuing.

'Gentlemen, I will not be persuaded on this point. You have saved my life and restored my liberty, for which I owe you a debt.

'Now, I will not lie to you, I am still very much convinced that the original purpose of the Order of Icarus is a noble one. A purpose which I hope to one day help restore. As such, I cannot abandon the sacred vows I have taken, even though the Order I formally served has lost its way.

'That said, I have decided, that while I cannot and will not assist you in the pursuit of your ultimate goal, I can help you in avoiding the misguided attentions of my former colleagues. This will be the price I pay for the debt I owe.'

It was clear to us all that Selene's mind was made up on this point, so we accepted her offer with gratitude, before she went on to describe how the Order would normally trace and track us.

'Naturally, the coastguard vessel will report their encounter with the two boats, and from what you have said, they came close enough to accurately identify Stephanos' boat.

'Consequently, the Order will ensure it has agents or operatives in as many of the ports in this part of the Mediterranean as they can. The sheer number of marinas is still far too great for each one to be monitored directly, so attempts will be made to enlist the help of the relevant authorities and information brokers in the different countries where you might land.

'Having said that, the Order will also understand that the route you were spotted on was also the shortest way out of Italian waters, and as such, you may sail south, around Sardinia, as soon as it is safe to do so.'

'I begin to understand why you suggested the Riviera would be a good place to charter a different boat,' observed Peter, thoughtfully.

'Yes,' replied Selene. 'Aboard Mr Alexandrakis' boat you will be comparatively easy to locate. As soon as he moors-up somewhere, he has to provide his details to the harbour master, and if the Order has already succeeded in adding his boat to that harbour master's watch list, it will take only an hour for a notice to be sent informing them of his arrival.

'Swap boats though, and you become much more difficult to trace.'

'And if we swap boats more than once?' queried Harry.

'Then you become practically invisible,' replied Selene simply.

'Well, it is a fairly short journey from here to the mainland,' observed Jean, thoughtfully. 'It would be easy to charter a vessel to take us there, I believe there is even a ferry service.'

'And Stephanos?' asked Marlow simply.

'He is a practical man,' replied Jean. 'He may even suggest something similar himself.'

'Do you think he would consider acting as a decoy for us?' asked Peter, after swallowing some food.

'I think he might like that,' replied Jean, smiling. 'He

certainly has a penchant for... how shall I put it, playing with the authorities!'

We discussed the options for a while longer and decided to stick with our initial plan of staying in Calvi for a couple of days, while we worked out the details, and discussed the situation with Stephanos. The extra time would also allow us to find out when the ferry departed, which Riviera ports it served, and to make any arrangements.

Selene informed us that while we stayed in Calvi she would contact one of the legal representatives she used, of which the Order knew nothing, to arrange for a replacement passport and other documentation to be sent to whichever port we headed for.

I'd expected that as an operative for the Order she would have some covert means of obtaining new travel and bank documents, but when she explained the ease with which this could all be legally obtained, and then deposited with a solicitor, ready for dispatch whenever it was needed, I felt like a wide-eyed school-child.

Sensing my wonder at her explanation, she looked at me thoughtfully for a moment over her coffee, before addressing all of us at the table.

'Perhaps when we stop in Ankara I could help you all to make these arrangements for yourselves?' she offered. 'As I'm sure you have all realised by now, a second identity can be very useful if you need to discreetly cross an international border.'

It was something which simply hadn't occurred to us, but it clearly made a great deal of sense, so as we finished our coffee we all readily agreed to accept Selene's help.

Later on that day I went with Jean and Peter to discuss our plans with Stephanos, while Androus and Harry returned to the hotel for a closer examination of the tablets.

After all the help and insight Stephanos had given us in getting away from Italy, we felt it wouldn't be right to settle on a plan of action without first consulting him.

As expected, he was already one step ahead of us, and when we sat down on his boat to discuss what action we should take going forward, he immediately suggested we might draw less attention if we were to find another boat.

He was happy to continue with us if we wished, but he'd quite obviously worked out, that if the people we were attempting to avoid could somehow call upon the services of the coastguard, then they must be powerful people who would have no difficulty in using their connections to find his boat and us with it.

With that decision made, the only thing that remained was to ask whether he'd be prepared to act as a decoy for us, by taking his boat to one of the other ports on the French mainland.

True to our suspicions, causing mischief for the authorities was something he was more than happy to do, especially as he might be able to pick up some additional work through one of his contacts based in Nice.

Later, when we'd had the opportunity to consult the concierge at our hotel, we discovered there was not only a regular ferry service from Calvi, but that there were several ferries, each serving a different destination, only one of which was Nice.

I popped into the hotel bar with Jean to talk through the different options which the concierge had listed, which included Livornio, Monte Carlo, Genoa and Ostia, if we were prepared to take a car over to the eastern edge of the island first.

By the time we'd ordered drinks I'd already ruled out the ports on the Italian mainland as simply asking for trouble, which left us with just Monte-Carlo and Nice, but if we asked Stephanos to go to Nice as a decoy, then it would make no sense for us to go there, so our choice was looking like a fairly easy one.

'So, George, what do you think of our options?' Jean asked, with that now familiar glint of amusement in his eye, which immediately told me he'd thought of something, but wanted to see if I could spot it also.

'You know Jean, I'm still quite tired from the trip, so my wits are not at their sharpest today,' I replied, stalling for time while I thought through the options.

'Oh nonsense, mon ami,' he replied, sitting back in his chair with that satisfied expression akin to well-fed cats the world over, as they attempt to persuade the mouse between their paws to continue trying to escape.

'Alright,' I replied reluctantly, taking a fortifying sip of my iced drink before I began.

'Genoa, Livornio and Ostia are clearly not options for the obvious reason,' I explained, still thinking furiously. 'While the Italian mainland would be the last place the Order would expect us to return to, it's the last place for good reason. Namely we'd have to show our passports in order to enter the country, and that would almost certainly result in our names being flagged on a watch-list. It would also be very difficult for Selene without any papers to enter the country, though being a fluent Italian speaker, she might be able to talk her way through without arousing any suspicions.

'Then of course, even if we did manage to get past the port authorities without being detained, the question of what we'd do next would be equally difficult. Heading north or south through the country would add to our risk of discovery, which would already be high with a group of our size, and would leave us with more border problems to face sooner or later.

'We could cross Italy and then find passage across the Aegean to Greece, Albania, Croatia, and then overland through Bulgaria to Istanbul, but this would be difficult travelling all the way if we wanted to keep a low profile, and I suspect the Order will have a lot of influence across this region if our past experience in Greece is any indication.'

'Very good, George,' encouraged Jean, still with that Cheshire cat glint to his eye. 'Your assessment is precisely the same as my own. But what of Monte-Carlo and Nice?'

This was encouraging, and meant that Jean must have thought of some reason to consider Nice. I couldn't put my finger on what it might be though, so decided to reason my way through, in the hope that inspiration might strike.

'Well, Monte Carlo is probably the obvious option,' I began, thinking hard. 'We'd still have the border issue getting into the country on the ferry. But while Monaco may be small enough and independent enough for the Icarii not to have much influence. It's also popular with the very wealthy and discretion goes hand in hand with people like that, so entering Monte Carlo, even for Selene without papers, is probably not too much of a concern.

'Once in, we could easily blend in with the multitude of foreigners, charter a boat to Istanbul and resume our original plan.'

Jean again nodded his acceptance of what I was saying, but clearly wasn't going to be drawn any further, and I still had no idea what he might have come up with about Nice.

Suspecting I'd shortly have to admit my defeat, I took another sip of my drink and then began to outline the option of travelling to Nice.

'Okay, the final option is Nice, where unlike the other options we won't have to contend with border controls because Corsica is a French territory, so we should be able to make the crossing without having to provide travel documents, which means the Icarii will have no way of knowing we're there.

'The drawback though is that Nice is where Stephanos was going to go to provide us with a diversion, and it wouldn't be much of a diversion if we were to then travel to Nice anyway. Yes, we could ask Stephanos to sail to a different port, but that would definitely be imposing on his good nature.'

'So you do not think Nice would be such a good option for us?' Jean asked, contentedly.

It was enough to give him away. He clearly thought Nice might be a good option after all, but it would be crazy to go to the same place you were trying to persuade someone that you'd gone to. What would be the point of the diversion in the first place if we actually went there?

Then it hit me. If Stephanos went there with an empty boat, anyone looking for us, would guess he was acting as a decoy to distract attention from where we'd really gone. Nobody would ever suspect we'd actually gone to Nice via different means, because that's just not how diversions worked.

'You think we should use Stephanos as a double bluff,' I guessed.

'Ah bravo, my friend,' he replied, with a genuine smile on his face. 'It is an elegant option is it not?'

'It's more than elegant, my friend, it's inspired,' I replied, still thinking through the different permutations. 'But you're thinking is clearly in advance of mine. Are you suggesting we ask Stephanos to arrive before us, or perhaps after? I can see advantages either way.'

'Very good, George, so quickly you move on to the critical detail,' he replied.

'I think we must certainly ask Stephanos to arrive in Nice half a day ahead of us if we wish to be sure that our adversaries will discover his arrival and focus their energies upon him.'

'Yes, of course,' I replied. 'At present they may still be monitoring the borders and observing who arrives on the ferry. Efforts they will surely cease once Stephanos arrives.'

We talked for a while longer to work out the exact details before taking the plan to the others.

The following day we arranged for the rest of our belongings to be unloaded from the boat and brought to our hotel, then settled our account with Stephanos, including an additional payment for the time he would spend providing us with a diversion in Nice, and something for his cousin who'd been so helpful in aiding us to reach

Corsica in the first place.

Stephanos would then leave Corsica in the afternoon to reach Nice in the early evening, and would ensure the local harbour authorities were in no doubt about the identity of his vessel when he docked.

The rest of us had booked passage on the ferry for the following morning, arriving in mid-afternoon.

I was sorry to be leaving Corsica so soon, as I'd hoped to stretch my legs amongst the wild mountain landscape that framed the port so picturesquely, but time was short. Reluctantly, I had to add yet another location to the list of places I'd someday like to return to at a more leisurely pace.

In the meantime, I had to settle for a shorter walk along the waterfront, around the great bay where the port was located, even though it meant walking back the same way in the fading evening light.

It had been a pleasant walk, albeit shorter than I would've like, but I just couldn't bear to head straight back to the hotel on such a pleasant evening, so decided to explore the streets around the old citadel where we'd had lunch on our first day.

My feet led me where they wished, and I walked around those high old walls, enjoying the view of the sunset over the water as the orange light slowly turned to a deeper shade of copper.

The last crescent of sun was dipping behind the watery horizon when I stumbled upon Marlow engaged in his evening habit of watching the sun set.

I didn't want to disturb him and wasn't particularly in the mood for company, so quietly turned around before finding another route through the streets.

A SUNSET TIDE

SAILING TO NICE on the ferry was like sailing into an advertising poster. The sea was placid and coloured purely in rich blues, as was the sky, which contained only a single picturesque white cloud directly above the town.

This made the city look like one of the reclining sunbathers that graced it's beaches, with long sandy legs stretched out to the west, and a slender bathing suit clad body, made up of the white marble hotels and old town houses, that reclined against the slope of Mount Boron to the east.

It was early afternoon when we arrived, and with the sun high in the sky the sea was illuminated at its best, creating an idyllic scene that was breathless in its serenity, and completely becalmed by the golden sunshine.

We'd booked a hotel on the lower slopes of Mount Boron, near to the marina to act as our base, it was a cool marble clad pile of a place, which reminded me of the hotel we'd just left in Rome, as we entered.

Here in Nice though, the style was evidently an abundance of cool greenery to offset the polished marble flooring, in the form of exotic potted plants, small lemon and orange trees, figs, palms, olives, all different sizes and shapes, creating a very grotto like feel in places.

While luxurious in its dimensions and appointment though, our hotel lacked the one thing that was required to be one of the popular, fashionable hotels, and that was location.

The lower slopes of Mount Boron lacked the wide

sea views provided by similar hotels on the fashionable Promenade Des Anglais, and as such, the Bacchus Hotel where we were staying was comparatively quiet, which suited us perfectly.

It was also convenient when it came to Stephanos, who had docked his boat in the nearby marina.

Selene, Jean and I had visited Stephanos before he set sail from Calvi, so we could talk him through the subtle ways in which the Icarii might approach him in order to extract information about us.

'It will seem like a perfectly innocent inquiry,' Selene had explained. 'A respectable looking young woman, possibly with a friend, will approach you and pretend to be looking for a boat to charter.

'Now, you will probably be approached by a great many attractive young women while in port,' she added, with a dry humour that Stephanos clearly appreciated. 'But this enquiry will stand out because they will be very interested in some specific details. In particular, whether your boat can comfortably accommodate six or seven people with baggage, and whether you've recently transported this size of group.

'They will ask their questions in this way in order to encourage you to talk about charters you've recently carried, how many people, where you picked them up and dropped them off, that kind of thing, but what they'll really want to know is whether you've just carried a very similar sized party to Nice.

'Make no mistake though, if you don't volunteer this information, the next question will almost certainly be more direct, asking what sized party you came to Nice with, or where you have just sailed from.'

Needless to say Stephanos understood what Selene was saying, and was happy to simply tell the truth, namely that he'd dropped us off in Calvi before heading over to Nice with an empty boat, in the hope of picking up another charter.

The idea of sending the authorities on a wild goose chase over to Corsica appealed to him, but the fact that he could do so without having to lie or mislead anyone made the deception all the more entertaining.

In the meantime, we would go about our business of finding a boat which could take us to Tunis via Menorca, where we planned to change vessels again before sailing on to Malta and Crete, then the Greek islands, the Turkish coast, Istanbul and ultimately on to one of the Turkish ports in the Black Sea.

At every step we'd try to find a new boat, just to take us on the next leg of the journey rather than the whole way, with five or even six changes in total before we disembarked in the Black Sea.

It would take much longer to reach our destination this way, but while it would be laborious to change boats so many times, we'd listened to what Selene had said about the different ways her colleagues could track us, so we were intent upon making it as difficult as possible for them.

This route would also keep us out of Italian waters for the all-important next week, during which time, Selene had confirmed it would become increasingly difficult for the Order to keep the Italian authorities interested in hunting us.

Jean was the only one of us who'd visited Nice before, so he offered to find a boat we could charter for the first leg of our odyssey around the Mediterranean. While he was visiting the marina, he was also going to discreetly meet Stephanos each day to find out whether anyone had been asking the type of questions which Selene had warned him about.

Marlow, Harry and Androus were to continue their study of the tablets, which initially involved the time-consuming business of transcribing the text into notebooks so that Androus could more easily work on them.

This work had been going well over the past couple of days in Calvi, now that Harry had brushed up on his understanding of cuneiform, and Marlow had applied himself to learning the script and the associated languages.

Harry and Marlow were still complete amateurs in contrast to Androus, but their command of the language was now good enough for them to act as his assistants, while Androus laboured over the more technically challenging aspects.

The rest of us had other jobs to do. Peter planned to find some maps for the countries around the Black Sea and Levant, as well as south-east Asia where Androus had previously indicated he thought the tablets were directing us. Selene had to meet the courier who was bringing her papers, visit her bank and equip herself for the journey ahead. All of which would leave me with enough time to get out for the long walk I'd been promising myself, as well as having some time to update my journal which I'd now neglected for a week.

I had a chat with the hotel manager to ask for his advice on possible walking routes, but came away with so many recommendations I was still undecided about which way to go. In the end it was Jean who simplified things for me.

He was setting out to meet Stephanos while everyone else was busy, so he invited me to tag along in order to help keep an eye out for any of our adversaries while he made his way through the marina.

The marina was a large, roughly rectangular area, which had been constructed by expanding a natural river mouth. It looked like an efficiently run place with hundreds of boats of all sizes moored along every side, though some areas appeared to be reserved for private residences, sailing clubs or boat yards.

The effect to the uninitiated like myself was one of chaos, with row upon row of boats each obscuring one another.

After a few minutes of confusion we gradually started to find our bearings, picking out the wooden jetties and the floating walkways running off them, then finally picking out boats of the same size and class as Stephanos' before ruling them out one by one.

We took our time, spending as long watching who was coming and going as we spent looking at the boats, before eventually spotting Stephanos' boat over on the western edge of the marina, docked almost at the end of a wooden jetty.

Having located the boat, we decided to find a good vantage point from which we could observe it for a short while just to make sure nobody else was doing the same.

A small bar not far from the ferry terminal provided the perfect vantage point for us, so we ordered a couple of cool drinks before sitting down to observe the marina and a chat.

'So you wish to go for a nice long walk,' observed Jean to my surprise.

'You heard me talking to the hotel manager?' I asked, knowing there must be some way he had guessed.

'Yes indeed,' he replied, smiling. 'I was at the reception desk, making a few enquiries of my own.'

'I feel like I need to get away from cities and towns for a while,' I admitted, answering his first question. 'I spent too long at home in Shropshire, too far removed from the wilderness, and I've been yearning for it ever since.'

'Ah yes. I believe I comprehend,' Jean sympathised. 'Once you have walked in the wild places of the earth for a while, it changes your soul, and makes life within the quiet boundaries of civilisation seem less complete.

'This is why you were looking so wistfully at the mountains as we passed through them on the way to Genoa?'

I confirmed it was, and explained how in my heart I had for a time resented the decision we'd made in Paris to continue our search, because we couldn't then stop as the inclination took us and explore the great natural places as we passed them.

'It is a difficult balance to find,' Jean continued, thoughtfully. 'And one which I do not believe I have yet fully achieved myself, but for what consolation it might be, I anticipate our future will involve us spending perhaps more time than we would like in the remote and wild places of the earth.'

In a strange way the thought of such things was comforting to me, though it didn't diminish my desire to stretch my legs.

Realising this, Jean suggested I head west along the Promenade Des Anglais, past the new airport and out towards Antibes, which had an attractive rocky peninsular that jutted out into the waters of the Mediterranean.

He was planning to head in the opposite direction, up the slopes of Mount Boron, with his sketchpad to do some drawing, but he had walked out to Antibes once on a previous visit and found it a very pleasant route.

'I would dearly love to take my watercolours up there with me,' he confessed. 'But foolishly I included them in the items we forwarded on to Ankara, so a pencil will have to do.

'Mount Boron has many pleasant walks, both through and around its wooded slopes, and I would enjoy your company even if only for a while, but I suspect you are wanting to walk further, and it is difficult to continue the route east beyond Mount Boron without walking along the roadsides.'

I admitted it was a long and tiring walk that I was really after, something that would make my legs ache afterwards, so I would accept his recommendation to head west, along the promenade.

We continued to chat and watch over Stephanos' boat for another half hour until we finished our drinks and then, having seen no indication that anyone else was snooping around the vessel, we made our way back to the jetty on which it was birthed, and while Jean wandered out to make contact with Stephanos, I walked over to the corner of a nearby bar where I could unobtrusively keep a look-out.

Jean only stopped to speak to Stephanos for a minute, looking for all the world like an old friend who had simply stopped by to say hello on his way to somewhere else.

As he walked back along the jetty, I set off to reach the edge of the marina at the same time he would, before we both walked off away from the hotel.

We walked a few steps apart for a short distance, just in case anyone was watching, until we rounded a corner, when I caught him up, and now walking alongside, confirmed I'd seen nobody paying undue attention.

Jean steered us away from the marina and our hotel, as a precaution against leading anyone back to where the rest of the group were staying. Now we turned our steps toward the grounds of the former Roman villa on the adjacent Cimiez hill, on the other side of the marina, a much lower vantage point than Mount Boron.

The area was only lightly wooded, with wide open spaces that would allow us to easily spot anyone attempting to follow us, while at the same time providing a natural circuit we could walk around on the way back to the hotel if all seemed quiet.

Once we were both confident we hadn't attracted the attentions of our adversaries, Jean explained what Stephanos had said to him.

'He hasn't had any suspicious questions from anyone yet,' Jean explained. 'But he did notice an official from the port authority on the jetty, with a young woman he was sure he'd seen previously in Corinth, when we travelled there with him.'

Even though this was what we were expecting, it was still a shock to hear that the Order had already managed to get an agent over to Nice.

'Did he give any further description of the young woman?' I asked, wondering whether it was Miriam or Thea.

'He did, he described her as being fair haired and a shorter than Selene.'

'That must be Thea,' I said, relieved that it wasn't Miriam.

'Precisely,' Jean responded. 'This should give our diversion a better chance of working. Thea being the youngest and least experienced Icarii operative we have encountered.'

'I was thinking just the same,' I replied. 'Hopefully Selene will agree with our assessment also.'

We meandered our way back to the marina and our hotel, checking our trail to ensure we weren't being followed, and then, expecting we would need to have a detailed discussion with the others, we asked the hotel concierge if he could recommend a restaurant which might have a private dining room available for a group of our size.

The concierge was only too happy to oblige, but as well as several restaurants he also mentioned the hotel had a couple of smaller, family sized dining suites, one of which he would be happy to reserve for us.

This sounded like an ideal option, which would not only give us the space to discuss our plans going forward, but would also help us keep a low profile.

We weren't sure when everyone would return to the hotel, so we booked the room for eight o'clock that evening. Then while Jean wrote out a couple of notes to push under Peter and Selene's doors, I popped up to see Harry, Androus and Marlow in Harry's suite where they'd been working on the tablets.

I knocked on the door hoping I wouldn't be interrupting anything important, and was surprised to see Peter opening the door and ushering me inside.

Harry had arranged a large suite, specifically to give them enough space to work on the translation of the tablets, but after we'd arrived he'd evidently also asked the hotel to set up a dining table in his rooms where he could lay out the maps and other documents.

'Hello, George, that was rather good timing,' Harry commented, looking up from a pile of documents he'd just been writing on. 'We've just finished the transcription and checking of the Alcathous tablets.'

'The Alcathous tablets?' I asked half guessing what he meant.

'Ah yes, that was Chuk's suggestion,' Harry explained. 'As we've got several similar sets of historic material now, we needed a shorthand name for each group of artefacts. As such we've now got the Faron tablets from Crete, which the Order retrieved from under our noses, as well as the Nelion tablets from Kenya, which they subsequently stole, the Gilgamesh tablets from Uruk, damaged in the bandit raid, the Alcathous tablets from Corinth heavily worn and broken after falling into the sea.'

'And let us not forget the transcription of the Ziusudra scroll,' Androus interjected from the other side of the room. 'Which I'm pleased to say the Order of Icarus overlooked when they destroyed the scroll itself.'

'Yes, I suppose it could all start to get confusing now we've got so much material to work with.'

'Confusing is an understatement,' replied Androus. 'The epigraphic riches we now have and are carrying around with us could keep teams of international researchers busy for years.

'Ordinarily in Jerusalem we would keep each of these collections of artefacts in separate rooms to prevent any possibility of cross contamination,' he continued, slipping easily back into his professorial mode.

'But we must make do with what we can, and for the moment that means keeping each item carefully and consistently labelled.'

I could see the faintest hint of a smile on both Marlow and Peter's faces as they patiently observed me receiving my lesson, no doubt having endured something very similar themselves.

'Were you just popping in to say hello,' Peter asked,

desperately trying to keep a straight face.

'Actually, I wanted to update you all on a couple of things, as well as to find out how you were getting on with the tablets.' I replied.

I then described what Stephanos had said to Jean about seeing both the harbour master and someone matching Thea's description near his boat. And then explained that we'd booked a private dining room at the hotel for the evening to discuss what we should do next.

They all clearly understood the implications of what I was telling them, and after we talked things over for a minute or two, both Peter and I left them to their work.

He had apparently only popped in to see them to drop off the maps he'd found, but had then got stuck while Harry and Androus had explained their new naming convention to him.

We still had a couple of hours before dinner, so I retired to my room to relax for a while before getting ready. I had a good-sized window overlooking the side street, and a comfortable armchair beside it which I turned around to allow me to watch the world go by. After a few minutes I must have dozed off, only waking up an hour later when a small child went wailing past in the arms of its mother, after presumably suffering a fall or some other great calamity.

If I hadn't been stirred by the crying child I have no idea how long I might have dozed for, but fortunately, I'd woken up with just enough time to get ready without rushing.

Everyone else was already there, and after sitting down, I joined in with the usual light and frothy banter, which continued while we made our various menu choices.

As soon as the waiting staff had brought us our drinks and then left us alone the conversation quickly turned to our situation, and the information which Stephanos had given to Jean.

Naturally Selene had considerably more insight into the situation than the rest of us.

'If Thea is here so quickly and alone, then the Order weren't seriously anticipating we'd come to Nice,' she explained. 'Which probably means they've sent Haleena and Miriam to ports in Spain and north Africa.

'They'll no doubt have other operatives that are familiar with all of you on the way. Perhaps some of the teams involved in the hunt for you in Kenya last year, or those that have been tasked with watching you since. Though many of them will still be covering the borders, known locations and your home networks, so it will take another few days before they're in position.

'In the meantime, we need to maintain our low profile,' she continued. 'Thea lacks the experience and confidence to act on her own initiative, so she'll probably just make her report and then wait for further instructions. That will take no more than a day, so by tomorrow afternoon she will probably be ordered over to Monaco, Cannes or Marseilles.'

'And if it had been a more senior operative, such as yourself?' asked Marlow neutrally.

'If it had been me,' Selene replied, dispassionately. 'I would report the arrival of Stephanos' boat without you and my intention to head to Cannes unless other instructions to the contrary were received.

'In many circumstances an operative's controller will simply be forced to make an arbitrary decision for the more junior operatives, even though the best person to decide where to go next is often the operative herself.'

'You don't think it's worthwhile for us to try and find out where Thea is staying, so we can be sure when she leaves?' Harry asked.

'No, she will almost certainly be staying at the Negresco,' replied Selene very matter-of-factly, before going on to explain further. 'Most large hotels reserve a small number of suites purely for the use of their owners or visiting dignitaries, people who may turn up without reservations, and who the hotel particularly wishes to impress or attract.

'The Vatican City owns interests in a wide range of commercial enterprises, including hotel chains, specifically to facilitate the work of the church and state. In the case of the Order, this allowed us to quickly and easily move locations without having to first make the usual arrangements. In many cases it also enables operatives to check-in as visiting diplomats without having to provide any form of name, identification or other documentation.'

'I can see how that could be very handy,' Harry replied, slightly wide-eyed.

'So, while we could perhaps attempt to monitor your former colleague's activities,' Jean asked. 'We could only do so by risking our own discovery.'

'Precisely,' Selene replied, simply. 'Nice is a popular and large city within which it is very easy for us to hide, provided we are not specifically being searched for.

'Thea may be young and inexperienced, but she is still a well-trained operative who will notice us no matter how unexpected our presence is, if we are careless.

'A day, perhaps two of staying away from the Negresco and the more popular attractions in the city, and she will have received her instructions from Mother Agostine and moved on.'

It seemed almost too easy, and during the rest of the meal it was clear I was not the only one thinking this, but we could find no holes in Selene's thinking, so the conversation eventually moved on to what we could each be doing while we were lying low.

For those working on the transcription of the tablets, including Peter who volunteered to help out with the maps he'd found, the time would no doubt pass fairly quickly. Meanwhile Jean would follow up on a couple of boat charters he'd found to secure our passage to Tunis, and then he'd be off to work on his sketching.

When it came to my own plans to do some walking, I was half expecting Selene to suggest I plan a different route, rather than walking down the main promenade past the Negresco, but all she suggested, if I was going to go that way, was that I walk along the beach at that point.

Our meal arrived and turned out to be excellent, particularly the fish dishes, which was probably to be expected on the French Riviera. But having a good restaurant in the hotel was also useful if we were going to have to hide-out for another day or two.

After the meal we continued to sit and chat for a few minutes over coffee and liqueurs, during which time the conversation gradually drifted back to more sociable topics. This included Jean's regret that we wouldn't get to explore Nice more fully while we were here. A sentiment which I was surprised to hear Selene echo and expand upon, by pointing out some highlights of the city, much to Jean's enjoyment.

It was in that moment I realised I'd been thinking of Selene the wrong way, as an Icarii operative first and last with nothing in between. Yet here she was not only talking with us about the situation we were in, but also expressing her own passions and enthusiasms, including a local art gallery she much admired, a building that was a striking example of its type, even a couple of other hotels which were renowned for stocking fine wines from some of the Riviera vineyards whose vintages she had much admired.

DANCE MACABRE

THE MORNING WAS FRESH and invigorating, as I walked along the beach toward Antibes. There was a sporadic onshore breeze that wafted my shirt and occasionally lifted the brim of my panama, but despite this, the clear sky and unrelenting sunshine clearly indicated it would be another warm day.

I'd left the others quite early the previous evening, just as they were heading to the bar for a nightcap. As a consequence I'd managed to get up and out of the hotel in time to blend in with the early morning workers on their way to their places of employment.

Anticipating a nice long walk, I'd left the hotel in my usual walking attire of stout shoes, loose fitting shirt, and lightweight trousers and jacket.

In my haversack I carried my journal, a couple of pens and an orange, to which I was intending to add a bottle of beer or cider, as well as some bread and cheese when I spied a likely looking grocery shop.

But I was in no rush, so an hour or so later, and with the Negresco well behind me, I wandered back up from the beach in search of a croissant or two for breakfast and some coffee, both of which I found almost straight away in a bakery, which looked old enough for every other building in the neighbourhood to have been constructed around it.

On the way back to the waterfront I spied a grocers where I probably could've picked up the provisions I wanted for lunch, but anything I bought now would have at least three hours in my bag getting warm, so, thinking better of it, I passed on by and made my way back to the long curving beach and gently lapping waves.

I allowed my feet to lead me while my eyes drank in the never-ending horizon of water and sky, and before I knew it I had passed the new airport and was well on my way to Antibes.

It was a pleasant route for the most part with only a few short sections that demanded I walk along the roads rather than some more natural pathway or track. I'd stopped once in a nice wooded area with some shade to enjoy my orange, but as I entered the outskirts of Antibes it was well past noon, and I was feeling ready for my lunch.

Antibes was a good-sized town, with many

attractive buildings, but they weren't quite so modern looking as Nice. The town centre had the usual selection of shops, in one of which I bought a couple of bread rolls along with some cold ham and a tiny jar of mustard, another orange and a small bottle of chilled beer, the last of which I could barely wait to open and quench my thirst.

I wasn't in the mood to stay in the town, despite passing a well-cared for park, so I continued on back toward the sea in the hope of finding somewhere I could have my lunch and then update my journal.

I was rewarded half an hour later as I drew close to the sea, by discovering the coast here was lightly wooded and led straight down to the water via some low cliffs.

The breeze was also more consistent here, but now the temperature of the day had risen, it was only enough to prevent the heat from becoming sticky.

The headland I walked to was clearly a popular spot with the locals, with a number of well-worn paths through the woods, and even a picnic bench in one sunny beauty spot, which I just had to stop and take advantage of.

Time slid by as I sat there, first enjoying my well-earned lunch, and then as I updated my journal with all that had happened since we'd decided to leave Calvi, so much so, that before I knew it the sun was descending toward the horizon, and I realised with a start that it was already six o'clock.

The others weren't expecting me back at any particular time, but if I hadn't returned by nightfall I knew they'd be concerned, so I re-packed my bag and headed back into the centre of Antibes, to find somewhere from which I could call the hotel, and let my friends know I wouldn't be back until later.

Unfortunately, by the time I made it back to the town the post office was already closed for the day, so I had to find a local hotel with a phone that wouldn't mind placing the call for me.

This at least was easily done, and I managed to get

a message sent with the minimum of fuss. Getting back to Nice in contrast proved to be more involved. I knew there was a train station in Antibes which had a direct line to Nice, but I'd only checked the times up until six o'clock, anticipating that I'd be returning well before then.

Now I discovered that after the last commuter train at seven o'clock the service wouldn't run again until ten-thirty because of some essential maintenance work, and as such I wouldn't arrive in Nice until just after eleven.

This was considerably later than I'd planned, but on the positive side, I could hardly keep a lower profile than being where I was.

Returning to the hotel where I'd called from, I explained the situation with the train, and firstly asked if I could use their phone again to update my friends about my even later return, and secondly, if they could recommend somewhere that I could obtain an evening meal. They were not only happy for me to make the call, they also offered me a table in their own rather elegant restaurant, despite my slightly dusty travelling clothes.

While the day hadn't ended as I'd planned, I arrived back in Nice a few hours later having had a delicious meal, and ample opportunity to digest it, before getting the train back to Gare de Nice-Ville, from where I strolled, good humouredly, through the quiet streets toward the marina and our nearby hotel.

I hadn't really explored much of the city centre in Nice, so I had to find my way from the station toward the water-front to get my bearings, even though I was sure this made the route much longer than it needed to be.

Despite staying nearby, we'd decided it would be best to avoid the actual marina as much as possible, in case Thea should return to observe the comings and goings at Stephanos' boat. But it was practically midnight by the time I reached the group of streets leading to the hotel, and as everywhere seemed so quiet, I decided to risk the slightly shorter route across the top of the marina.

As I crossed the road leading past the water I couldn't help but glance across to where Stephanos' boat was moored, which was a good sixty yards away.

There were actually a handful of people on the jetty leading to Stephanos' boat. But while I wasn't close enough to see them clearly, they were obviously all men, or at least individuals well above Thea's height, so, assuming they were just the crew from one the larger boats, I didn't give them a second thought.

Feeling increasingly ready to rest my now pleasantly aching legs I rounded the corner at the top of the marina, and was just about to turn down Boulevard Stalingrad toward the hotel when I heard the shots.

They were shockingly loud in the quiet night streets, and for a moment in my tiredness, I thought it must be some inconsiderate partygoer letting off fire-crackers, but then my weary brain recognised the sound as that of several guns being fired in quick succession.

I don't know why I then thought of the group of men that I'd seen on the jetty leading to Stephanos' boat, but fearing the worst I turned and ran back to the marina in time to see countless people emerging from the buildings and boats, some of whom were yelling for help and the police.

The people that were emerging from their boats prevented me from seeing whether Stephanos or his boat were affected, so, running back around the top of the marina to get over to the jetty on which he was moored, I began pushing my way through the crowd until I finally caught a glimpse of a boat with broken windows, through which a thin line of smoke appeared to be escaping, and I realised it was Stephanos' boat.

My legs nearly buckled beneath me at the sight of it, but I somehow managed to keep moving, until I found my way onto the now full jetty.

Slowly barging my way through the crowd until I reached a group of other boat owners, who had gathered around the stern of Stephanos' boat, I saw a couple of them board it and peer inside, before coming back out looking quite shocked.

Without hesitating I jumped onto the familiar stern of the vessel, the place where I'd sat only a few days before, and then moved to the hatch which led below into the main cabin area.

Stephanos was there with a couple of other men slumped over the dining table which took up most of the space, they were all riddled with ugly holes from numerous entry and exit wounds. Blood covered the entire scene, and a cigarette which had been dropped on the floor smouldered the newspaper it had landed on, and would clearly have caught fire if the blood hadn't also started to be soaked up by the paper.

They were all dead, each man having been shot well over half a dozen times through the walls of the cabin, which were also splintered and cracked on the inside in dozens of places.

In shock, I staggered back out of the cabin, and somehow managed to find my way back to the seat I'd occupied on the journey over from the Italian mainland.

I've no idea how long I sat there until I was gently coaxed off the boat by one of the other boat captains and given a seat further down the jetty toward the edge of the marina.

The police and doctors arrived at some point, but none of them bothered me, and then I heard Jean's familiar voice talking to someone not far away, before he came over with Marlow to help move me out of the way.

We made it back to the hotel, where I was given a stiff drink by someone, which slowly brought me out of my shock.

My friends were no doubt desperate to understand what had happened, and how, if at all, I'd been involved, but they waited until my wits returned before they pressed me for information.

Still part dazed, I explained about the train, and how on my way back to the hotel, I'd decided to duck along the side of the marina.

Then, while I was passing, how I'd noticed the group of men I'd seen walking along the same jetty where Stephanos was moored, but how I'd assumed it was just the crew of some bigger boat returning after an evening on the town.

'Is that as close as you approached, my friend?' Jean asked, quietly. 'You walked along the top of the marina and just glanced across?'

'Yes, I just thought nothing of it at the time,' I replied. 'Several of the boats, including Stephanos' still had lights burning in the cabins, so I just assumed they were...'

'Perfectly understandable,' Jean reassured me. 'But at that distance, you could not have made out their faces or other distinguishing features I suppose.'

'No, they were just shapes,' I explained. 'I could tell they were all quite tall, which made me think they were men, or more specifically that Thea was not amongst them, but that was all.'

We continued to talk, though it was clear we all suspected the Order was somehow behind this grotesque act, even if I hadn't seen Thea amongst them wielding a gun herself.

Eventually, the tiredness and shock got the better of me and I had to go to bed, though until my head hit the pillow I wasn't sure whether I could sleep.

AFTERMATH

THE CITY WAS IN UPROAR. Outraged by what had happened to an ordinary boat owner, who appeared to have just been entertaining a couple of acquaintances, when they were all gunned down.

The gendarmes were everywhere, trying to interview as many witnesses as they could, from amongst the legions of visitors who had decided to leave Nice, and were consequently making their way to the train station, the ferry terminals, marina or via car out of the city. It wasn't panicked, but nobody wanted to stay in a city where ordinary people could be so brutally gunned down.

I'd slept straight through till morning, but as I awoke the memories of the night before came back to me, along with a terrible weariness and guilt that Stephanos and his friends were now dead, murdered, because of his association with us.

There was a note on the floor beneath my door from Jean, suggesting we should all have breakfast in Harry's suite in the morning, in order to "discuss the tragic events of the previous evening", before heading down to see if we could be of any assistance to the authorities.

It was innocently worded, as always, in the event that it went astray, but it would be clear to everyone in our group that he was suggesting we meet to get our stories straight, before we got asked any awkward questions by the police.

There was no time suggested on the note, so as soon as I was dressed and ready for the day, I went upstairs to Harry's rooms and quietly knocked.

Jean answered the door, bidding me a good morning and asking how I was.

Harry was dressed, but looked like he hadn't slept very much, and Selene was there also, but was just sitting watchfully, with all trace of the ease she'd started exhibiting around us, now gone.

There was still no sign of Peter, Androus or Marlow, but taking his lead perhaps from the arrangements which Jean had made in Rome, Harry had arranged for a pot of coffee and another of tea to be brought up to his room, and placed on the large dining table which he'd previously been using to work on the tablets, of which there was now conspicuously no sign.

'You look better, George,' Harry observed, handing me a cup of tea. 'Have you slept?'

I confirmed I had, but then admitted I wasn't feeling too good about the entire situation.

'I can't help but feel this is all our fault,' I confessed, clumsily. 'If we'd just let him go his own way after he dropped us off in Corsica.'

'It would have made absolutely no difference, I'm afraid,' Selene replied, rather coldly. 'Stephanos wasn't targeted because the Order thought he was here with us, he was added to a burn list, and a price put on his head, in order to stop him being of use to us again in the future.'

I couldn't believe what she'd just said, and was about to say as much when she continued.

'I'll know more when I've had a chance to work the crowds and the people that may have seen the killers leaving,' she explained, clinically. 'But if I were to speculate, I'd say the job was done by one of the mercenary teams routinely employed by the Order, judging by the clumsiness and overkill.'

I didn't care for her tone one bit. This was one of our friends she was talking about, and she talked about his death so dispassionately I couldn't help but lash out at her in response.

'And I suppose if the job had been done by you, it would've been one bullet for each person and nobody would've noticed until the morning?'

'No, Mr Whittaker,' she replied, coolly. 'If I or a group of operatives from the Order had murdered these men then it would've looked like an accident. A gas leak from the kitchen stove, or a bottle of wine fatally contaminated with some naturally occurring toxin. We would never leave a job of this kind looking like someone had been deliberately killed.'

I drank my tea and went to stand by one of the windows, seething at her response.

'I know it's not pleasant information for any of you to hear,' she continued, finally with a hint of genuine human emotion in her voice. 'But you have to understand what this means. The Reverend Mothers have decided to exterminate the threat you represent at all costs, and that means neutralising everyone who might help you.

'If you show any sign of going back to Africa then everyone who worked with you before will be killed. If the Order thinks you will return to Athens, Corinth or Crete, then anyone who might lend you aid there will be extinguished. Your servants, your employees, your family, any kind of contact that doesn't benefit the Order will result in a series of terrible accidents. As will each of you if you are ever found or discovered by them.'

'Surely, such actions would attract a great deal of attention to your former colleagues,' Harry asked, incredulous. 'Something they would never risk?'

'You underestimate how the people that judged me in that chamber think,' she said wearily, before adding. 'Even I underestimated them this time.

'Yes, they would normally shun such attention, but there are a number of well-established mechanisms which the Order can use to confuse and distract the authorities.

'Drugs or other illicit material is a popular example,' she continued. 'Do not be surprised, if, during the course of their investigations, it is discovered that your friend had a stash of illegal drugs aboard his vessel, or firearms, or documents which could be used to blackmail persons of influence. All these things can be faked or planted to make it look like your friend may have been killed by criminals because of a disagreement.'

Eventually I realised that what Selene was saying to us was not only true, but also something we had to hear, so I apologised to her for my earlier behaviour and promised to think before I spoke in future.

After the others arrived, we explained the matter to them before moving on to what we would say to the police or other authorities, should they question us.

Regarding my own behaviour that night, it was agreed that the simplest option was for me to just tell the truth, but it was when we started discussing what we could say to the authorities about how we knew Stephanos, that we ran into a stumbling block.

Eventually Selene came to our rescue.

'In these circumstances, it's generally best for amateurs to stick as close to the truth as they possibly can,' she explained, as though we were a class of school children. 'You have hired Stephanos' boat before during a visit you all made to the Holy Land, when you wanted to visit some of the islands in that part of the world.

'If asked you can then explain that having recently arrived from Rome, you're now planning to do a bit of island hopping to Menorca and Majorca and were wanting to charter a boat for the voyage. You'd stumbled across Stephanos again, and had asked about his availability, but he'd explained he had a business meeting arranged for last night which may affect when his boat would be available.

'The authorities here will be very unlikely to check into your stories, but even in the event they do, they won't discover anything amiss, because you have been in Rome recently and you have been asking around the harbour for a charter to take you to Menorca and on to Tunis.'

'But surely they will know that Stephanos has recently been to the port of Calvi on Corsica, and if they find out that we have just been there?' Androus asked uncertainly.

'Then it is just a coincidence and you didn't run into one another.' Selene reassured him.

'But they could easily go to Corsica and find someone who saw us with him there,' suggested Peter.

'Perhaps, but they won't,' came Selene's unflappably confident response. 'The authorities will also interview the bar staff and management here, from which they will learn that the majority of us, were here in the hotel, in the bar having a drink when we heard the gunshots. The waiter and barman could both attest to this, as could the concierge and the reception. So even if the authorities did begin to suspect us for some reason, they would quickly rule us out as possible assassins long before they started to contemplate travelling to Corsica.

'And of course, you are forgetting that the Order will also attempt to confuse the real motives for the killing by planting some kind of evidence of criminality to mislead the police.

'So, as I was saying, just keep the story simple and close to the truth. We all became acquainted last year while travelling around the eastern Mediterranean on holiday, and as such decided to do the same again this year around the western Mediterranean.'

When Selene had finished her explanation, I must admit I felt more comfortable with the idea of talking to the authorities, though I'd completely forgotten that we were supposed to be keeping a low profile and subsequently leaving Nice within the next few days, thankfully Jean and Marlow still had their wits about them.

'Selene, please forgive me for labouring the point, and assuming you may have any knowledge of these things,' Marlow began. 'But is there any chance that the Reverend Mothers will be able to access the police reports and discover that we're in Nice?'

'Please ask any questions you like, if I don't know the answers I will tell you,' she replied with a gentle smile. 'Yes, the Order could arrange access to the police investigation, but to do so would be to create an additional risk for them. They will of course be able to obtain the high-level information without any difficulty or risk, which they will almost certainly do just to confirm the investigation isn't going anywhere near Thea, or any of their other operatives.

'Needless to say, the likelihood of anyone who has been ruled out of the list of suspects featuring in those high-level reports is zero.'

'And one question also from me, if you will permit?' Jean interjected. 'Yesterday I arranged to meet the skipper of a local boat to discuss taking us to Tunis via Menorca. Unless you advise otherwise I would like to keep this appointment?'

'Yes of course,' Selene replied. 'There are a great many people leaving Nice at the moment, so now would be the perfect time for us to do the same.'

WAKE

WE'D BEEN SO CAUGHT UP discussing things in Harry's rooms we'd neglected to order any breakfast, so after Selene had offered her guidance, we went downstairs to the restaurant for something to eat.

The police had not yet arrived, but they had sent a request for all guests to be present in the hotel dining room at half past nine, so they could talk to us about the dreadful incident in the marina.

The concierge came over to relay the request to us as we sat down at the table, reassuring us that nobody yet knew the motive for the attack, but that Nice, he was sure, was still a safe place for visitors.

When the police did arrive, it was clear they were mainly there to reassure visitors about the safety of the city, despite the terrible incident of the previous evening.

It was here again that Selene came into her own, asking polite but probing questions of the detective when he came to talk to us, presumably with questions of his own.

'I'm sure you're doing everything you can inspector,' she began, once the pleasantries and introductions were out of the way. 'But I would feel far more reassured about staying longer in Nice, or coming back another time, if you had some idea who the killer was, and why he or she had committed such a terrible act.'

'I assure you, Madame, all these things will be discovered by us in the fullness of time,' the inspector replied very calmly, no doubt having answered many similar questions in the other hotels he'd visited that morning.

'But I can tell you it wasn't an individual, it was a group of five or six men, who we suspect must have had a specific grudge against at least one of the inhabitants of the boat.'

'Oh, I see,' replied Selene, frowning slightly.

'So these are presumably local French men that you're looking for?' she asked, as though she were reassured it was some local grievance grown out of control.

'That we are less sure of, Madame,' the officer corrected her. 'One of the men, probably the leader of the group, was heard to speak to the other men in one of the Scandinavian languages.'

'And the men on the boat, were they Scandinavian also?' she continued to press, albeit rather gently.

'No, that is why we're having such difficulty in identifying the motivation for the incident. The captain of the boat was of Greek extraction, but the other two men on the boat were French and English in origin.'

Still Selene pressed for more, albeit apparently irrelevant details until eventually the poor inspector managed to excuse himself, without ever asking us a single thing, so that he could continue his round of hotel visits.

'Ms Autieri… Selene,' Jean said, as soon as the inspector had departed. 'I feel I must applaud your skill in the handling of that poor detective, while also begging to be enlightened about the questions you were asking.'

Despite the inspector not having much to announce to most of the guests, the general hubbub of conversation in the dining room where he had spoken to us, was enough to allow us to talk openly, without any real risk of anyone overhearing.

'Why thank you, Jean,' she replied. 'You are very kind. As for the questions, some of them were merely to confirm the details which George had already mentioned, others were just the usual nonsensical questions that people ask in these situations, and a small number which you picked up on were to help me identify the mercenaries who did the killing.'

I had to bite my tongue at the casual, almost off-hand way, in which Selene spoke about the death of our friend, but I forced myself to remember that she wasn't being deliberately callous, this was just the detached way that people in her world would discuss such things, much like a doctor or surgeon might have to talk about life threatening ailments or conditions with the person suffering from them.

'And may I ask if you succeeded in identifying them?' Jean asked simply.

'Yes, I believe so. To the best of my knowledge there are only a handful of Scandinavian assets used by the Order, most are solitary operators who are commissioned for specific types of contracts and whose work is as good if not better than any which the Order handles itself.

There is a husband and wife team who specialise in

information gathering, and a couple of larger burglary or demolition teams. But there is only one six-person mercenary team which would be prepared to handle an overt killing such as this one.'

'And now you know this?' Harry asked, looking unsure about whether he wanted the answer.

'It should be relatively easy for me to confirm my suspicions,' Selene replied, with a polite smile despite Harry's tone.

'Along with the details of where the team will re-locate to next, so that we can ensure we avoid any further contact with them,' she added almost as an afterthought.

Realising he might have offended her with his inference that she might take matters into her own hands with the mercenaries, Harry apologised for his clumsiness, but while he was talking there was a part of me that was thinking what it would be like to find these individuals and deliver some justice of our own.

I was lost in my own thoughts, until I realised that Marlow was looking straight at me with that penetrating gaze of his.

Not that he'd need to read my mind to guess what it was I was thinking.

Pretending I hadn't noticed his gaze, I blinked my eyes a couple of times and reached forward for a glass of water before looking around the table to some of the others.

The conversation had made its way back to what we were going to do next, and after only a short debate we agreed to arrange a boat charter to take us away from Nice, either later on that day or early the following morning.

It was Jean who'd been making the arrangements with a local skipper to take us away to Tunis, and feeling like I wanted to discuss things further with someone, I offered to accompany him.

We walked around to the marina to see the boat captain that Jean had been talking to, and found him working on his vessel.

He was a Frenchman with very little English, so while Jean talked to him I went for a walk along the jetty, looking at some of the other boats, and trying not to just stare across the marina toward where Stephanos' boat was still moored, though thankfully now covered in a tarpaulin by the police.

I'd only left them to it for five minutes when Jean walked over to join me, after surprisingly concluding his business with the captain already.

'It appears several of the boat owners are quite keen to be away from Nice,' Jean explained, in response to my clearly surprised look. 'Our captain being one of them, so he is more than happy to take us to Menorca for a very reasonable price. We depart tomorrow morning as early as we wish.'

'I suppose they must all be quite nervous as well,' I observed.

'Of course,' replied Jean, sympathetically. 'But I suspect you did not accompany me just to discuss our travel arrangements.'

'No,' I admitted, knowing he would already know the subject I wanted to broach with him. 'I wanted to talk to you about these men who killed Stephanos.'

'You wish to deliver some justice of your own?' he asked, knowingly.

'I do. I know it won't bring Stephanos back or make things right with his family, but I'd like to do something.' I replied, as we walked back around the marina.

He was quiet for a while as we walked. I wasn't sure where Jean was leading me, and didn't much care, I just allowed him to pick the direction and then waited for his response.

'I would like to see this justice you desire also,' he eventually replied. 'But I will not lower myself to their level. I will not simply gun these people down while they are defenceless.'

'What else can we do?' I asked, hoping my friend

would come up with something.'

He steered our footsteps up the castle hill again, where there were very few people walking.

'Perhaps nothing, perhaps we can play them at their own game,' Jean replied, indicating the next path to follow through some thicker trees.

'If the Order are hoping to use these individuals against us again,' he continued. 'They will direct these mercenaries to one of the places they think we might be likely to visit. Perhaps Tunis or Malta, Tripoli, Misrata or Benghazi.

'That's the bottle neck if we travel by sea, the gap between Sicily and the north African coast. It's a long stretch to sail through, with Italian waters to the north, which we'd have to be most foolhardy to enter.'

'But, what if they just send these people back to Scandinavia instead?' I asked, concerned that Jean's assumption may not be correct.

'In that instance, we would be powerless to pursue them without giving up on our current goals, and that would in itself be too much of a victory for our adversaries.'

I didn't want to think about that option, so I changed the subject to what we could do if we did find them.

'Now that is an altogether more interesting question,' Jean added, as he thought.

'Ideally we would not only strike a blow for justice against those individuals who fired the bullets, we would strike at those behind the curtain also.'

The path we were following became steeper at this point, so we walked in silence for a while until it levelled off again, and led us out of the trees and back into the sunlight. We'd climbed part way up the hill, and as we came out of the trees we spotted one of the viewpoint platforms, which were built out from the hillside so that visitors could enjoy the scenery of Nice. In this case looking back toward the marina and Mount Boron.

There was a bench on the platform, so we took a seat for a while to get our breath back before continuing our discussion.

'I feel as though we could do with some more guidance from Selene,' I suggested.

'Yes, Mademoiselle Autieri is very knowledgeable in such matters,' he replied. 'But I feel in this particular circumstance, it would be better if we were first to consider what it is we actually want to achieve, not in the heat of the moment, but as rational and just people.'

I couldn't help but think back to the bloody scene which I'd witnessed inside Stephanos' boat when I'd entered the cabin shortly after the shots had been fired. For a moment with that terrible image in my mind, I almost felt I could bring myself to murder the people that had committed the deed, but in my heart I knew I couldn't do it, and said the same to Jean.

'I don't think I could gun them down in cold blood in the same way they killed Stephanos and his friends,' I said, after a momentary pause.

'That is as it should be my friend. To fight with another man on the field of conflict or in response to some other dispute is one thing. To kill a defenceless person is quite another,' Jean replied.

'But I wonder if we might not simply lend the authorities a hand in dispensing the justice we seek,' Jean mused aloud, before continuing.

'Suppose we could find a way to not only lead the authorities to where these men are, but also ensured they were found with sufficient evidence to incriminate them?'

'I doubt they would be foolish enough to hang on to anything so obvious,' I observed, doubtfully.

'Precisely, my friend,' Jean replied, with a mischievous glint in his eye. 'But what is to stop us from supplying that material and planting it upon them. Assuming of course that they haven't already fled.'

That got my attention.

'If that were possible,' I mused. 'We could also incriminate Thea at the same time. Perhaps make it look like she'd been careless to her colleagues within the Icarii. Use it to sow a bit of disharmony within their ranks, while at the same time forcing them to come out of the shadows in order to deal with the authorities.'

'Exactement!' Jean replied, gleefully. 'A letter or perhaps a few scribbled notes, which mention Stephanos' boat, its location in the harbour and an unambiguous phrase about killing everyone on board. We might even add a newspaper clipping just to make doubly sure the local authorities had absolutely no doubt about who they might have in custody, before they made contact with the police here in Nice to report what they'd found.

'Now we have enough to have a conversation with Ms Autieri, and the rest of the group,' he said, nodding his approval while he filled his pipe.

We didn't dally in getting back to the hotel, both to tell everyone about the charter which Jean had arranged for the following morning, so everyone had time to pack, but also to float the idea which we'd discussed for striking back at the Icarii and the mercenaries they'd hired to kill Stephanos.

Perhaps expecting that we wouldn't have much more time in Nice, the others were still out when we got back, so we fell back on our default contact method of slipping notes under their doors to let them know about the arrangements, and suggesting we meet later on in Harry's rooms to discuss our travel itinerary.

I doubt anyone would have a lot of packing to do, with the possible exception of Selene who'd had to obtain new clothes, luggage and everything else after leaving the Icarii complex in just the clothes she stood up in.

Not knowing how long the others would be out, Jean suggested we do our own packing before heading out for a late lunch somewhere.

This sounded perfect, as I definitely didn't want to

dwell on Stephanos' death any more than I already had, and Jean was, above all else, good company.

Unusually for him though, he didn't suggest a restaurant he'd been to before when we headed out of the hotel an hour later, because on this occasion he wished 'to explore'.

'I know you perhaps think of me as always being ready with a recommendation for a good restaurant, when I have been fortunate enough to visit somewhere before,' he explained, as we wandered aimlessly through the streets. 'But in truth it requires a great deal of research and dedication.'

For a moment I thought he was being serious, but when he finally turned to me with that familiar twinkle in his eye, I knew he was once more playing with me.

Deciding a humorous afternoon of nonsense was probably what I needed, I decided to play along.

'Of course, of course,' I replied, almost earnestly. 'Is there any kind of method you apply to this research.'

'Method? Naturally there is a method,' Jean responded. 'I apply the most rigorous scientific practices to this arduous task. Would you like me to illustrate?'

So it was, we wandered the streets like mad men for over an hour, discovering and then discounting a handful of promising bistros until finally settling upon a tiny out of the way place around the corner from the train station, which we also discovered there was indeed a much more direct route to, than the one I'd taken on my way back from Antibes.

It was a delightful place, owned by a local man, who prided himself not only upon the lovely food he created, but also upon the quality of the local produce he used, which were supplied, as far as I could gather, by his brother-in-law.

The food was good and the conversation a little nonsensical, but our afternoon passed quickly, and by the time we'd ambled our way back to the hotel the others had congregated in Harry's rooms over more pots of tea and coffee.

Moving from such a silly conversation to such a serious one, should have been difficult. But while my afternoon with Jean had been filled with frivolous and light-hearted conversation, I'd known all along it was a deliberate effort, on both our parts, to distract ourselves from the terrible events of the past twenty-four hours.

We didn't beat around the bush when it came to the reason that we'd asked everyone to meet.

'We've asked you all here in order to discuss something which I feel we've not touched upon,' I began. 'I know our adversaries are capable and dangerous people, but I'm not satisfied that Stephanos' family will ever receive the justice they deserve, if we don't help to deliver it.'

Harry and Peter both looked as though they wanted to interrupt me, but I held up my hands to stop them before they started, so I could continue.

'I'm not suggesting we attempt to find them and kill them in the way they murdered Stephanos. After discussing the options with Jean, I'd like to suggest we simply help the authorities to find these men, and then ensure there is enough evidence on them, to make it clear that they're the people responsible for the cruel murder of our friend and the men with him.'

I'd ploughed on, in order to explain as much as I could before giving them the opportunity to respond, but now I'd finished they all sat there quietly.

Selene was completely unreadable, simply sitting there and watching me very carefully.

Marlow, said nothing, but appeared to have the faintest trace of a smile on his face.

Androus finally voiced the question which I knew was coming.

'George, I think we would all be happy to help the authorities to track these men down so that justice can be dispensed, and I know Ms Autieri is confident she can find out where they were going next. But leading the authorities to these men will surely be very difficult and dangerous. Are you confident we can accomplish what you suggest?'

'Well, Androus,' I replied, quite bluntly. 'That all depends on whether Selene has managed to track them down and whether she is also prepared to help us incriminate and deliver them to the authorities?'

She seemed as though she wasn't going to respond for a moment, but then after taking her eyes off me, and slowly looking around the room she spoke.

'The men you're talking about are on their way to Tangier,' she began. 'Where they will attempt to find out if we have been there or are still there, after which they will make their way back along the north African coast, performing a sweep to establish where we went to after leaving Corsica.

'As for whether I can, or will, help you to deliver them to the authorities,' she continued. 'That depends entirely upon what you have in mind?'

Jean and I outlined our plan to fabricate a letter or some notes, along with a newspaper clipping of the brutal murder in Nice, and then to leave them where they could be discovered amongst the belongings of the killers, before tipping off the local police.

Together we explained our thinking of using the letters or notes to implicate Thea, but in a way which might make the Order think she had just been a bit careless. In that way we might sow dissent in our adversaries ranks, and force them to use their influence to cover up or divert attention away from one of their own number.

Finally, I saw a cool smile creep across Selene's previously neutral features.

'Mr Whittaker, Monsieur de Gris, I begin to see why this group was so troublesome for us to keep track of. We completely underestimated your natural talents for strategic thinking.

'Yes, I will help you to execute your plan and try to deliver these people into the hands of the authorities.

'I suggest we stick with your existing plan of heading to Tunis, and then to make arrangements to ensnare these mercenaries while we're there. It will probably take four or five days before they arrive, which should give us ample time to prepare our trap.'

SMOKE AND FIRE

TUNIS WAS A CITY OF CONTRASTS and diversity, of antiquity and modernity, it was cosmopolitan with streets full of visitors from all over the world, and yet it was also traditional, even conservative in its demeanour and its public habits. In many ways it was the epitome of the great French concept of savoir faire, it was appropriate and welcoming to all, and I loved it instantly.

We'd arrived after a long but thankfully uneventful voyage, briefly stopping in Menorca, as planned, on the way.

Our captain was amiable and talkative, though only with Selene, Jean and Androus who had a good command of French, so the rest of us were limited in our ability to join in. This left us as easy prey for Harry, who it turned out had wanted to visit Tunis, or more accurately the ruins of ancient Carthage for a great many years.

Now, with Androus distracted by his conversation with the captain, Harry of course took it upon himself to educate us about the remains of the city so famously razed to the ground by the Romans.

Thankfully we also had some work to do en-route, in the form of the fake letters and notes which we needed to incriminate the mercenaries if we finally managed to track them down.

We took Selene's advice on these, and faked pocket

books of random information dated to weeks and months before the murder of Androus in Nice. She even gave us the details of a kidnapping which the same men had been involved in several months earlier in Germany. We also made shopping lists of weapons, contacts within the Icarii who had commissioned the jobs, costs and payments received, and in the case of Stephanos the all too incriminating name and mooring details for his boat, the name of the hotel where the men had stayed, even a quickly drawn sketch showing where each man would take up his position before they all opened fire.

We used different pens and pencils, added coffee stains and smudges, we even managed to dredge up a couple of receipts for the occasional odd small item, which we then diligently created side notes for.

By the time we were finished, everything looked quite authentic, down to the scuffs and creases in the various documents we'd picked up. Not that everything was complete, there were a few bits of information which we just didn't have, the address to which the letter was addressed by Thea, hiring them to do the killing, the bank details in which the money was supposed to have been paid. These few bits of information we would need to fill in to make the documents seem as authentic as we wanted them to be.

Selene had also outlined a deceptively simple plan, using a technique which the Icarii had used before. Essentially, we would track the mercenaries to where they were staying and then render them unconscious in their own beds using one of several, almost untraceable methods, which she would enlighten us about when the time came.

With our plans made, it seemed like no time at all before we were stepping ashore outside Tunis and making our way into the city. Again, with Selene's help we managed to reserve rooms in different hotels under names which I was sure nobody would be able to connect to our group.

To begin with Selene and Androus checked in

together under the pretence of being father and daughter on holiday in North Africa. Meanwhile Jean and Harry checked in to a different hotel for a single night only as visiting academics, Selene and Marlow checked into a third hotel as a married couple, and Peter and I checked into a fourth hotel an hour apart as two individual travellers.

A couple of days later and we'd all joined Androus and Selene in the first hotel, albeit checking in a day or two later, so that we looked like several disparate groups, further helped by the other guests who had quite naturally checked in or out in the meantime.

As for our plan, it was simplicity itself. We knew the mercenaries, who were Finns, had no reason to hide their arrival, so we simply staked out the port, the railway station and a couple of the local Dar guest house apartments, which Selene had known other 'assets' of the Order to use in the past for low key stays in the city.

Apparently it was common practice for both operatives and hired mercenaries to use the same handful of accommodations, in order to streamline any preparations that needed to be made, while at the same time facilitating communications, and enabling the locations to be referred to by seemingly innocuous features that nobody else would recognise.

Selene had also encouraged us to start changing our appearances slightly by growing moustaches and beards, purchasing sunglasses and hats.

This resulted in Androus, who was very reluctant to shave his elegant moustache, growing a small pointed goatee and buying a rather opulent looking fez, which he quickly became so attached to that he went out and bought another while he could.

The rest of us became gradually more disreputable looking, and noticeably less like our normal selves. Jean even had a brief flirtation with a traditional turban until Harry reminded him, that the idea was to disguise ourselves, not to attract as much attention as humanly possible.

We also relaxed into a routine of watching the different locations. Each person keeping lookout from a nearby café or bench for an hour or two before being relieved by someone else.

If the café owners noticed us they asked no questions, happy enough to have the additional custom, even if it was slightly odd to see the same person coming back to their establishments several times each day, seemingly just to complete a crossword, read a book or watch the world go by.

Finally, on the third day, just as the routine was beginning to get tiresome, we spotted them.

I was sat in a street-side hotel café overlooking the railway station, and all of a sudden I noticed a group of tallish men making their way out of the station toward the taxi rank.

Leaving some money on the table where I'd been having my coffee I crossed the street and walked toward where they were standing, hoping my disguise, which included a battered old sun hat, some dark glasses, a newish camera hanging from a strap around my neck and a walking cane, would do the trick.

I'd also acquired a slight limp to go with the cane, curtesy of a sharp stone which I'd deliberately placed in one of my shoes, making it quite uncomfortable to put my weight fully on my right foot. Hobbling forward I managed to approach without any of them paying me any attention, and was practically amongst them just as their luggage was brought through to the front of the station by a couple of station porters.

A train had obviously just arrived, so there were a good number of people milling around the entrance to the station with the group of men I'd spotted.

Now that I got close to them, I pretended to be looking for someone arriving on the same train. Then as one of the porters finished loading the luggage into the two taxis which the men were taking, I simply walked over and asked him whether this was the train from Beja which had just arrived.

We'd already researched the various destinations which the station served and deduced which direction the mercenaries would be coming from, if they were travelling by train.

As a consequence, I was stood right next to the taxi as one of the men spoke to the driver asking to be taken to the Rue du Tamis, where I knew one of the traditional Dar guesthouses we'd been watching was located.

Having obtained the information I wanted, I decided not to push the effectiveness of my disguise any further, so walked off into the crowd, still for all the world looking as though I were searching for someone who had arrived on the train.

A few moments later when I thought it likely the mercenaries would have departed, I walked back to the entrance of the station, and after crossing back over the road, made my way to the guesthouse we'd been watching on the Rue du Tamis, to confirm their arrival.

I found Peter sat on a bench located a bit further down the street from the guesthouse, dressed in his now habitual loose work clothes holding a newspaper in one hand and what appeared to be a delicate honeyed pastry in the other.

He'd picked up an old sun-bleached canvas cap from somewhere, along with a pair of wire rimmed spectacles, which made him look every inch the young intellectual worker, on his way back from a morning's labour.

There was another bench backing onto the one which he was sat on, and to my great delight, I managed to approach and sit down on the bench behind him without him noticing.

'Now that's what I call a disguise,' I suddenly commented from behind him, just as he was biting into his pastry, resulting in a small cloud of powdered sugar, as he coughed in surprise.

'George! You did that on purpose,' he protested around a mouthful of the pastry, after turning briefly to look at me.

I confessed my guilt, and then asked him if he'd seen our quarry arrive a few minutes ago.

'I did indeed,' he confirmed. 'Six of the most ordinary looking men I've ever seen in my life, arrived here about five minutes ago, along with a good number of bags and cases, all of which were ferried straight into the courtyard of the apartments. Since then there's been no sign.'

'Excellent,' I replied. 'Time to leave them to it while we let everyone else know.'

Selene had thoroughly briefed us over the past few days on exactly what to do when the mercenaries were spotted, how to find out where they were heading rather than trying to follow them, how to confirm their arrival, and then how to let everyone else know, so that we could move forward with the next stage of our plan.

She had also explained that while these mercenaries weren't up to the standards of the Order's own operatives, they were still professionals, so they would spend no more than two days in Tunis trying to find us before moving on, so if we were going to trap them we'd have to do it quickly.

With our instructions clearly in mind, and having now confirmed the arrival of the mercenaries at the apartments, Peter and I went in separate directions to collect the others. I would go via the other guesthouse where Jean should be, while Peter walked over to the marina where Selene was stationed.

We'd then rendezvous back at the hotel in Selene and Androus' suite, which had a spacious and airy lounge.

Despite the stone in my shoe I definitely had a bit of a spring in my step as I made my way over to meet Jean, and then from there back to the hotel.

I found Jean simply reading a book in the window

seat of a cafe just down the street from the apartment block he was watching, but unlike Peter, he saw me coming from a mile away, and guessing why I'd come, he'd already made his way out of the shop by the time I got there.

We walked in silence for a while, until we got to a quiet back street that twisted its way out of the old town and toward the broad boulevards of the modern city, where our hotel was located.

'So, George,' Jean began. 'They are here then. What is your impression of these mercenaries, will our plan stand a chance?'

'In truth,' I replied. 'They seemed so normal, just talking amiably amongst themselves about how nice it was to be back in Tunis. If it weren't for the fact that I was watching out for a group of exactly that size, I could easily have mistaken them for regular holiday or business travellers.'

'That is a little disconcerting, my friend,' Jean replied, clearly expecting they would've stood out more. 'Did they at least appear to be bringing a gun case or two with them?'

'Yes,' I was glad to reply, with something positive. 'The luggage they brought with them was fairly substantial including several hard cases that would've been big enough to carry rifles.'

'And in terms of their speech, could you tell they were Scandinavian?'

'Barely,' I admitted. 'They all spoke to one another in English, to the porter and the taxi driver in French, and while my own command of your native language is poor, it was spoken with confidence and precision from what I could tell. The English was a bit more variable. Two of the men spoke the language flawlessly with no accent, the others were fluent, but with a noticeable accent of their own tongue.'

'Hmm, this confirms what Selene has said about these men,' Jean mused in response. 'They are evidently well travelled and are experienced enough not to stand out if they don't need to. It will be interesting to hear how we are to deal with them.'

An hour later and we'd convened in Androus and Selene's suite to hear from Selene about how we should go about the next stage of our plan.

I'd suggested ordering more tea and coffee, as had become our habit over the previous few weeks, until Selene had quietly but emphatically pointed out, that it was just such a detail, which could tip off the hotel staff that we were acquainted, but trying to hide our association.

Which in turn, would be exactly the kind of information our adversaries would be looking for.

It was such a seemingly insignificant detail, but I could see straight away how it could've completely given us away.

Following this timely advice, Selene began to outline what would happen next.

'Over the next two days these men will use their apartment as a base of operations from which to coordinate their search for us.

'They will check the hotels for any recent arrivals or departures which could be us, and they will monitor the marina and railway station, even the aeroport to see if they can find any trace of us arriving or departing.

'In order to cover the entire city as quickly as possible they will split up, and probably won't return to their apartment until the early evening, when they will piece together whatever information they have picked up.'

'Could they find out we're here?' I asked, feeling nervous after our near mistake with the drinks, especially after hearing about just how efficient these men would be in their searching.

'If we're careful about how we come and go, then no it isn't likely,' she responded, with an unshakeable confidence. 'They may identify some of the brief hotel room bookings we made upon first arriving in Tunis as possibilities, but don't forget they're expecting us to be further ahead of them, because they think we may have travelled this way when Stephanos travelled to Nice, so they'll be looking for hotel bookings that started several days before we actually arrived.'

'Ah, but of course,' Jean concurred. 'They will be searching for a group of our size that arrived here in Tunis on roughly the same date that we actually arrived in Nice, not realising we were there at the same time they were, and then followed on behind them after that.'

'Precisely,' replied Selene. 'But make no mistake, second teams will start trailing the first before long, checking the less likely locations which were skipped by the first teams, so we cannot hide behind them indefinitely.'

'So we infiltrate their apartment sometime tomorrow?' asked Marlow, bringing us back to our plan.

'Correct,' replied Selene. 'I have already obtained the drug, which I will place in the lamps around their rooms during the day. This will remain inert and ineffective until the lamps become hot, at which point it will burn off and spread through their rooms, anaesthetising the occupants in a very similar fashion to a carbon monoxide or gas build-up.'

'So will they know they've been drugged when they wake up?' Peter asked.

'No,' Selene replied. 'The drug in question renders them unconscious by inhibiting their ability to absorb oxygen into their blood-stream. This will cause headaches and nausea in exactly the same way as carbon monoxide poisoning, and will be just as difficult to trace in a blood sample.'

'So they might not realise we've been here,' Peter followed up.

'That is less likely,' Selene replied. 'The use of this drug in this way is a well-known technique within the Icarii. As such it won't take long for them to realise this was probably my work.'

'By which time we will need to be well on our way,' Harry suggested.

'Yes,' Selene agreed.

'We know there's a ferry service between here and Malta, and Malta has a much larger port and marina,' she continued. 'So I suggest we simply lay our trap, plant the evidence, and then travel on either the overnight or early morning ferry. Once, that is, we've alerted the authorities to the unfortunate accident which will have incapacitated the men, just as they were about to destroy the evidence of the crime they committed in Nice.

'It means you will all have to read about the justice you have delivered in the newspapers over the next few days, but hopefully that will still satisfy everyone?'

We were all happy with this arrangement, provided that justice was indeed served.

'And is there any risk to the lives of these killers from using this drug?' Androus asked, as the voice of our conscience.

'Too much of the drug, or allowing these men to be exposed to it for too long, will result in either death or permanent brain damage,' Selene responded, clinically. 'But provided we open the doors or windows within two hours of them being exposed, the danger of either is small.'

'So we simply watch their apartment, and wait for a few minutes after the lights go on?' Peter asked.

'Exactly,' was Selene's simple reply. 'The reason that this guesthouse is so popular with people wishing to be discreet is because they allow open access to the apartments via a very simple financial test. Fail to bribe the doorman appropriately on your way in and you will be denied entry. Offer the correct compensation and the doorman will notice and remember nothing, and won't even ask which apartment you wish to visit.'

I was slightly appalled at how easy it all sounded, and couldn't help but wonder how many innocent individuals may have been framed using exactly the same method we were about to use. But these were definitely not guiltless men, so putting such thoughts out of my mind, I focused on what Selene was saying.

Tomorrow we had to arrange our passage on the ferry to Malta, but we needed to do this discreetly because the mercenaries would also be scouring the city for any trace of us, and that would surely include the ferry terminal and its travel office in the centre of the city.

At Selene's suggestion we would book our own passages on two separate ferries, and using as many different ways of booking as we could. Through the hotel concierge, by visiting the terminal in person, and by visiting the travel office in the centre of Tunis, all to conceal the fact that we were travelling as a group. We'd also book a mixture of first class and standard class passages for the same reason.

It was quite likely the mercenaries would be planning to watch the ferry terminal in the evening in order to observe who was boarding the overnight service to Malta, but with luck they'd all be either incapacitated or in police custardy by then.

Even if everything went according to plan, tomorrow would be an interesting day.

WATCHERS

I HATED NOT HAVING a proper shave in the morning, especially in the humid weather which permanently surrounded Tunis. I could, of course, get used to the heat if we stayed here, just as I had done in Kenya, but for now I'd have given anything to be able to have a decent shave and get rid of the moustache I'd slowly been growing since we left Nice.

The sharp pebble I'd placed in my shoe every morning was something else I'd be glad to see the back of, but I needed to keep both the stone and the stubble for the moment, so went through my new morning routine of little irritations before going down to the hotel breakfast room.

It was an odd experience going down for breakfast, but not being able to sit with anyone from the rest of the group. Instead choosing either an empty table, if there was one, or to sit at a table with strangers if there wasn't.

Having only a poor command of French and Italian, and almost no German or Spanish, limited me to breakfasting with the English or American holiday makers and businessmen in the hotel, which usually resulted in a fairly polite if predictable conversation to start the day.

After breakfast, my first task was to relieve Peter from his position in the tea shop overlooking the apartment where the mercenaries were staying.

We didn't need to know where they were going during the day, and it would have been dangerous to follow them, but we did need to know when the apartment was empty so that Selene could place the drug in the lamps.

Peter had gone out just before dawn, to get a seat in the window of the tea shop, before the place filled with people on their way to work.

While the majority of the early morning customers would only be interested in a quick tea or coffee, and perhaps a pastry, the place also provided a light Arabic breakfast for any of its patrons who had more time, which Peter was intending to order, to make his longer stay seem more natural.

I arrived at the tea house just as all the other shops on the street were opening, and bought a glass of my preferred mint tea from the counter, before heading over to join him, hoping he was about to inform me that all six of the mercenaries had already left the apartment to begin their day of searching.

'Five of them went out about twenty minutes ago,' he explained, once I was sat down. 'But no sign of the sixth yet.'

'That could mess things up for us if he stays in the apartment all day,' I commented.

'Precisely, though from what Selene was saying that sounds…' he replied, stopping half way through what he was saying to indicate a figure walking down the road from the other end.

'Miriam,' I found myself saying, as I watched the unmistakable figure of the tall red haired Icarii operative walk down the road and disappear into the courtyard which served the guesthouse.

This was an unexpected and dangerous turn of events, which we hadn't anticipated.

'She must be here to monitor their progress, like Thea was in Nice,' Peter speculated.

'We need to know where she goes,' I observed, thinking hard. 'As soon as she's finished here with the mercenary, one of us will have to follow her while the other goes to update Selene.'

'Following her will be risky,' Peter replied, nodding his approval. 'These disguises are good enough to fool anyone who hasn't met us before, but it wouldn't take much for Miriam to see through them.'

'We'll just have to take the risk, we've got to know where she goes.'

Twenty minutes or so later and both Miriam and the last mercenary appeared back on the street in front of the apartment, and after exchanging some final words they walked off in opposite directions.

As soon as the mercenary had passed the tea shop, we left our hiding place and started to walk after Miriam, but as we reached the next junction Peter peeled off, as agreed, to go and inform Selene, while I hobbled in the direction that Miriam had gone.

I knew I was completely outclassed by Miriam when

it came to this kind of thing, but I'd managed to follow her into the bookshop in Rome and out again without being noticed, so I just kept reminding myself that no matter how skilled an operative she may be, she had limits.

She was already a long way down the street by the time I started after her, and in the winding streets of the old town I lost track of her countless times, in and amongst the crowd of people and the stacks of goods, which filled the streets.

But here, her blaze of red hair was her undoing, for even when I thought I'd completely lost her, I would catch a flicker of her hair, that would put me back on her track.

The route she was taking gradually started to lead through quieter streets, and I was convinced I wouldn't be able to follow her for much longer, when suddenly she stopped at an ornate doorway, and after knocking on the door she was admitted.

This was as far as I could go and still hope to get away unobserved, so after hobbling down the road to the doorway to make a note of the address, I returned to the apartment where the mercenaries were staying, and where I hoped to meet Selene.

Although in the stress of the moment it had seemed like I'd followed Miriam for miles, it only took me a few minutes to find my way back to Rue du Tamis where the mercenaries were staying. I didn't want to return to the tea shop straight away, so walked a few yards further up the street to the front of a bookshop, which also had a few inexpensive books in a box just outside the door.

I was keeping an eye out up and down the street while pretending to rummage through the box, but had somehow completely missed Selene's approach until she spoke to me.

'On the hunt for a bargain, Mr Williamson?' she said, addressing me by the name I was registered under at the hotel.

'Ah, Ms Bath,' I played along. 'Yes, I can't resist

looking through to see what hidden treasures there might be.'

'Well, as chance would have it, I'm just on my way to have a look around a local apartment I'm thinking of renting, for a longer stay here in Tunis. Would you care to join me?'

'Yes, I'd be delighted,' I said, falling into step beside her.

Getting into the apartment which the mercenaries were using took a matter of minutes. Selene quickly dipped into the doorman's office to provide the expected bribe, and without even exchanging a word, stepped out again and led the way up the stairs.

There were about a dozen apartments in the building, but only one was used routinely by the Icarii, so Selene led me straight to the door, and with barely a moment's hiatus, picked the lock to let us in.

Seeing my amazement at this feat, she pointed out that it was a lock she'd picked several times before.

Inside we found an elegant apartment that had been transformed into a centre of operations by the mercenaries, including good quality photographs and biographies for each of us, pinned along one wall. A large map of the city lay spread over one of the table tops, with circles drawn around all the places which the men would be searching to see if there was any sign of us.

Along another wall were the open gun cases, displaying an assortment of weapons, from rifles and pistols to explosives, knives and a series of chemical containers which I guessed were either poisons or drugs of some other variety.

While I was slightly over-awed by the arsenal laid out around me, Selene appeared to take it all very much within her stride, and was already through impregnating the first lamp with the drug before I even realised she was talking to me.

'George… George!' she was saying, looking over

her shoulder at me while she continued to put the lamp back together again. 'I was asking where it was you followed Miriam to?'

'Oh, sorry,' I said, pulling myself together and digging out my notebook. 'It was a house about twenty minutes away on a street called… the Rue Abba.'

'A traditional building?' Selene asked frowning slightly. 'With a large iron-studded street-gate painted a solid black?'

'Yes, that's the one,' I replied, finally getting my wits back enough to carefully take down another lamp and remove its glass shade, so that it was ready for Selene to add the drug to.

'Do you know who lives there?' I asked, bringing another couple of lamps out of the bedrooms.

'Well, most of the local crime in this area is smuggling related, and the family that controls that trade in Tunis are the Gosseyn's. From what you've said, it sounds like Miriam was visiting their family home.'

'Do you think she could be trying to enlist their help in some way?' I asked, wondering whether Miriam's presence in Tunis might have nothing to do with looking for us.

'I don't know,' Selene admitted. 'I'll have to think about it once we're done here.'

It took about thirty minutes in total to place the drug in, or on, all the lamps in such a way that it would be vaporised once they got hot. Selene then, apparently for the first time, looked around the room for anything else which might be of interest.

'We'll have to remove these files when we come back later on,' she said, indicating the photographs and biographies which were taped to the wall.

'Careless,' she muttered, holding up one of the other files which the men had brought with them.

It was Stephanos' details and photograph, along with his boat details and berth in the Nice marina.

'We can plant the letter from Thea here, along with the newspaper clipping and it will look like they've kept it as part of a portfolio.'

We also found a stock of passports from different countries, some of them with names but no photographs, and some completely blank.

'These could come in handy as well,' she observed, carefully putting them back where she'd found them.

Lastly, we discovered several large bundles of currency, American dollars, British pounds, French and Swiss Francs, Italian Lira, and even three small bars of gold. All-in-all enough money to allow these men not to need to visit a bank for several years.

Ensuring everything was as it should be, we quietly left the apartment, locking it behind us, and then exited the building back onto the street as though it were the most natural thing in the world.

Selene then led us deep into one of the crowded souks and the back room of a secluded coffee house, where I was pleased to find the others already sat waiting.

'It has all gone according to plan at the apartment?' Jean asked, looking concerned.

We both indicated it had, and that the lamps were now primed and ready. We then went on to describe what we'd found within the apartment, both in terms of the information about us, but also in terms of the weapons, money and other, slightly more incriminating material about Stephanos.

'You know, if everything goes according to plan this evening,' Harry began, looking around the room. 'It would be nice if we could find a way to get that gold to Stephanos' family.'

'I agree,' chipped in Peter. 'And I'm sure one of the newspaper articles mentioned something about Stephanos leaving behind a wife and daughter.'

'If you wish to take this money and send it to the family, I would suggest you send it via a newspaper office,'

Selene offered. 'They're generally open at odd hours, and are receptive to accepting anonymous packages provided you address them to a specific member of staff.'

'Would it not give us away as having been in Tunis though,' Jean asked.

'Yes, it would, but the Order will figure that out fairly quickly anyway,' Selene replied.

Looking around the room, it was clear we were all thinking it was worth the added risk. Peter had already bought his ferry passage, so agreed to research which of the big French newspapers had offices in Tunis, who it would be best to address the package of money to, and to prepare a suitable letter that we could include with the parcel explaining who the money was intended for.

The rest of us still had to arrange our ferry passages, and then at least one person had to get back to the bench or the tea house on the Rue du Tamis to watch for the mercenaries returning. This wasn't likely to be early, because of the sheer number of locations they'd be trying to cover during the course of the day, but equally, they'd need some time in the evening to compare notes and make their plans for the following day.

'The main risk to the success of our plan,' Selene conceded. 'Is that the lamps will be lit before all the men have returned, and those returning later will see what has happened and open the doors and windows to dispel the drug.'

We'd have to take shifts watching the apartment to make sure that all the men had made it back to the apartment before the lights went on. If that was the case we knew there was a chance the plan would work.

The final piece of advice from Selene before we left the souk, was to think and act slowly during the course of the day, while we were making our arrangements to travel to Malta.

'Remember, these men are in a hurry, they have dozens of hotels to visit and even more people to try to get information out of, including banks, restaurants, boat captains in the marina, the ferry offices and terminal, the railway station and aeroport, not to mention numerous local contacts and information dealers. This means they won't have much time at any one location before they need to be somewhere else.'

I wasn't sure whether we were the cats or the mice, as I made my way down through the souk after leaving the coffee shop, ignoring the attentions of the traders on either side of me. I had to focus on the job at hand, and right now that meant booking my ferry passage to Malta.

We were sticking with our plan of not appearing to travel as a group, so this time Selene, Androus and Harry were travelling on the overnight ferry, while the rest of us would travel in the morning.

I knew Peter had already sorted his ticket, by visiting the travel office in the city centre, so I decided to go to the ferry terminal to purchase mine. It would still be a while until midday, when the sun would be at its hottest, so I decided to stroll out to the terminal and then maybe hop on a tram to get back during the afternoon.

Approaching the terminal in this way would also allow me to scout the area for any of the mercenaries that might be staking the place out.

It was just over a mile and a half, as the crow flies, but with all the twisting streets and a sharp stone in my shoe, it felt more like ten, so by the time I arrived I was thoroughly regretting my decision to walk rather than simply getting the tram both ways.

The area around the terminal was a hive of activity, like all ports. There was a modest sized marina for private vessels, one of several which served Tunis, as well as a dock for larger commercial ships, warehouses and boat yards, hotels and guest-houses, small restaurants, coffee and tea shops, a bar or two, and, as with everywhere in Tunis, there was a souk type market place selling everything from jewellery to spices.

I was in need of a good sit down and something cold to drink, so was paying particular attention to the tea-shops, one of which had overflowed onto the broad boulevard overlooking the marina and the ferry terminal, with a dozen tables and chairs below a cotton canopy, that fluttered on the meagre sea breeze, between tall wooden poles.

Forgetting everything else I made for one of the shaded tables, several of which were free, but it was only as I got close that I noticed a very ordinary looking fair-haired man, sat alone on one of the tables toward the back of the open area, nearest to the shop.

I couldn't tell whether he was one of the men I'd seen at the railway station, and for a moment I considered stopping short of the table I was heading for. But realising that would look suspicious I decided to bluff my way through, and deliberately steered myself to the table right next to him, which meant practically having to squeeze past him.

The waiter arrived a few moments later, while I was rubbing the knee of the leg I'd been limping on, hopefully making my use of the cane seem more convincing. I ordered some tea and a sandwich, making no attempt to hide my accent, and then as an afterthought, asked the waiter if I could also have a glass of cold water as well.

I wanted to see if the man at the next table would pay any more attention once he heard I was an Englishman, but I hadn't accounted for quite how cool a character he might be.

'You're from England?' he asked, with just a hint of a Scandinavian accent.

'Yes, that's right,' I replied, still massaging my knee. 'You sound like you may be from just over the water in Holland.'

'Very close,' he replied, naturally. 'I'm from the other side of the Baltic in Finland. Is your leg giving you some trouble?'

'Oh this, yes. I had a bit of a fall going over a fence on New Year's Day,' I lied, using my prepared story. 'Been on the mend ever since.'

'And is that why you're here in Tunis?' he asked quite openly.

'Yes, my doctor thought the Mediterranean climate might help, so I'm doing a small tour of the north African coast. And you?' I asked, after thanking the waiter who'd just brought my tea and water.

'Work unfortunately,' he replied amiably. 'Which direction are you heading, along the coast I mean?'

'Oh, I had a couple of weeks in Cairo and Alexandria, then a few days in some smaller places, Tobruk, Benghazi, Sirte, with a bit longer in Tripoli, but I'm a bit stuck for where to go next.' I rambled on, as I stirred some sugar into my tea. Trying my best to sound like a solitary traveller who'd been a bit starved of conversation. 'I'd like to visit Tangier of course, but I'd like another stop or two along the way if I can, perhaps Algiers.

'I don't suppose you have any recommendations,' I probed, anywhere your work might've taken you?'

'Well, Algiers is attractive,' he replied beginning to sound less interested in the conversation. 'But I've only ever been there for work.'

I was almost tempted to ask him what type of work he did, just to see what he might come up with, but then it occurred to me that I might be able to hasten his departure by being more interested in myself than in anything he was saying.

'Oh, that's a shame,' I replied, before changing the subject completely, in a way which I've always found completely infuriating when other people have done so to me.

'I don't suppose you have much in the way of hunting in Denmark,' I asked, deliberately mistaking his nationality. 'A bit too flat to make it interesting.'

'No,' he replied, looking increasingly irritated by my

conversation.

'But you do ride I take it?' I asked, barely giving him the chance to get a word in sideways, before barrelling on with my self-centred conversation so that he couldn't get away. He was clearly looking for a way to escape from me, when my waiter brought my sandwich.

'Well, I should leave you to enjoy your food,' he said standing up quickly and placing some money on the table to pay for his drink, despite my again rather selfish offer to eat my sandwich while we chatted.

I'd got so into my character of a boorish tourist that I'd quite forgotten my nerves, and it was only as I watched the man walking back along the water-front toward the town, that I realised my heart was beating quite fast.

I finished my sandwich while I calmed down, drank my glass of tea, and then remembering Selene's instructions about thinking slowly, I ordered and drank a second glass of tea before finally venturing over to the travel offices located near the ferry terminal.

It was only as I entered the sales office that it occurred to me how I'd not only fooled one of the mercenaries, I'd also given myself the perfect alibi for visiting the travel office, in the unlikely event that one of his compatriots should also be watching over the site.

In any eventuality, I bought my one-way ticket on the morning ferry and then hopped on a conveniently timed tram to travel back into the centre of Tunis.

Selene had encouraged us all to be especially vigilant when making our way back to our hotel, both in terms of the route we took to get there, and of the time at which we returned. With a suggestion that none of us should return until at least seven thirty, by which time anyone observing the hotel would be likely to have given up on it as a bad idea.

This gave us all quite a bit of time to kill, but the coffee shops and bars were everywhere in the modern part of the city, so it was easy to find a shady corner for a while, where I could sit down with a newspaper and a coffee to while away a few hours.

EXPOSURE

I STAYED IN A NEARBY BAR for the rest of the afternoon and early evening, in a no-man's land of uncertainty. If Miriam or the mercenaries had found out where we were staying, or what we were up to, then the people we hunted could well be preparing a trap for us, similar to the one they'd sprung on poor Stephanos.

However, if they hadn't discovered us, then it was our trap that would be sprung that evening, and it was they, who were about to lose a significant portion of their lives to a prison cell rather than the grave.

There was no knowing one way or the other, though because of Selene's help the odds at least seemed in our favour.

Marlow had agreed to take the first watch in the tea house, near the apartment, where the mercenaries were staying, followed by Jean, who was relieving him.

I now rendezvoused with Selene, before we both went to join him, when we would find out how many of the men had returned to the apartment, and whether there was yet any sign of the lamps being lit.

I was sure Selene knew what I was thinking, and possibly also heard my heart hammering in my chest as we walked along the broad boulevards of the new city, before heading into the twisting and much narrower streets of the medina, but she said nothing, both of us content to walk in silence.

We'd taken a slightly different and more indirect route to the tea house, but as we rounded a corner onto a road that would bring us out near the apartment, Selene suddenly stopped, and took hold of my arm to halt me, before motioning me back to the corner.

'Carefully, look around the corner and down the street, just before where it joins the Rue du Tamis,' she said, stepping back from the corner to do the same.

'Just beyond that group of people on the left there's another figure almost at the corner.'

'Yes, I see them, a tallish figure with a confident stride, and…' I commented, just as the figure stepped out into the cross street and a low shaft of sunlight that bathed that street.

The figure had the unmistakable deep auburn hair of Miriam, and she was obviously walking toward the apartment where the mercenaries were staying.

We hurried along the street, hoping not to see her come back around the corner, and then carefully turned the corner onto the road where the apartment and tea shop were located.

It was only a matter of yards in one direction to the courtyard entrance that gave access to the apartment, and a bit further in the opposite direction to the tea shop which looked down the street.

I would've quite happily run those few yards to the tea shop just to get off the street before Miriam could come back out of the courtyard, but Selene walked at her usual, unflustered pace without even looking around.

When we finally made it into the tea shop I was sure I was on the verge of a heart attack, and judging by Jean's slightly strained expression, he felt the same.

'My friends, your timing is really quite alarming,' he observed quietly, as soon as we had sat down. 'Did you know you were so closely following Ms Sabbadini?'

'Yes, we happened to stumble across her a few minutes ago, just before she turned into this street,' Selene replied, calmly.

'Fortunate indeed that you were not two minutes

earlier and it was her that followed you down the street,' Jean commented, still wide-eyed.

'I believe chance affects everything we do, Jean,' Selene replied, still slightly hesitant to address him so informally. 'All we can do is accept the good with the bad.

'The more important question is whether all of the mercenaries have returned from their day of searching for us.'

'They have indeed,' Jean replied, nodding his approval at Selene's philosophical perspective. 'The last of them returned about twenty minutes ago, shortly after I swapped places with Robert.'

'So we're just waiting to see if the lights come on,' I asked, looking up at the apartment windows at the front of the building.

'It is perhaps still a little too light outside,' Jean suggested. Though as he spoke these words the tea shop owner moved to the back of his shop and lit a couple of decorative oil lamps to make the shadowy seats furthest away from the window seem more inviting as the evening approached.

For a few minutes it seemed as though the light outside was barely dimming at all, and then, just as I'd seen it do countless times in Kenya, the light suddenly faded, and lights started to appear behind the windows and balconies up and down the street, including those that fronted onto the apartment where the mercenaries and Miriam were.

'Now, is the moment of truth,' Selene commented beside me, while she looked up at the now gently glowing windows. 'If all remains quiet for the next five minutes and none of the men or Miriam appear from the courtyard, then the drug may have worked.'

We sat in tense silence for a further ten minutes, while the tea shop owner walked around his premises lighting his own lamps, and a steady flow of customers came and went through the door, until finally Selene indicated it was time to move.

It felt like time had slowed to a crawl, as we left the tea shop and strolled down the street to the archway which led to the guesthouse courtyard, and then up the stairs to the apartment where we hoped everyone was now unconscious.

Selene paid the expected bribe to the door manager, once again without need for a single word to be exchanged, and then we unhurriedly made our way up the staircase to the apartment.

With every step I half expected Miriam to appear, springing a trap of her own, but we got closer and closer to the doorway of the apartment.

Each apartment looked out over the central courtyard, which was open to the now distinctly dark sky, but all was quiet, save a young boy who had recently started to light the courtyard and staircase lamps on the ground floor.

When I looked back, Selene had drawn a small snub-nosed revolver from somewhere beneath her clothing, as had Jean, and then with a final look between us we all took deep breaths as she reached out and silently tried the door handle.

She opened the door in one smooth motion, her gun hand hidden behind her body, and then entered the short corridor which led to the lounge.

As soon as I entered the apartment, my heart still racing, I could see the unconscious form of one of the mercenaries lying across the floor. Selene and Jean were ahead, opening the windows at the front and back of the apartment, while I closed the front door and moved through into the two bedrooms which had windows opening out onto the courtyard.

Despite having only just entered the apartment, I couldn't open the first window quickly enough, and I felt my lungs burning, as I returned to the front door to get another breath of clean air, before going back in to open the second window.

With all the windows open to their fullest, I walked through to the lounge to find Jean and Selene stood next to the open balcony window at the front of the building, while the seven unconscious forms of the mercenaries and Miriam lay where they'd passed out.

As I joined them at the window I could feel the hint of a breeze wafting through the apartment, changing the air for us.

'They're all unharmed,' Selene confirmed, as I joined them at the window. 'Though they'll have terrible headaches in the morning when they come around.

'We should start with the evidence, removing all the documents which contain any information that could lead the authorities to us,' Selene suggested.

'George, you remove everything down from the walls and the table.

'Jean, there's a stack of other documents which these men have brought with them, see if you can find one that could plausibly be a second target for these men in Tunis. A local dignitary, religious leader or crime boss.

'If we can I'd like to make it look as though these men were not only responsible for your friend's death in Nice, but have been hired again by Miriam to kill someone else here.'

'Of course,' Jean replied. 'We must make the most of our unexpected extra catch.'

It felt strange moving around the apartment with all those unconscious people there, but we got down to work. We bagged everything that could incriminate us, while Jean found the details of a couple of local journalists, with photographs which we put up on the wall, along with the various details contained in their files, to make it look like they were being followed.

The money was removed from its hiding place, as were the blank passports, while some of the fake passports were placed in prominent places for the authorities to find. To these we added the newspaper clippings and details of

Stephanos' brutal murder, along with the letter we'd faked from Thea requesting the kill. As an added bonus, we also discovered files on Miriam, Thea and Haleena in another pile of documents which the men had obviously collated on their customers, which surprised even Selene.

'I don't know why they would take the risk of collecting this information,' Selene commented, shaking her head slightly. 'Certainly, if we'd had any suspicion they were doing this it would not have ended well for them.

'As it is, the fallout from this information being uncovered will be very large.'

Selene then wrote a second note, apparently in Miriam's handwriting, requesting a meeting this evening to discuss the elimination of a local troublemaker. In it she specified the location of the meet to be at the apartment, and the need for the death to appear as an accident. It also specified a three-thousand-dollar cash deposit which would be handed over as a down payment against the job being successfully completed, the balance of a further two thousand dollars to be paid upon completion.

We then used three thousand dollars of the money from the stash which the men had, placed it in a blank envelope, which Selene then put into one of Miriam's pockets.

It was almost like watching a piece of art being created as Selene carefully staged the scene, so that the authorities would immediately realise these people were criminals.

It took us two hours to arrange everything so that the scene was as convincing as possible, and then we simply walked away closing the windows and doors behind us, after rigging one of the gas lamps to make it look as though it hadn't been burning properly and it was this that had led to the occupants of the apartment falling unconscious because of carbon monoxide poisoning.

We stopped off at the local office for one of the big French newspapers with the box of gold and the rest of the dollars, all carefully sealed and labelled for the attention of the editor, along with a letter explaining that the money was from a group of visiting businessmen, who had recently heard about the terrible killing in Nice, and would like to donate the enclosed money to help out the victim's widow and child.

Then it was finally a question of making the phone call to the authorities, which Selene did from a private telephone booth in one of the hotels we were passing.

In the call, she pretended to have overheard a violent commotion between a group of foreigners in the apartment while visiting a neighbouring flat, and what she thought was the sound of a fight and a muffled gunshot.

This, she informed us on the way back to our own hotel was guaranteed to get the authorities to investigate straight away.

'In any country you visit you are guaranteed to get more attention from the authorities than a local resident,' she explained. 'That combined with the mention of firearms in a densely populated city frequented by tourists, and the response from the authorities will always err on the side of being heavy handed.'

ON THE BREEZE

NOT KNOWING WHAT WAS GOING ON, or how the authorities were responding to the tip off we'd provided, was far more tortuous than I'd expected. Several times before we left Tunis in the morning I wanted to take a stroll back to the Rue du Tamis to see what was happening, but this was something which Selene had warned specifically against.

'It won't happen immediately, but as soon as the authorities start to realise what they've discovered, a great many people will visit the scene, just to see who shows up in the area,' she explained. 'And I'm not talking about the police or other parts of the establishment, there will be journalists and criminals and information brokers of every type.

So we'd stayed away, and involuntarily awake until our ferry departed in the morning.

There was a part of me that was hoping we'd be able to relax once the furore started, when the newspapers and the authorities started to ask awkward questions about Thea and Miriam and the group of assassins which they appeared to have hired on two separate occasions.

If we were lucky, the files which the mercenaries had compiled on their clients would come out as well, and these killers would try to incriminate as many other people and organisations as they could, in order to get away with lighter sentences for themselves. But we'd only find out about that once the story made its way into the newspapers, and just as importantly the newspapers made their way to wherever we ended up.

In the meantime we kept a low profile, moving from Malta quite quickly after arriving by chartering a couple of smaller boats to take us to Crete, and from there a single larger boat to the Turkish coast via several smaller Greek islands.

Finally, we arrived at a anonymous Turkish town on the southern coast called Antalya, where we finally felt safe enough to stop for a few days and find out how the authorities had dealt with the tip off we'd given them in Tunis, before we figured out how to proceed now that we'd reached Turkey.

To say that the impact was bigger and more widespread than we'd expected would be a huge understatement.

In tipping off the police to the presence of the

mercenaries, with all the incriminating evidence in their apartment, both fake and real, we'd unwittingly exposed a scandal the like of which the civilised world had never seen, igniting a chain of consequences that reached across the political, economic and judicial infrastructure of Europe like wildfire.

The authorities may not have realised quite what they had when they found the obvious clues which we'd laid out for them, but perhaps because the atrocity which had occurred in Nice was so recent, they didn't hesitate in announcing to the press that they had apprehended several people they suspected of being involved in the murder at the marina. They couldn't have even examined all the evidence they had when they issued this statement later on the same day we'd left Tunis, let alone started to piece everything together in order to reveal the bigger picture

Within another day the story of the killer's capture was on the front page of every newspaper, followed by late editions hinting at the possibility of an even larger story to come, as details of the documentation found with the mercenaries started to be talked about. The following morning they'd discovered the killers had been hired to kill Stephanos by a mysterious young woman with ties to Italy and more specifically the Vatican City.

Because of this evidence, the police had tracked Stephanos' boat back to Ostia, and had somehow managed to discover that his cousin had also sailed that day, and had observed the strange way in which the Italian authorities had followed their boats as they sailed toward Corsica, both by boat and by plane.

This focused attention on the regime of Mussolini, with the French and Greek governments in particular demanding to know why the Italian authorities appeared to have been so interested in this boat just before the owner had been so brutally killed.

Having missed over a week's worth of newspapers by this point, when we finally started to catch up with them it seemed as though the authorities and journalists could barely print the newspapers quickly enough to keep up with the steady stream of information flowing from the investigation.

Thea was tracked down and arrested in Marseilles after her picture appeared on the front of several French newspapers, which was surprising enough in itself until she foolishly tried to assert her diplomatic immunity to avoid arrest, only for the Italian state to deny any knowledge of her or that she was even one of their citizens.

Miriam and the mercenaries being more experienced tried to play things cooler, by simply refusing to answer any questions.

This only delayed things when it came to the mercenaries, who, after their pictures and descriptions were shared with the Finnish authorities, were quickly identified by their real names and exposed. Interviews followed with their shocked families and friends, who clearly had no idea what these men were doing for a living.

Hand in hand with the criminal investigation came the news of the cash and gold, which had been donated to Stephanos' widow by an anonymous group of businessmen.

This story also ran for several days, with pictures of the grieving widow and her thanks to the donors being closely followed by a public appeal for the benefactors to come forward, and then some wild speculation about a possible connection with the royal family of Monaco.

We were staying in a small villa, set back slightly from the coast, but the natural splendours of the shoreline were routinely forgotten for several hours each day as one batch of newspapers after another was delivered to the door, only to be devoured by us en-masse.

After scrutinising every newspaper we could lay our hands on for several days, it finally seemed as though the story might be dying down, but with their true identities now revealed and the condemnation of the world trickling in through their prison bars, the mercenaries finally agreed to cooperate with the authorities in order to try and cut a deal.

Other stashes of documents were retrieved from safety deposit boxes in Finland and in Switzerland, revealing incredible information about the clients for whom the mercenaries had worked, the criminals and corrupt politicians, the pseudo government agencies and of course the other secret organisations like the Icarii, the existence of which the world had never guessed.

Even Selene was shocked by the wealth of detail these men had secretly amassed, presumably for the express purpose of giving themselves additional leverage, should the authorities ever catch up with them.

One enterprising Spanish journalist went through all the information which had been released about the countless jobs these men had been commissioned to do, and had estimated their total income, which was more than enough to have allowed them to retire in great luxury. It appeared from what they had said during their police interviews that they'd continued working well beyond the point where they needed the money, because…they enjoyed their work.

Whether the authorities uncovered any information about us during their investigation we had no idea. There was certainly no sign in any of the newspaper reports, but one thing was for sure, and that was that the Icarii would be retreating back into the deepest and darkest shadows they could find.

According to Selene, all communications would stop, all operatives would simply hunker down wherever they were and wait. The mother superiors like Agostine, and the Reverend Mothers would simply retreat to their own fiefdoms until the world, including the mainstream Catholic church, simply moved its attention elsewhere.

While the scandal of the century ran on, the flames now fanned by the press as much as by any new revelations, we took the opportunity to move inland from the coast and then start the long journey overland by car and train to Ankara.

With each mile we travelled across the vast and natural countryside of Turkey, we all began to relax, even Selene, who had remained constantly vigilant until then. At times we travelled through such quiet rural landscapes we barely knew where we were.

Two weeks later, after many a winding road and not a small number of wrong turns we finally reached Ankara, and the quiet obscurity of the hotel Anubis run by Androus' cousin Osman.

With the Order leaving us alone, and the luxury of once more being able to stay in the same place, we finally had time to grieve for Stephanos, before turning our attention back to the lapis tablets, and the translation of those cryptic directions, which would hopefully lead us to the first great temple of Ziusudra.

The Adventure Continues in:
The Ashes of Time

I hope you enjoyed reading this book, if so please visit my website and sign up for my newsletter so I can let you know about other titles when I publish them.

You can find my site at
www.knytewrytng.com

All comments and feedback are welcome.

Thank you.

Peter Knyte

And finally:

In the next few pages you'll find a taster of the third and final book in this trilogy: The Ashes of Time.

Here's the back-page blurb, followed by a sample chapter.

'With only an ancient set of cryptic directions as a guide, and the murderous Order of Icarus trying to find them, our group of adventurers must decide what to do next.

If they break cover from where they have been hiding in Turkey it won't take long before their enemies begin their pursuit. But the only map they have to follow is so ancient the world it once described may no longer exist.

There can be no going back, and no shortcuts to find what they seek. Perhaps only the strange dreams and visions that visit them on the sound of distant drums can help them reach their goal.

To find out what happens, read The Ashes of Time, the third and final instalment in the Flames of Time trilogy.'

THE
ASHES
OF
TIME!
BOOK
THREE
PETER
KNYTE
THE VASTNESS OF INDIA HIDES MANY SECRETS, SOME IN PLAIN SIGHT
FOR ANYONE WHO CARES TO SEE OTHERS THAT WILL ONLY EVER
BE REVEALED SLOWLY, ONE FRAGMENT AT A TIME!

THE ASHES OF TIME

LANDS OF THE DJINN

SAMARKAND IS A GHOSTLY SILHOUETTE on the horizon, partly comprised of heat haze and partly imagination. It is a pale grey-blue outline of a city below the gold and orange clouds of evening, which almost reach the tops of the fading minarets and shimmering domes.

Between the clouds and the city are the even fainter shapes of the Tien Shan, the mountains of heaven, and one of several possible routes that we must follow beyond the city before us.

We are close to the city, perhaps an hour's walk, so the great snaking caravan of people, wagons and animals which stretch out behind us will reach their final destination in the central market by mid evening.

Samarkand is finally in sight though, and in celebration some of the merchants begin to give thanks and prayers for the safe completion of yet another journey.

Moments later I hear the first high-pitched sounds of the Zurna, the traditional clarinet-like instruments played by folk musicians and snake-charmers in this part of the world, spreading the news of our arrival down the length of the caravan.

Despite the sun having set, it is still warm, and the festivities of the caravan quickens as we approach the city, growing louder and more insistent each time the road turns to reveal the city a little closer, before dying down as we weave back through the orchards and woodland which line the road and obscure our view.

Adding to the sights and sounds of the caravan, and filling the warm autumnal air with their gentle fragrance are the ripening peaches on the trees all about us.

Why are we walking this long route to this most ancient of cities? The question is so familiar to me. It seems almost the only thing I have thought about for each day of our incredible journey.

These last six months have been the hardest of my life, but with the hardships have come rewards and a strange sense of fulfilment. Each day we have walked, not ridden, twenty miles or more. Hard miles with heavy packs over often rough terrain. Days that were tiring beyond belief to begin with, but which are now just our normal routine. So much so that rest days with no walking seem unnatural, even uncomfortable.

There have been times in my life when I have wished for nothing more than to get away from the boundaries of civilisation and out into the wild, but now, having sampled a wilder form of life than I even knew existed, the idea of craving more of it brings a brief smile to my heavily tanned face.

For nearly a year we stayed in Ankara, licking our wounds at the Anubis Hotel owned by the ever present and benevolent Osman, one of Androus's many cousins.

It is another home away from home, like Nyrobi, Jerusalem and Corinth, where I felt instantly more comfortable than I ever did at my house back in Shropshire.

After reaching Ankara, we take some time to mourn the loss of Stephanos, and to digest the events of the previous weeks, but before long the need to stop looking backward arises, so we hire another couple of rooms in the hotel where we can study and research the route ahead.

The research is familiar work for us now, and it provides an excellent distraction from the grief we each feel over the loss of our friend in Nice, so before long we are making good progress again.

Our skill and understanding when working with the cryptic directions found on the tablets has also developed considerably over the last year, since our first amateurish attempts at deciphering the lapis lazuli tablets, and then transposing their directions onto our maps.

Both Marlow and Harry have become much more conversant in reading Sumerian cuneiform, but more importantly, we have all become much more experienced at matching the directions which the tablets contain, to the world as it is today.

It is this experience, a few months later, that persuades us to commit to the long and gruelling overland walk.

The problems are familiar to us. So much time has passed since the directions were written that not only the names of places have changed, but also the very landscape itself.

Eventually it is Androus who calls us all together to break the stalemate.

'As you all know,' he explains, after we have struggled with the finished translations of the tablet text for several months. 'Between them, the different sets of tablets contain several possible routes to the first great temple of Ziusudra, which is clearly located somewhere in Asia.

'Unfortunately, the lowland routes through Iraq and Iran have changed so much over time they will be almost impossible to trace.'

'More so than the routes through the mountain passes and the high country?' Peter asks, sceptically.

'Yes, I'm afraid so,' replied Androus. 'You see, the arid landscape which we are now all familiar with, after our trip to Uruk, was once a fertile and green place. But that fertility was man-made, created by harnessing the annual flood waters from the Tigris and Euphrates. In much the same way that the Nile was later managed, by constructing canals and smaller waterways to take the flood water further into the dry land of the open plains, creating a huge amount of cultivated land.'

'And, the directions we have, date from when this irrigation was at its height?' Peter asks.

'Ah, no. If that were the case, we might still stand a chance,' Androus, replies. 'The directions on the tablets date to the time before the waters of these two great rivers were first tamed by the extensive irrigation of the landscape. Irrigations which have subsequently been abandoned and allowed to fill in, changing the landscape significantly for a second time.'

'Of course,' nodded Jean, 'And while we might recognise the landscape after one such manipulation of the topography, the chances of doing so after a second such change is much lower.'

'Precisely,' continued Androus. 'What hope can we have of finding some of the places mentioned like Meluhha or Meyan, Anan or Markush when we know the geographic features surrounding them might have been changed by subsequent cultivation and then drought. Even such places as Agade, the ancestral home of the Akkadians, has still to be discovered for the same reasons, and that was lost far more recently than the features we seek.'

'But the mountains you don't think will have changed as much?' asked Marlow, simply.

'In truth, I do not know,' Androus admitted. 'Rock slides and avalanches could well have transformed large sections of the route described through the mountains, but when these routes were established, they were made in stone, and the environmental factors like sand and dust, which can completely cover and hide all trace of a lowland settlement within just a few dozen years, are much slower to take effect in the mountains, often leaving historic sites completely unobscured for centuries.

'In addition, the directions we have for the routes through the mountains are more numerous, but also a little more cryptic, and to my reading will only be intelligible to us by following the route on foot.'

'The mountains of Turkey alone would take us weeks of walking to cover,' observed Harry, with dismay.

'Yes,' conceded Androus.

'But you think it would be enough to set us on the right track,' Harry asked, more hopefully.

'Of that I am not certain,' confirmed Androus, holding up his hands at seeing Harry's alarmed expression.

'One of the biggest problems we have with the directions are the features which *aren't* described. Geographic features which for us give essential indications of distance and direction.

'In this case, as you are all aware, no mention in the directions is made of the Caspian Sea, that huge body of water to the east of Turkey.

'Now in reality this is to be expected,' he explained, placing a large map of the region on top of the other paperwork which covered a nearby table.

'You see, while it may appear unavoidable on a large-scale map, the walking routes through that area all focus on the valleys and low mountain passes, from which the Caspian Sea is not visible, due to the high mountains which surround much of its western edge and all of the sea to the south.'

'So, just how much of this route do you think we'll need to cover on foot?' Jean asked.

'In truth, my friends, I do not know.

'If the directions take us to the north of the Caspian then we will need to stop and begin our research again, as the directions will be taking us across the Russian Steppes, of which we have only very poor maps and information.

'If, on the other hand the directions take us south of the Caspian, then we will almost certainly need to find our way along the old silk and spice routes to the east, south and north, and match the directions we have to the many ancient settlements that cover that area from Herat, Farah and Kandahar to the south, to Mashad, Merv, Bukhara, Samarkand and even Tashkent to the north, and Kabul and the Khyber Pass in the east.

'Until we positively identify one of these places from the directions, the route will not be clear.'

Of the long walk through Turkey to the south of the Caspian Sea, the directions seem to indicate we should begin travelling in the spring, so we make our preparations and leave Ankara at the end of March.

Over the next three months Androus's suspicion that the path will have changed less, proves to be correct, and while the walking is quite hard at times, we quickly get a feel for the route, and just as importantly, develop a sense for when we should continue following the path, and when we should be looking for the next feature described on the tablets.

We are also fortunate to be walking through a mild and dry spring. So while the route still physically toughens us up, by the time we approach Tehran we have seen very little of the snow and ice that could still blanket the mountains at this time of year.

In contrast, the second part of our journey with the trade caravan eastward and then north, up the other side of the Caspian Sea, goes less well.

The route this way seems easy to follow as we wind our way eastward, skirting the curving mountain range which surrounds the bottom edge of the Caspian Sea on our way to Mashhad, but of sprawling Mashhad itself there is no mention in the tablets, nor any mention of the features from the surrounding territory.

After leaving Mashhad we encounter a series of sand storms. Small by the standards of this part of the world, but severe enough for us, in our western travel clothes, to be painfully uncomfortable for several days, until one of the merchants travelling with the caravan takes pity on us, and offers us some of the all engulfing Bedouin robes and turbans that almost everyone else in the caravan is wearing.

As the sand storms cease we walk out of them transformed. We had entered wearing our usual light-weight travelling attire of sturdy boots, canvas trousers and cotton shirts, beneath heavier waxed jackets and wide brimmed hats. Now these things have been exchanged for the looser fitting sarong trousers, thobe and cloak-like overcoats, which we have learned to wear in several different ways along with the turbans, depending upon the conditions, and whether protection is needed from the sun, sand or wind.

During our time in Ankara we had all become fluent in Turkish, as it not only made every aspect of life easier, from buying new research materials, clothing and food, but also because it made us less conspicuous.

As a bonus, when we leave Turkey and begin travelling along the great silk roads, we discover a variation of the Turkish we all speak is used interchangeably with the local dialects along the route.

This in its countless local variations is known simply as Turkic, and is spoken by all.

Consequently, now as we approach Samarkand in our new clothing, hardened and tanned by the incessant walking, and speaking to the merchants in the Turkic language of the spice routes, we are no longer recognisable as westerners.

The leader of the caravan, a hard, but fair Afghan known only as Paylin or Master Paylin, explains to us that upon entering the city the caravan will wind its way through the streets before taking up residence in the merchants quarter amongst the local warehouses, shops and bazaars, where there will be much feasting and celebration of our safe arrival, and which he would like us to enjoy as his guests.

It would be impolite, if not impossible for us to decline such a gracious offer, so as the lamps and fires are lit across the merchants quarter, we find ourselves following along amongst the noise and hubbub of it all, stopping eventually beside one of the big auction platforms that will used over the next few days, as the caravan merchants sell the goods they had brought with them, and then buy new merchandise to take back to Tehran.

A tea seller stops to provide us all with hot mint tea in small glass cups, courtesy of Master Paylin.

Beneath the folds of our carefully wound turbans I see my friends smiling at one another in the lamplight, as we point out acrobats and jugglers, greet fellow members of the caravan, or receive the polite salutations from the local people, everyone is content to simply enjoy life for the moment.

Selene is one of us now, more relaxed and at one with herself than I have ever seen her, and for a moment she even looks like she is going to dance with Jean, as the spiralling notes of the clarinet like Zurna once again begin to fill the night air.

After finishing our tea and returning the glasses I feel in the mood to investigate the sights and sounds of this most ancient city, and am just about to take my leave of my friends, when the hair on the back of my neck prickles, and I become aware of a faint, half-heard sound mingling with notes of the Zuma.

The sound is unmistakable. It is the sound of the distant drums from back in Africa, once again floating in on the night air. That writhing serpentine sound which so effortlessly curls around the corners of my mind, reminding me once again of the shamanic ceremony and the strange insight filled dreams which followed.

Before I can even begin to doubt what I am hearing I see recognition dawning on my friends faces, even Selene and Androus appear to hear the strange whispering rhythm.

To find out how the adventure ends, read the third and
final book in the trilogy:
The Ashes of Time
Available from all good retailers

Or:
For more information visit:
www.knytewrytng.com

www.ingramcontent.com/pod-product-compliance
Lightning Source LLC
Chambersburg PA
CBHW021644110726
47902CB00007B/1818

9 780993 087486